KYLIAN

An Urban Fantsy

ANN GIMPEL

CONTENTS

KYLIAN
CIRCLE OF ASSASSINS, BOOK FOUR

Urban Fantasy

By
Ann Gimpel

Tumble off reality's edge into a twisted world fueled by lore and magic

Copyright Page

Power is intoxicating. Anyone who says you can overdo it is either incompetent or a very good liar. I've chased down every scrap of additional magic that crossed my path, drained it, and started the hunt anew. My obsession hasn't made me much of a companion. I wouldn't have blamed my bondmate for leaving, but the snow leopard has stuck by my side.

It pains me to admit he's my sole connection to my better nature. He tempers my penchant for blowing holes in the world and asking questions later. Not that he has a soft side. He doesn't, but we've taken care of each other for all the years in my memory.

Information just fell into my lap. Critical material I should have picked up on if I'd been paying attention. My next stop is Grigori, the werewolf who heads up a gang of paranormal assassins. Once I was part his Circle, but I left to sharpen my seer skills. No matter how adept I became, scrying the future—or the past—didn't augment my power, so I moved on. Flitting from this to that to the other has been the story of my obscenely long life.

No more. It's back to the Circle for the leopard and me. We'll remain as long as we're needed.

Between Covid-19 and the California fires, I've had a lot of time to dream up ideas for books. Watching too much *Blacklist* and *Warehouse 13* and *Stranger Things* probably didn't help. And the last season of *Supernatural*. I will miss Sam and Dean...

Meanwhile, a concept shaped up for me. Assassins have always held a fascination factor. Death is a job for them, but what kind of people are they beneath their knives and guns and poison? Toss a few bond animals into the mix, and the bones for a darkish urban fantasy series took shape.

Within its pages, you'll ride alongside men and women who found their way to an age-old profession. Every king worth his salt had a court assassin, and so has every ruler from olden times to modern. If you're shaking your head saying such things can't happen today, take a look at "suicides" that are swept under a whole bunch of rugs. Oddly enough, all those suspicious deaths had stories to tell, stories someone wanted silenced—forever.

Kylian is a different type of assassin. In a fruitless search for peace, he withdrew from everything long ago. Enforced solitude isn't all it's cracked up to be, though.

PROLOGUE

Ice cracked ominously. Another epic chunk peeled off from the glacier above and divebombed our position. A surreptitious shot of magic diverted it, not so far away as to cause suspicion, though. The thousand-pound missile thumped to the ground, narrowly missing one of our precious snowmobiles. We used them to ferry supplies, and I'd be damned if I'd leave shit for the Russians to steal parts from.

"Dame Fortune loves us," one of my companions shrieked and fist-pumped the air.

I stifled a wry grin, amused at how quickly mortals attribute random events to some special intervention. Would he still be hanging his hat on Dame Fortune, who doesn't exist, if the block of ice had landed on his helmet?

My earpiece crackled with instructions to move out. The falling seracs suggested the day had grown too warm for maneuvers on Ellesmere Island, a scrap of rocky land next to Baffin Island north of the Arctic Circle. The Russians had snuck in an outpost here, violating of a bunch of international treaties. Because it was so remote, they refused to admit it existed.

My group of mercenaries had been dispatched to take it out. So far, we hadn't made a hell of a lot of progress.

I try not to lead expeditions like this one. Too much temptation to toss magic about and out myself. But I'm not shy about voicing opinions. I located Frank, our *de facto* team leader, with a thread of seeking magic and hustled to his side before anyone acted on his pull-the-plug command.

A big man with a full black beard and the build of a linebacker, he shot me an annoyed glance. "We're pulling out," he said. "Something wrong with your communicator?"

Because I could, I scraped the surface of his mind to see what was really going on. Surprise, surprise. He wasn't annoyed, he was scared. The last batch of falling ice must have gotten to him.

"We can finish this," I said, holding to a neutral, non-confrontational tone. Before he ginned up a reply, I went on. "Then we won't have to keep coming back."

No need to point out we were going on two weeks and so far hadn't gotten near enough to the Russian installation to be much more than a nuisance. They'd wisely sunk their building deep in the ice with its foundation resting on bedrock. It protected them from avalanches, and damn near everything else. It was how they'd gotten away with denying its existence. The only thing that stuck up above ground—or in this case, ice—level was their com equipment.

The satellite apparatus protruding from the roof was all we'd managed to destroy. Since I was certain they had duplicate machinery inside, we hadn't made a dent in their defenses.

Frank wasn't all that swift on the uptake, but he did manage to grunt, "How?" in response to my comment about finishing things.

I considered it a win. He could have told me to shut up and get moving. Line of command and all that shit. "So far, the problem has been we can't get inside."

"Tell me something I don't know," he growled.

Time to lie my fucking head off. "I did some poking around," I told him. "I believe I can breach the barrier, and then the rest of you can follow. We'll finish off whomever we find, and then we can go home."

"Not seeing it. We've been around and around the target ten times."

Another volley of automatic weapons spewing bullets split the eerie quiet of the Arctic. We returned fire. Waste of good ammo, if you ask me. The rattle of weaponry was the only noise other than the perpetual pounding of the ocean on ice that rimmed the shore. We had a ship moored quite a way out in Baffin Bay. Danish troops were keeping an eye on it for us. Amazingly, our fleet of Zodiac rafts lined the ice, untouched.

But then, we had our target pinned in their building. It might be considered an accomplishment, but the Russians are masters at stonewalling enemies. They barricaded themselves into Leningrad during World War II and beat the Germans by default.

"Let me worry about the where part," I told Frank seeding my words with enough calming magic to, hopefully, settle him down. I could launch my plan without his blessing, but I try to be a team player on these missions. I only sign up to amuse myself. If I got a rep for being tough to work with, no one would tap me for anything.

Keeping my various aliases straight was a challenge. Most mercenaries stash go bags in key locations. I craft what I need on the spot with magic. It beats pulling out a set of creds I haven't used in so long they've expired. Had that happen with money too when one of the squabbling Eastern European counties deep-sixed their currency in favor of the Euro. I miss gold—and silver. They never fell out of fashion.

"What are we doing, boss?" hissed through my headset.

It made sense. After Frank's pronouncement we were leaving, he hadn't fleshed out any details. The troops were growing restless, all fifteen of us. Including me.

I made a decision, one that might cost me, but I was tired of dicking around. Dropping a hand onto his shoulder, I said, "Maybe you were right the first time. Fall back to the rafts. Don't wait on me." Along with my persuasive suggestion, I did some rearranging so he wouldn't remember our earlier conversation.

Or me, until I materialized.

Hopefully, when I saw him next aboard the ship, he'd go along with my version of reality, the one where I reminded him he'd assigned me to go in solo. A secret mission only the two of us knew about. As fact-planting went, it should be simple enough to accomplish.

Frank keyed his mic. "Pack up. Move out."

Excellent. My wee bit of compulsion had taken root. I didn't wait around for him to ask questions. Our team was on the move, revving up the snowmobiles and stowing gear. Drawing invisibility around myself, I headed for the Russian installation. Ione joined me well out of sight of the others.

He's a snow leopard and my bondmate. He's always along on these expeditions, but he knows to stay out of sight. His kind aren't exactly native to this area, but that's not the worst of it. He's easily double the size of a normal snow leopard, and would draw the wrong kind of attention.

Wind had been brisk since daybreak, but it picked up still more. Bits of ice thwacked my face, the only place I had exposed skin. Ione sported bloody smears near his mouth. "What'd you kill?" I asked.

He licked his whiskers, but it didn't obliterate the evidence. "Seal," he mumbled.

I muffled a snort. "You ate a whole seal? That's going to slow you down."

"Only half." He sounded miffed. "Saved the rest for our next trip here."

"Ha! You may have to do battle with a polar bear."

Ione growled. He and I both knew he was more than a match for any polar bear, but not many were left. On the other hand, seals were ubiquitous. "What are we doing?" he asked.

"We're teleporting inside and killing everyone. Then I'll dismantle everything useful, and we'll return to the ship."

"You'll return to the ship. I'll wait…elsewhere."

"Not here. We'll be done here."

He rolled his big shoulders as he trotted next to me. "Fine. I'll go home. Which one?"

I'd been thinking about it. "Maybe you will want to remain here if the hunting is plentiful. I have to stop by the villa. Haven't been there in years."

Ione made a snarly face. He hated the villa by the Adriatic; the climate was far too warm for his taste. Mine too, truth be known, but I couldn't abandon it. Someone had to ensure the warding was still intact.

We reached the perimeter of the Russian installation. A muted electronic whirring suggested someone knew we were here. Guessing at the interior layout, I snatched a spell out of my bag of tricks and teleported to the lowest level of the building, making certain Ione and I were well concealed.

In stark contrast to the outside, the building was overheated. At least the small room forming around us was deserted. As I'd hoped, it contained banks of computer equipment. Ione padded toward the door.

"Wait," I told him and redirected power to assess exactly what we faced. I scanned once, and then again with the same results. Eighteen men, two women, and one Dark Fae. What in the hell was a magic-wielder doing here? Was he passing for human? They were capable of that if they employed a glamour to hide their wings. And their ears.

Until I shot my wad, the mortals would remain oblivious to my presence. But the Fae could find me the same way I located him. In truth, he probably already knew we were here. It meshed with the sense of having been discovered that had buffeted me when we stood outside. I'd been going back and forth on a strategy, but the Fae's presence decided things. I wouldn't have nearly as much fun, but I'd be efficient.

I hustled to Ione and consolidated our ability. Once I had both magics well in hand, I sent lethal power in a wide arc. It would seek out life and destroy whatever crossed its path. Except the Dark Fae. He'd require a direct approach. Lab animals were one floor up. They'd die too, but weeding them out would take more time. Lots more.

Besides, once the humans were gone, there'd be no one to

take care of them. The rats, mice, cats, and monkeys wouldn't stand a chance at survival if I loosed them. Maybe death was a backhanded favor.

"You're ruining the fun," Ione groused as the sound and scent of death surrounded us.

"I know. I'll make it up to you."

"How?"

I nudged him. "Wait for it." Untangling our power, I formed small lightning bolts and contained them as they arced between my hands.

"Fae?" Ione snarled. Hackles shot up along the length of his back. "How'd he get here?"

It was the question of the hour, but one I lacked an answer to.

The door to our cramped quarters blew open, carried by a gust of magic. Interesting. This must be one of the stronger Fae. Usually, their White counterparts were the ones with the most magic.

Pinning him and draining his power was tempting, but I wanted information. He probably wouldn't volunteer jack, but I have ways of getting around that. Power poured from him, pelting Ione and me.

"Is that the best you can muster?" I asked. "Hell, blowing ice chunks were worse."

The Fae grunted and swept long white hair over broad shoulders. He was tall for his kind and naked from the waist up. Silver wings mottled with jewel tones were folded against his shoulders. His skin held a coppery tint, which was odd. Most of his kinsmen were fair to the point of looking bleached out. At least his pointed chin and sculpted cheekbones looked like they should. His legs were encased in khaki pants, and he wore shiny leather boots. Another oddity. All the Fae I've known have preferred to go barefoot. It amplifies their connection with the earth.

"You killed my beasties," he gritted and hurled more power our way. Had he figured out what I am? If he did, he'd have conserved his resources. Or maybe he already knew he was a dead mage.

I tried to place his accent and pegged him for one of Faery's residents. Even more curious. What in the hell was he doing here?

"Stand down." I infused command into my words. A shocked look crossed his face, eyes wide, fair eyebrows raised. But he dropped his hands and stared at me.

Yup. Thrall works extremely well, especially for those with weaker magic than mine, which is damn near everyone.

Ione padded closer, his amber eyes brimming with disgust. "What were you doing with those beasties?"

The Fae averted his silver eyes. Not many can stare Ione down and live to tell about it.

"Making them better," he mumbled.

I could play twenty questions, or I could hurry things up. He was the last loose end. Nothing alive stirred on the floors above. If I'd been feeling generous, I might have opted for something that wouldn't hurt him, but he was on his way out anyway.

Shaping a spell, I shoved it into his memories as I mined for all the details I could come up with. He groaned and grabbed his head. My estimation of him shot up a few notches. He wasn't squealing or begging for mercy.

Ione trotted through the door. Good. He'd check on the rest of the facility and make damn good and sure no one was left. Where there was one Fae, there might be others who'd been hidden to my probing.

I'd passed through surface layers and was trolling deeper. Once I was convinced I'd moved past his association with the Russians, I cut the connection. The Fae dropped to his knees, keening softly. He knew the jig was up. It was only a matter of how I chose to drain his power.

Not much shocks me, but this mess held a worrisome sophistication. "You violated our covenant," I shouted. The Fae didn't even bother to look up.

Ione was back, furry face twisted in disgust. "His beasties are unnatural monsters." He swiped a paw down the side of the Fae's face, leaving bloody tracks.

"I know. I saw everything in his mind," I told my bondmate. "Keep an eye on him. I'll have a look for myself, and then we'll blow this place up."

I hadn't planned on taking out the installation, but I wasn't about to leave the twisted specimens I figured I'd find above. A crafty scientist could probably harvest their DNA and save themselves a whole lot of steps recreating this Frankenstein's palace.

Crap. No wonder the Ruskies had denied all knowledge of the place. I hurried down a concrete corridor and up the first set of stairs I came to. The next floor up was one big room with cages of varying sizes. I'd picked up on the animals when I scanned. But I'd missed the hybrids because they didn't pigeonhole neatly into any categories.

How long had this project been underway? More importantly, was it the only one? The Russians were clearly breeding soldiers by splicing animal DNA in with human, with obvious advantages. They'd grow to fighting size in less than half the time humans took, and they'd have cunning and strength and more of an animal intelligence than a human one. It might mean warriors who obeyed without question.

Or not.

I'd seen things like this before, and the results usually backfired. Animals rely on instinct. Unlike men, they have principles. The comparison amused me, which was a relief after the bleakness of the lab. Draping everything that had protoplasm with the unmaking spell, I kindled it and watched bodies turn to dust.

To be on the safe side, I ran through the upper two floors. Other than dead bodies and a greenhouse, I didn't find anything noteworthy. On my way back to Ione and the Fae, I congratulated myself for making a sound decision. Frank and the troops wouldn't have added anything. This was definitely a one-man operation. The sounds of chewing reached me before I bolted back into the computer room. Ione was crouched over the Fae working on one of his legs.

"Time to go," I said cheerily.

The snow leopard offered a bloody grin and trotted to my side.

The Fae was clinging to life. I took pity on him and drilled a hole in his magic center. Brilliant light spilled into the dingy space as his essence bled out. This had almost been too easy, but then very little challenges me. It's a curse in a way. I'd really love to sink my teeth into a situation where the outcome's not a foregone conclusion.

"Why?" Ione asked once we were outside in what had turned into a raging blizzard.

I understood what he wanted to know. "They did those experiments to breed a race of warriors."

"Not fair to the animals."

"Not fair to anyone." I set a good pace. When we were a hundred yards away, I called on the sea. It's never far away on these Arctic islands. Its answer was instantaneous. Flowing through bedrock, it crashed upward through the remains of the Russian installation, annihilating it.

Being Poseidon's son has a few perks. That's one of them.

All in all, a good day's work.

"Still going to the villa?" Ione asked.

"I don't want to, but yes."

"Find me when you need me." My bondmate swiped my face with a bloody sandpaper tongue that smelled of Fae. Power sheeted from him, and he was gone. What we'd found had disturbed him enough he wanted to put space between himself and Ellesmere Island.

I girded myself to return to the ship. My first stop would be Frank, where I'd convince him our super-secret mission had been a total success. I'd have skipped it, but if I didn't do something, the team would suit up and show up.

And find the installation gone, a crater leading to the sea in its stead. Tough to explain shit like that.

First, I built a ward, and then I set a course for the ship and the corridor right outside Frank's quarters. Hopefully, he'd be there and not shooting the breeze with the Danes in the bar. I wouldn't bother mentioning the human experimentation side of the equation. Frank would run to his bosses in the CIA, and it would spawn an international incident. I'd stymied the DNA lab efforts for now; it would have to be good enough.

The cramped corridor formed around me. A sailor bumped into my shoulder and stumbled off mumbling about having had too much to drink. I waited until the corridor was empty. It took a while. In one fluid motion, I dropped my ward and knocked on Frank's door.

"Come."

I turned the latch and walked inside, miming a jaunty salute. "Mission accomplished."

"Huh?"

I tossed believe-me magic all over the place and said, "You know."

"Know what? For Christ's sake, spit it out, man."

I pushed the door shut. "The installation is gone. Very few were manning it. They're all dead. We can go home." I pushed more power his way, rearranging a few brain cells, and hoped for the best.

His mystified expression yielded to a broad grin. He high-fived me. Then he slapped me across the back. "Strong work. Find anything inside?"

"Nah. People. A greenhouse. Computers."

A sly look crossed his face. "We'll split the bonus."

If money mattered to me, I'd have stopped his heart for suggesting such a dick move. Lucky for him, it doesn't. "Generous of you," I mumbled and walked out of the cabin. Teleporting away from here was tempting, but I had to stick it out until we made port. I'd catch a flight from Reykjavik, and then I'd be free.

If I cared a twit about mortals, I'd have hunted for additional clone labs. I didn't. Let mortals solve their own damned problems.

One of the team ran toward me. "Frank gave us the good news. Come to the bar, man. We all want to buy you a drink."

Breath hissed from me. I hadn't expected Frank to finger

me, but then he was focused on the bonus, money that should rightfully be divided among the entire team. Maybe there'd be a way to guilt trip him into doing just that.

"On my way," I said. "Right after I change into something that doesn't stink of blood and cordite."

"Take your time," he said. "Booze will still be there."

Laughing, I ducked into my cabin and plotted how I could manipulate Frank into sharing the bounty.

❦   I   ❦

A *Village Near Rimini, Italy*

Distant laughter rumbled through alabaster walls. Or maybe it was thunder. Sometimes it's tough to sort these things out when I'm, shall we say, otherwise occupied. A bevy of Nereids fluttered about. One rubbed fragrant oil into my feet while another worked on my shoulders. The beat of their wings was hypnotic. Long hair brushed my skin as they moved this way and that.

The ones who weren't massaging me nipped and kissed and stroked. Being the center of this much attention was intoxicating. I'd started out standing, chasing this one and that, but they'd convinced me to lie on a low-slung bed.

They'd swept into my home a little while ago, giggling and purring. Usually, they wait until I've been here for a few days before showing up. Maybe they missed me. More likely, they were bored. Poseidon keeps a tight rein on his minions.

Something's been going on with him for a few years now.

He's always in a rotten mood. So much so, I've avoided contact. Out of all my homes, this is the only one near water, and I haven't been here often. It was why I'd shown up a few hours before. To check on the place and make certain the magic concealing its existence hadn't eroded.

Laughter sounded again, and the sea nymphs froze.

"We shouldn't be here," my foot savior trilled.

I roused myself enough to ask, "Why not?"

"Master likes us in the sea," another said in hushed tones.

"So, he's still in a snit?" I asked.

"Worse, if it's even possible," she murmured, sounding genuinely distressed. I extended a hand and smoothed violet hair away from her gamine face. I felt for them, but they didn't need my pity. A way out of their predicament would go a whole lot further than me feeling sorry for them.

I have power to burn, but separating the sea folk from their god was beyond even my skillset. Poseidon would sic the Kraken on me if I tried. Depending on how it shook out, he might even hound me himself. He can't kill me, but he could make me so miserable I longed for death.

The same laugh sounded again, except this time it sounded menacing. The Nereids clutched at one another, their attention on me forgotten. "The sea," one cried in shrill tones.

Breath rustled from my mouth. "The Adriatic is so close, you can see it from the window."

"Not the same." The shapely nymph who'd been massaging my shoulders muttered. "We love you, Kylian—" she began.

"Adore you," the others chimed in.

"But you're leaving, anyway," I growled about the time

they frittered to globs of sea foam splattered on the red tile floor.

Lying on my stomach, a nicely rigid member beneath me, I was beyond pissed. I'd had plans. Delectable, sensual ones. This group of nymphs could do amazing trade-offs with fingers, mouths, wings, and their bodies. We'd indulged in group play many times before. Poseidon always rebuked me sternly, made it clear the Nereids were off limits, but I don't answer to him.

The Nereids did, though. If I'd earned the rough side of his tongue, he'd probably flogged them. I clenched my fists. If I were god of the seas, I'd manage my people differently.

Big words. Who knew how anything would go? Maybe after a million years of ruling I'd be as sour and ill-tempered as my sire.

He was a part of my making, but only part. Mother was an elemental mage. I'm actually the reason the Celts decided to pull the plug on them. For gods, they're an insecure lot, but they're far from stupid. They understood a few mages like me would spell the end of their godhood. Tough to cling to the top dog spot if someone else runs magical rings around you.

Rolling to a sit, I stared at my cock. All my mental meanderings should have quashed its enthusiasm. No such luck. I reached for it, but my heart wasn't in a solo jerk-off session. I'd been enjoying the nymphs. Their briny scent lingered along with the pungent smells of sea flowers and coral.

I could walk to the village. Surely, one of the women would look appealing. My errant member throbbed happily. I told it to take a hike. A sensual romp with half a dozen nymphs held appeal. One on one with a mortal, not so much.

Eh, maybe next time.

I got back into tan cargo pants, scuffed boots, and a white linen shirt with full sleeves. A quick tour through the bathroom, where I splashed cool water on face and hands, reduced the carnal heat keeping my erection alive.

The mirror reminded me to resurrect the glamour that makes me look more human. Golden hair shaded to blonde. Bronze eyes turned a neutral blue. I shaved the stark edges off my pronounced cheekbones and square chin and added some stubble.

My cock pressed against the front of my trousers, still lobbying for a trip to the village. It's not as particular as I am. The Nereids would have been nice, but any port in a storm. A walk would reallocate my blood supply. I considered it while I glided to the kitchen to pour myself a glass of port.

I built this villa in the 1500s back when Poseidon and I were on better terms. Needless to say, it's been remodeled several times, but I've done all the work myself. The house, courtyard, and outer walls are concealed behind veils. Keeps mortals from stumbling in trying to sell me this, that, or the other thing. Also keeps squatters at bay. The lure of a perennially empty home would be tough to resist.

Like many homes in the area, this one is built of thick adobe walls. It's small. Beyond the living room, there's a kitchen, two bedrooms, and a bath. Because I prefer keeping things simple, everything is in natural tones. Whites, beiges, browns.

So far, I've avoided most of the scourges of civilization. Nothing electronic here. Hell, not even electricity to power the welter of devices everyone takes for granted. I do have running water, but it's cold.

I may have mentioned I'm not here all that often. Magic takes care of whatever I need when I am. My bondmate prefers cooler climes. Ione's pelt is so thick my fingers get lost in it. Italy isn't his cup of tea.

After a bit of sleight-of-hand where I moved food from a nearby corner market to my kitchen, I sliced ripe cheese, olives, and fresh bread onto a board. I'd just taken it and my port outside to a veranda overlooking the sea when Poseidon's head broke through the surf.

He threaded his way through people dotting the busy beach. No one even noticed his passing. I could have summoned a travel spell and left. Plenty of time to finesse it. He might be pissed enough to follow me, but his power degrades quickly when he leaves the sea.

Thanks be to all the gods I didn't inherit that little flaw.

Better to stick around and determine what he wanted. Running from problems isn't my style. All it does is put them off and give them an opportunity to grow into even bigger complications. You'd think we'd be friendlier, him and me, but he's not close to anyone I know of. Except the Kraken, a brain-damaged heap of scales that can scarcely cobble two thoughts together.

I put a lid on my opinions and spun a ward around my mind. Daddy-O was already angry. No percentage in stoking the flames by projecting ill will toward his pet. I had a few minutes to kill, so I grabbed another glass and filled it.

I'd offer food and drink but didn't expect him to eat with me. If nothing had changed, he ate alone after food had been sampled by a phalanx of tasters. For some reason, he was paranoid about being poisoned. My suspicion was it had already happened and was unpleasant enough he wanted to avoid a replay.

Poseidon sprang from the beach to the veranda, clearing the rail handily. He always looks the same. I suppose I inherited my height and broad-shouldered build from him. Tall with a full head of silver hair that spilled to his knees, he was handsome in an imperious sort of way. Essential to his power, a trident staff was held loosely in one hand. He's always favored robes. Today's was black sashed in white with embroidered tridents.

I flapped a hand at the chair across from mine. "Take a load off. I poured you a drink."

A grimace distorted his even features, and he skewered me with dark-blue eyes. "Must you spew modern phrases? Take a load off? You can do better than that, Kylian."

I shrugged. "You knew what I meant. Isn't that the whole point of verbal discourse?" He perched on the edge of a chair, and I decided to hurry things along. "To what do I owe the pleasure?"

"As if you need to ask. I've told you to leave my Nereids alone."

I shrugged again and adopted a salacious leer. "Is that all? They came to me."

"You could have chased them off."

"Why would I want to do that?" I held up a hand. "That's not why you're here. What is?"

My words earned me a grudging smile. "Occasionally, I'm proud to call you mine."

I ground my teeth and corralled an urge to punch him square in his patrician nose. "Only occasionally?"

"It happens I do have a small favor to ask." He tried to spread out the smile, but it made him appear grotesque.

"I'm really busy," I began.

"Then what are you doing cavorting with the Nereids?"

My temper has never taken much prodding without exploding. I banged a fist on the table and hissed, "I told you. They came to me. Why is me leaving them alone so all-fired important?"

Rather than answering me, he glanced around. "Where is that cat of yours?"

Breath streamed from between my teeth. "You are damned lucky Ione isn't here. He'd take exception to being called that cat of mine."

"Where is he?" Poseidon pressed.

"Somewhere the climate suits him better."

"Since you insisted on bonding with an animal, why not a dolphin or a whale?"

So much for being pleasant. I shot to my feet. "We've had this conversation so many times I've lost count. Tell me why you're here so you can leave."

"A wee bit on the rude side. And to your own father."

"It takes more than sperm to be a father," I growled.

"How would you know?"

My hands were balled into fists; I turned away and struggled to get hold of myself. I shouldn't let him get to me, but he does. Every. Single. Time.

When I faced him again, I repeated, "What is this small favor?"

Apparently tired of sparring with me, he nodded. "Do you remember Rhiana?"

I had to muck around in my memory to come up with an attractive elemental mage. "Aye. I remember her. Why?"

"Her unicorn tried to kill the Kraken. I want you to find them both and bring them to me."

I frowned. Rhiana was old, seasoned. An unprovoked attack seemed very unlikely. "What did the Kraken do to them?" I dropped a truth spell over Poseidon.

He flinched but didn't waste power cutting through it. "I'd asked Rhiana to do something for me. She refused."

"So you sent the Kraken to convince her, and she and her bondmate fought back." At Poseidon's nod, I went on. "Do your own dirty work."

"You know I can't travel far from the sea."

"How is that my problem?" I unclenched my fists. "Send someone else, like the Kraken."

Poseidon lifted his upper lip and showed me his teeth.

I smiled sourly. "See? That's precisely why I'm not bonded to a creature who can't operate outside of the sea."

He picked up the glass I'd poured for him and drained it, muttering to himself. I couldn't make anything out, but I didn't try very hard. After pushing to his feet, he asked, "Do you remember Ciara?"

I didn't have to search through my memories for her. With her fair coloring and Valkyrie build, she was quite the attraction. Nodding, I said, "Why?"

"She's missing. Perhaps you could keep an eye out for her."

"Have you checked with the sea witch? They used to be close." I winced. Poor choice of words since no one was close to the witch. She and Ciara had both killed for Poseidon, though.

"If you see her, bring her back."

A pattern was emerging. If I mentioned it, I'd really piss him off but I didn't care. "Having trouble keeping track of folks lately?" I inquired sweetly.

"Ciara is mine," he gritted.

"Probably not the way she sees it," I retorted.

"I'll allow the Nereids to return if you find her." A sly tone had crept into his voice.

"Fine. Send them back right now. They're terrified of you. What the hell have you done to them?"

He stood, drawing himself up tall. "They are not terrified of me."

"Yeah. They are." I made a show of glancing about. "Where are they?"

"Bring me Ciara, and you can spend as much time with them as you want." A satisfied cant to his chin suggested he was confident he'd zeroed in on a bargaining chip. One that would bring me to heel.

Not likely. I knew where Ciara was. And I could find Rhiana if I set my mind to it. Elemental mages can always locate one another. But I'd be damned if I'd be party to his petty games.

I poured more port into my glass and waggled the bottle in his direction. He shook his head. After I'd taken a long swallow, savoring the piquant brew, I walked closer to him and kept my voice soft.

"I don't expect you to change, but you've turned alienating people into an art form. Rhiana tried to tell you she wasn't interested in your proposal. You sent the Kraken after her. If Ciara is gone, and it appears you believe her absence is permanent, she had reasons for leaving."

I paused for emphasis before saying, "You have to respect both of them."

"What about them respecting me?" he blustered.

I didn't have an answer. Everything wasn't always about him, but he'd never understand. "If I run across either woman, I will mention our conversation. What I won't do is ensorcel them and drag them into the sea against their will."

"But you kill for sport." He hooded his eyes but didn't take them off me.

I shook my head. "Wrong. I select assignments that appeal to me. When I kill, it's to take a bite out of evil. I've never been Grigori's errand boy, and I sure as hell am not going to be yours."

"Speaking of the werewolf. How is he?"

"Not sure. I haven't been back there in a while."

"So you're freelancing?" The sly note was back.

"You might say so." I girded myself for his next shot out of the box.

"Why not work for me? I pay as well as anyone."

"It's not about money. Or Nereids. Were you listening when I mentioned being selective about the jobs I take on? Besides, Ione has to agree."

"The cat has always liked me." Poseidon smirked.

I bit my tongue. Nothing could be further from the truth. My snow leopard loathed Poseidon. Telling him as much would accomplish nothing, though.

I drank the last of the port and stood facing the god of the sea. "Fresh out of conversation," I told him, hoping he'd take the hint and leave. He didn't, but the self-absorbed are like that. Ultra-sensitive when the ox that's gored belongs to them; totally oblivious if it's someone else's.

After a few minutes dribbled by, I tried again. "I need to get moving."

"Didn't you just arrive?"

"Yes, but I hadn't planned on staying." I considered asking about the Nereids again, but I didn't want to be in his debt. For anything.

"Come to dinner tonight. We can discuss these matters at our leisure."

Before I responded, he sketched a glowing blue portal, walked through it, and was gone. He hadn't wanted an answer. Hadn't expected one. His parting invitation was a way for him to save face, to pretend we laid claim to a normal relationship. He didn't expect me at the underwater palace this evening.

Good thing because I'd be long gone by then.

He also had no intention of sending the Nereids back, but it didn't matter. I didn't want them that way. Having them mob me was a carnal treat. If they showed up because Poseidon ordered them to service me, our playtime would have an entirely different feel.

I carted the glasses inside and rinsed them before putting them back in a cupboard. The illusion keeping the villa hidden was intact. No more reason to remain—except I was still here.

One of the benefits of my mixed parentage is a double helping of sea magic. Nothing like water to reveal mysteries. Running on autopilot and sheer instinct, I wove watery enchantment into a scrying spell and filled the kitchen sink with water, shaping it to my needs.

Until I began, I didn't realize what was driving me. If I had, I might have directed the same power at getting the fuck out of Italy. Reading the past is simple enough. It's already happened. Interpreting the future is far more difficult. Various events flirt with one another. It takes skill and practice to determine which ones will actually come to pass.

Imagery came alive beneath the surface of my impromptu pool. The questions driving my vision all revolved around Poseidon and what the future held for him. I wanted to know if his downhill slide would be permanent, or if he'd somehow pull out of his self-imposed tailspin.

I've never scryed anything about my sire. It's always felt too personal, too close to home, like I was snooping where I didn't belong. Compunctions be damned. I should have been more vigilant. Shock riddled me. A hail of bullets opened my eyes to what should have been obvious if I'd taken the time to read the signs rather than making one excuse after the next.

Sweat dripped down my sides, and I was breathing hard when I cut the flow of power to my vision. Even so, it took a while before the water was nothing but water again. At least I understood what had to happen next. I'd find Ione, and we'd head straight for the nearest Circle of Assassins guild house. They'd know where Grigori was, and I had to talk with him.

Warn him what was about to come down all around him and his mages.

I didn't entertain even a fleeting thought about misplaced loyalties. Some would insist Poseidon was my blood and therefore deserving of unquestioning allegiance. I disagree. Vehemently. Blood or not, he'd signed a pact with evil. How could I have been so blind?

Worse, why didn't I ask more questions?

Did the Kraken know? The beast didn't have many scruples, but even it wouldn't willingly be a party to what Poseidon was embroiled in.

I fine-tuned my travel spell and kicked myself for not pulling a jacket out of my closet in the villa I'd just vacated. Power can be redirected to keep me warm, but it's magic that isn't available in case I run into something unexpected.

An unending vista of white glistened around me. I must be more agitated than I thought to have arrived here to quickly. I shouted for Ione in telepathy and hoped I'd guessed right. The Ross Ice Shelf was one of the snow leopard's favorite hunting grounds. I've argued it's scarcely fair to kill penguins. They have no ability to protect themselves. At least seals fight back.

But Ione adores penguin meat. His justification is there are so many, no one would ever miss a few. When I mentioned those birds had mothers and fathers and other relatives, all I got was a growl for my feeble attempt at compassion.

Yeah, not one of my stronger suits.

My spell dissipated leaving me in the center of an unbroken vista of snow and ice. No trees here, nothing to cut the wind. I wrapped myself in a magical cocoon before I started to shiver.

I yelled for Ione again, and then launched a seeking spell. No reason to remain if he was elsewhere. If this didn't pan out, I'd track him through our bond. Meanwhile, time was drizzling through the glass. Some of the horrors I'd seen in my kitchen sink could have already come to pass.

Was Grigori still alive?

If he'd been forced over the veil because of something my sire had done, I'd dig until I found a way to end him. Maybe one of the Celts would help. Poseidon didn't have many friends among his peers. They'd been furious he'd lain with my mother. To their way of thinking, he should have known better than to create powerful offspring.

Those arguments had peppered my childhood. I remembered some of them vividly, mostly because I'd been afraid the Celts were going to snatch me up and drop me into a pit on a distant world. Mother apparently thought the same because she'd taken me and hidden us away until I came into my own, my magic on a par with anyone's.

I added juice to my seeking spell. If I didn't find Ione in the next five minutes, I was out of here. Finally, a weak ping vibrated against my casting. Waiting for him to come to me would burn up time I didn't have, so I took off at a dead run and welcomed the heat of blood pumping through my muscles. Like many of the bond animals, Ione is much larger than other snow leopards. With his ivory pelt and black markings, he's beauty incarnate.

Impossible to miss racing toward me, he grew larger by the moment. He'd been feeding. Something black hung from his jaws. Seal blubber if I'm any judge. At least it wasn't feathers. Eh, for all I knew, the seal was dessert.

We collided, and I wrapped my arms around his neck. Heat from his study body warmed me. Aiming his amber gaze my way, he dropped the partially dismembered seal in front of us, and said, "Thought you'd be gone longer. Whatever this is must be important."

My bondmate knew me all too well. "It is," I replied. "We have to leave now."

"Are you going to tell me where we're going?"

"Once we're on our way. Are you ready?"

He snatched up his kill in powerful jaws and stood by my side. I built a spell to move us to the primary guild house. It was located off world and would take a while to get to.

"Why are we going there?" Ione switched to telepathy since he was eating.

I started at the beginning and told him about Poseidon's visit. "Anyway," I went on, "I've always trusted my instincts. They were screaming at me to scry Poseidon's future."

"Found something you didn't care for, eh?"

Talk about understatements. "You might say so."

Ione swallowed the last of the seal meat. "Before you start on that, why did your sire want you to go after Rhiana and Ciara?"

"Don't forget Dorcha, the unicorn," I mumbled sourly.

"Was it revenge?" Ione sidestepped my snarky comment, probably since the unicorn was unforgettable. "How about Ciara's bondmate? Did Poseidon mention the eagle?"

"He did not. I'm guessing he has no idea Ciara is part of the Circle of Assassins. When she left the sea, she didn't have a bondmate."

Ione growled low. The bond animals stuck together, and he was probably feeling protective of both unicorn and eagle.

"I suspect he's plotting revenge, yes." I answered.

"We haven't been to a guild house for a long while," Ione observed.

It was true. Ciara was newly arrived and just getting to know her eagle the last time I'd stopped in. Grigori hadn't seemed to need us, so we'd left and pissed away the next eighty years or so visiting borderworlds. And getting sucked into other people's wars.

"We're looking for Grigori," I told Ione. "There's a serious plot against him, and Poseidon is in it up to his neck."

The snow leopard growled again. Hackles fluffed up around his neck. "Who else?"

"Satan. Demons. And a surprising number of disgruntled mages."

The growling intensified. "Not fond of the Kraken, but I can't envision him siding with Satan—not even on a bad day."

Same impression I'd had. Maybe we'd hunt him down. He might turn into an unlikely ally.

"Why Grigori?" Ione asked. With his hackles still furled, he looked like a lion.

"Sorry. I wasn't clear. It's the Circle they're after, assumption being if they disable Grigori, the Circle will crumple."

"Is he all right?"

I screwed my face into a grimace. "No idea."

"We shouldn't have stayed gone for so long. Pack is everything."

"Now you sound like a wolf."

"It's true," he insisted.

I crouched next to him and threaded a hand into his rough outer coat. Beneath was fluff that had always reminded me of a sheep, but I've never told him that. They're his second favorite meal after penguins.

We passed the remainder of my travel junket in companionable silence. Nothing I could do to hurry the transit. I've never waited well. This was no exception. When the spell dropped us into a familiar courtyard, afternoon was ceding to evening. I rolled to my feet and sent power in an arc to determine if Grigori was there.

He saved me the trouble of an extensive hunt and bounded down the steps with a female werewolf by his side. "Kylian," he boomed. "Welcome home."

About my height with flame-red hair streaming down his back and blue eyes, he moved with the grace of his wolf. Dark trousers, a white shirt, and battered leather boots hung off his muscled frame.

Relief streamed through me. I wasn't too late. Clasping his extended hand, I shook it hard. I'd never viewed the Circle as my home, but it warmed me to hear him greet me in that fashion.

The female werewolf knelt in front of Ione. Dressed in jeans and a multicolored sweater, she'd clearly been turned later than most. Medium height with gray-streaked blonde hair, she had hazel eyes that sparkled with curiosity. "You are so beautiful," she crooned to Ione. "I'm Rhea. May I touch you?"

The snow leopard purred and leaned into her hands. His read on mages is impeccable. I took it to mean the woman met muster. Behind them both, her werewolf flickered into a soft outline.

Grigori smiled at the tableau of werewolf and snow leopard. "Rhea joined us recently," he told me. "She literally saved my life."

Crap. He'd already run into problems. I wasn't as on top of the trouble as I'd hoped. "What happened?" I asked.

"You first." Grigori made a come-along gesture with one hand.

I started to build a sound shield, but he shook his head. "We'll go to the grove. It's more private."

"Are you good here?" I asked Ione.

Still purring up a storm as Rhea scratched behind his ears, the big cat nodded.

"She'll take good care of him," Grigori assured me and set off at a brisk trot for a place I knew well. A grove of white oak trees linked to his magic came into view. We slipped into the center, and he turned to face me. "You've been gone a long while," he said. "Whatever brings you here must be important."

"It is." I sketched out the bones of my scrying session, ending with, "I was concerned I'd be too late."

"Too late is relative," he said with the same understated humor I remembered. "I've fielded two attempts on my life, but as you can see, I'm still here."

"Your people love you."

He dropped his bantering tone. "You used to be part of the Circle. What happened?"

It was a serious question and deserving of something other than me blowing him off. "I honestly don't know," I said slowly. "When I left initially, I told myself it was to hone my seer skills."

"And?"

"Spent a few years doing that. And another few years doing other things. Nothing satisfied me."

"And your bondmate?"

"He's fine. Sometimes we're together. Sometimes not."

"Does he ever talk about missing the other bond animals?"

The question took me by surprise. "No, but he's not one to complain."

Grigori nodded. "He's in the same boat as Aidyrth and Dorcha."

"No, he isn't. They can find other dragons and unicorns. Ione is the only magical snow leopard."

Grigori raised a russet brow. "Are you certain of that?"

"No, but we've never run across any others."

"It's off topic, but remind me how you and he selected each other." Grigori made a wry face. "You were together when I vetted you for the Circle, but I'm not remembering exactly how it happened. The first time they tried to kill me, they targeted the virus that makes me a werewolf. My memory still has a few holes, but they're filling in with time."

I leaned against a generous tree bole, appalled by his disclosure. Who would stoop so low? If they'd been successful, he would have lost his wolf and died in agony.

"Kylian?" Grigori prodded, reminding me he'd asked a question.

He wasn't angling for sympathy, so I didn't offer any. I'm not good at cooing over people, anyway. After clearing my throat, I said, "You didn't forget because you never knew about Ione. No one does except Mother." A ripple of guilt tracked up my spine. Grigori wasn't the only one I'd given short shrift to. I'm not much of a social critter when you cut to the meat of things. It was another reason I'd left the Circle. Being alone appeals to me.

"Thanks," he murmured. "Makes me feel better, but I still want to know."

"Remember all the years the Celts argued both sides of the coin? To make more elemental mages or not?"

Grigori nodded. "How could I forget?"

"I was at the center of that controversy."

His eyebrows shot up. "How so?"

"They may have been thinking about pulling the plug for a while, but I was the lynchpin that clinched things." I shrugged. "Too much power concentrated in one mage annoyed them."

"Worried is the word you want. Not annoyed. How does this circle back to Ione?"

His question made me smile. Grigori was a good one for remaining on point. "Getting there," I said and continued, "I was young. Still in my first hundred years. The other elemental mages blamed me for the Celts' threats. One day, Mother plopped down from a lengthy absence with Ione by her side. Each type of bond animal, including shifters, have special places. Mother knew them all. She used to spin me tales of enchanted forests and magical vistas where they lived."

"She brought the leopard as a companion for you."

I nodded agreement. "She did since I'd turned into quite the pariah. He was young too, barely past kittenhood. Because she'd selected him, he was a perfect match for my magic."

I hesitated before adding, "We grew up together, he and I."

"Have you kept in contact with your mother?"

Something about Grigori's attention flagged my attention. "'Fraid not. Why?"

"Talk with Rhiana and Quinn and Ciara. We've battled elemental mages. Many crossed over."

I straightened from where I was slumped against a tree. "Crossed over as in died? Or joined Satan's army?"

"Both." Grigori bit off the word. "If they hadn't been part of the evil arrayed against us, we'd never have fought them."

The guilt that had pricked me earlier turned into a storm of sharp javelins. "How long ago?"

"Not long. If you need to see if she's still alive, I understand."

I shook my head. "She left Earth with a group of others like her. I wasn't welcome in their midst. Nothing's changed, and—"

"Aye, much has changed," Grigori cut in. "Only a handful

are left. They have bigger problems than blaming you for their downfall."

"Mother offered to remain behind with me. I wouldn't allow her to make such a gargantuan sacrifice. She encouraged me to visit. Both of us knew I never would. Too awkward. That part is the same." My jaw muscles tightened.

"People change," Grigori insisted.

I'd been studying a point somewhere to the left of his shoulders, but I swung my gaze to meet his. "If they joined Satan and his ilk, they did more than change. They lost their fucking minds."

"Poseidon was always a self-absorbed jerk, but I'd never have envisioned him taking up with evil, either." Grigori's tone was neutral.

"What have you done to retaliate?" I scooted past his all-too-accurate assessment of my sire.

"Dropped several bombs in Hell. Fought a few battles. Rhiana wasn't looking for other elemental mages. They found her and tried to hang onto her and Dorcha."

"Bet that didn't go over well." An image of Dorcha, a coal-black unicorn, rearing and bringing her hoofs down on a hapless victim made me smile. The bond animals are bloodthirsty and relentless. It's an honor to have Ione by my side—most of the time. He can be contrary and strong-willed, but then so can I.

"It gets deeper," Grigori said cheerfully. "Dorcha gored the Kraken."

"Aye. I know. It's why Father wanted me to run her and Rhiana to ground, truss them up, and deliver them. He was asking after Ciana too."

"She knows he's upped the fight to retrieve her. Rhiana

delivered that bit of news, but he'll never find her. The White Fae and I cooked up a spell to cloak her blood."

"Good. Any other skirmishes you didn't mention?"

"Aye. We put the word out I was sinking. It was soon enough after the second attack to be believable."

My ears perked up. "Did it work? Did they spring the trap?"

"They did, and we killed them all. It was only a few days ago. My guess is they'll be a while regrouping."

"Gives us planning time." I rubbed my palms together in anticipation. Planning destruction is almost as satisfying as meting it out.

"Us?" Grigori arched both brows. "Does that mean you and Ione are staying?"

"It does."

Grigori adopted a formal tone. "Your vows to the Circle still apply."

"Why wouldn't they? Blood oaths never expire." I flinched inwardly. I hadn't exactly always put the Circle first, but I had guarded its secrets. I'd never lifted power against anyone within its folds, either.

Magic swirled around me, moving nearer until I breathed in the clean forest scent unique to werewolves. I recognized the spell. Grigori was refreshing my linkage to both him and the Circle mages.

A sense of peace descended. I hadn't expected to feel any different, but I did. "Settle in," Grigori suggested. "Renew old acquaintances. I'll see you at dinner."

"Thank you."

He'd started out of the grove but glanced over a shoulder. "For what?"

"Keeping the hearth fires burning. It's good to have a home to come back to even if I didn't understand I needed one."

"You have other homes," he pointed out.

"All of them are empty." I pushed my shoulders back. "I'd convinced myself I preferred solitude, but maybe I was mistaken."

He grinned. "The guild houses can be overwhelming with competing magic and energy at cross-purposes, but the best thing I've ever done was forming the Circle. Sometimes on bad days, I remind myself of the alternatives."

"Such as no Circle? No roving bands of bond animals? No mages arguing among themselves?" I tossed out.

"Something like that. See you at supper." A black-and-silver wolf stood in his stead. After fluffing out his tail, he loped away.

Night had fallen. Stars dotted the midnight sky. I lingered in the grove for a while before setting a path for the guild house. Ione was hunting with two wolves, two eagles, and a hawk. From the sound of things, he was having a grand time.

I still had doubts about how easily I'd slip back into communal life with other magic-wielders, but I quashed them. My freelance days were over—for now. Once the Circle was safe, and her enemies dispatched, I'd regroup.

Power is a harsh mistress and fate a fickle bitch. I'd been caught in the crossfire many times, but for now, I was where I needed to be. I'd damn well jump into the deep end and make this work.

Even after my rah-rah pep talk, I lingered in the small room I'd selected. In a corner, on the top floor, its coved ceiling was tucked under the eaves. After cursing myself for being a coward, I pushed out the door and wended toward the mouthwatering smells of dinner. Seafood casserole if I was any judge, in a dill-laced cream sauce with fresh bread and probably potatoes or rice.

I've always been unique with my combination of two disparate magics. Plenty of other blends in mage-land. Fae-Sidhe mixes are common. And Druids do their damnedest to mate with those more powerful to enhance their ability.

Because my sire is a god, I've never exactly fit in anywhere, but some of that could be me assuming the worst and running with it. I've welcomed confrontation—but not from others working the good sides of power. To be fair, the only ill-wishes directed my way from that quarter came from Mother's kinsmen.

I didn't blame them. If the tables were turned, I'd have shunned me too.

Striding through empty hallways to the nearest staircase, I soaked in the spartan feel of the guild house. Grigori has never been one for overdoing decorations, and I'm with him. They have no place in a warriors' hall.

The dining room was on the main floor. Hoping to slip in unnoticed was unrealistic. Impossible once I discovered Ione was already there crouched over a trencher of raw something or other. Dorcha and a couple of wolves were sharing the bounty.

Cries of, "Kylian!" rang in my ears. I raised a hand in greeting, mildly embarrassed by the attention. Ione glanced up from his meal long enough to wink broadly with one amber eye, its vertical slit pupil narrow in the brightly lit chamber.

Grigori was on his feet. He motioned me to a table with him, the female werewolf, another male werewolf, and Rhiana. She rose, dark hair tumbling to waist level, and hugged me once I was near.

"Good to see you," she said.

"You as well," I returned her greeting.

The male werewolf got to his feet and extended a hand. "Xander. Nice to meet you, Kylian." With close-cropped silver hair, he projected an old-world elegance. Odd eyes, one blue, the other green crinkled at their corners when he smiled at me.

I took his hand before settling into one of two empty seats. Faeries rustled in from the kitchen and laid full plates in front of me. I remembered meals being buffet style.

Perhaps most of them still were. I selected a crisp white wine to complement the fish.

"Been growing the werewolf contingent?" I asked Grigori. For all the years of the Circle's existence, he'd been the only one, and now it appeared there were three.

"Not on purpose." Grigori chuckled.

"I showed up under my own steam," Xander explained.

"Grigori rescued me," Rhea said. "Taught me how to manage my power and get along with my wolf."

I set my wine glass down. "Are newly bonded werewolves no longer teaching the mortal portion what they need to know?"

"Long story," Grigori answered.

"Not in my case," Rhea murmured. "I was shanghaied. The pack nearly killed me before the wolf bite part."

I glanced from Grigori to Xander, confused, but not willing to come out and say what I was thinking, which was werewolves must have fallen a long way to turn the unwilling.

"We fixed the problem," Xander cut in smoothly. "It's been brought to the attention of the werewolf council, and it won't happen again."

"My wolf's pack had been banished," Rhea explained, "but they snuck back. Guess they didn't think the rules applied to them."

I'd started in on my meal. As usual, the food here was exquisitely prepared. What a nice break from eating cold cuts, raw kill, or takeout. A few surreptitious glances revealed familiar faces and others I didn't know. Probably some had been part of the Circle, but I'd never stuck around long enough to get to know many of my fellows.

"Do you suppose we caught a break?" Rhiana asked.

"Not much of one," Grigori replied. "If you two had stayed gone much longer, I'd have sent someone after you."

Hmmm. You two must mean her and Xander. "Where were you?" I asked.

Rhiana's fair skin developed a rosy tinge. "North of Lake Baikal with Xander's pack. He's their alpha, and I'm, um, I'm his mate."

I'm good at hiding my reactions. Not this time. I looked from one to the other, dumbfounded. "But you're not a werewolf," I blurted followed by, "Eh, never mind. Wishing you much happiness."

Rhiana grinned. "I expected his pack to draw and quarter me. Instead, they welcomed me, made me feel at home."

"Because they'd given up on Xander ever mating. With anyone," Grigori rumbled.

Rhea had her hand on his arm. They were a couple as well, and I hadn't even noticed. I must be slipping. Badly. "Any other happily mated pairs since I left?" I tried for a bantering tone and almost made it stick. Grigori knows me as well as anyone, though.

He sent a pointed look my way. "Interesting question."

I met his gaze and waited for an answer. During my brief stints at guild houses, sex had been an occasional event, and there'd been a handful of committed couples, trios, and quads. Emphasis on handful. Most drifted apart after a few decades.

"Quinn and Ciara," Rhiana answered for Grigori. "And Shira and Jake."

"Should I know those last two?" I asked.

"No. Shira is Aidyrth's new bondmate, and she recruited Jake."

My turn to smile. "A wee bit on the self-serving side."

"You don't know her," Grigori said.

A tall woman with pink-and-purple hair glided to our table. "Thought I heard my name." She focused her attention on me, and her eyebrows shot up. "Whoa. The sea god and an elemental mage. Shit, you must run rings around us all."

"Take my chair," Grigori suggested and got to his feet. "Time to take advantage of everyone being in one spot." He turned and strode toward the front of the room.

"Do you mind?" Shira asked before she slid into the vacant chair.

A powerfully built dark-haired man dragged another chair next to her. Must be Jake. His magic wasn't anything to write home about, but he carried himself as if he owned the world. Believing in yourself is over half the battle. What he lacked in raw ability, he made up for with sheer confidence.

So long as I was checking out my tablemates, Xander had power to burn but made a conscious effort to conceal the extent of his talent.

Grigori clapped his hands together, and everyone fell silent, waiting for him to speak. "Two weeks have elapsed since the battle we fought here," he began. "We must strike again soon. No reason to offer them more time to rise against us. Kylian has returned with news."

He gestured, and I hurried to his side. I hadn't expected to say anything, but I'd figure it out. "For those of you who don't know," I began, "Poseidon sired me. He's never been a father in any way, and he views me the same way as his other minions."

"Which is to say inconsequential," Grigori spoke up.

"Or worse," I agreed and forged ahead. "I was checking on

a villa I keep near the Adriatic. A few Nereids joined me. Since he believes he owns them too, he chased them off and showed up to berate me. When that didn't gain him anything, he tossed assignments about. I refused him. Once he was gone, something lit a fire under me, and I scryed his future.

"My seer ability is solid, and he's part of the group working to end the Circle." I blew out a breath, and then another. "In Poseidon's mind, I'm certain he believes he's in charge."

"News to Satan," someone called from the center of the room.

"Ya think?" someone else tossed out.

Rhianna stood. "We had our suspicions about him," she said in a clear, ringing voice. "Good to have them corroborated."

"Anything to add?" Grigori asked me.

I shook my head and jumped down from the dais intent on returning to the remains of my meal.

"We will split into several teams," Grigori said. "Similar to our previous skirmishes, the objective is to get in, exact maximum damage, and exit as quickly as possible. One contingent will take on Poseidon. Kylian will head up that group, along with Rhiana, Quinn, and Ciara."

"But he's looking for her," Quinn protested.

"I say let him find me." Ciara's fair good looks took on savage overtones. "I'm a sea mage. My power is better suited to this assignment than anyone's. Except maybe Kylian's."

Grigori rattled off five more teams, pinpointing assignments. Jake and Shira left. Quinn and Ciara joined us. Small talk at our table changed to strategizing. I assumed we'd leave right away, or not later than the following morning. No reason to put things off. Ione and Dorcha ambled over with eagles perched on their backs. The unicorn's appearance was timely because I had a question for her.

"You gored the Kraken?"

She whinnied enthusiastically. "I could have killed him."

"Looks like you'll get a second chance," Rhiana told her bondmate.

"I'd like to explore another avenue," I told the group. "The Kraken isn't overly bright, but he was never evil."

"The same could be said about Poseidon," Rhiana pointed out, followed by, "Sorry, no offense meant."

"None taken. I'm not under any illusions about him, and I agree with your assessment."

"What's your idea about the Kraken?" Xander asked.

I assumed he was coming with us, which worked for me. Old werewolves are strong magically, and their power is a good complement to mine. "One of us—probably me—will talk with him, explore how much he knows about his master's new affiliation."

"How could he not know?" Quinn demanded.

"It would be simple to hide things from him," Rhiana pointed out.

"Rather than speculate, I'll find out," I said.

"What if he doesn't know?" Xander pressed.

A corner of my mouth twitched downward. "Then I'll try to recruit him to help us. He's a logical choice to lure Poseidon, and he's strong enough to imprison him. No one has ever escaped from Poseidon's dungeon."

"I like it," Quinn growled.

"Which part?" Ciara nudged him.

"The poetic justice part where he's hoisted by his own petard."

She snickered. "I love it when you talk dirty to me."

The smaller of the eagles squawked and moved from Ione's back to her shoulders.

"This is where Ione and I will be." I sent coordinates telepathically. "We'll leave as soon as we break for the night. Join us in a few hours."

"How many?" Xander gazed at me out of his bicolor eyes.

I thought about it. "Six. It should be enough."

"How do you know the Kraken will be near enough to interrogate?" Ciara asked.

"Because he's never far from his master, and I just left there."

"One of us should accompany you," Quinn said. "Probably me. Ciara is too big a distraction."

"He's on the warpath over Dorcha and me too," Rhiana muttered.

"I should go," Xander said.

I nodded agreement. "Sorry, Quinn, but the werewolf is right. His power is different enough from ours, it could make a difference if I'm wrong about the Kraken and he turns on us." I paused before adding, "Full disclosure. He's never cared for me."

"He doesn't like anyone," Ciara mumbled.

"I get along with him," Ione purred. "I've brought him fish."

"Really? You're chock-full of surprises," I told him.

The snow leopard snarled. "He had it in for me when I was small, so I gave him reasons to leave me be."

"A regular ambassador of goodwill." Xander nodded approvingly.

I voted with Xander's assessment. Ione had never mentioned word one about the Kraken making his life miserable. Instead, he'd quietly dealt with the problem. It made me wonder how many other issues he'd quelled without bothering to let me know.

"Not much love lost between Poseidon and his minions," I said. "Mostly, they do what he wants our of fear of retribution if they don't."

"So, if we knock him out of the game, the sea folk won't be a threat." Ciara finished my thought for me.

"They never were," I agreed. "Mostly, all they want is to be left alone and for humans to quit pumping poison into the oceans."

"I resisted leaving for the longest time," Ciara murmured. "Until finally one day I'd had enough."

"You lasted longer than I did, by centuries," I told her. Turning to Xander, I asked, "When can you be ready to depart?"

"Anytime."

"My villa, the location I gave as our meeting place, is invisible to mortals," I told everyone. "No need to ward yourselves."

"Will we have problems getting inside?" Ciara asked.

"No because I'll dismantle my protections." I got to my feet, told Xander we'd meet him in the courtyard, and left with Ione padding by my side. The big cat's energy was welcome, and he was itching to be gone.

I sketched the bones of a transport spell. Xander stepped

into it, and we were on our way. "Thanks for volunteering," I said.

"Not exactly a leap of faith," he replied. "Your power is pure."

He stopped there, but I read between the lines and added, "Despite my parentage?"

"No one is responsible for who sired them. We face enough enemies. No need to create more where they don't exist."

"It's good to be back." Ione's words came out of left field, but then I remembered Grigori's question about whether the leopard had missed the other bond animals.

"It is," I agreed.

Xander cocked his head to one side. "Were you expecting otherwise?"

"Not sure I carried any expectations, but I had to let Grigori know what I'd unearthed. Turns out he already knew —or suspected—everything."

"Are you sorry you didn't save yourself a trip?"

I narrowed my eyes. Xander didn't miss much since the thought had crossed my mind. "No, not exactly." I left it at that, and he didn't pry.

"Once we get there, I'll go after the Kraken right away," Ione said.

"I should be close, somewhere in the background," I told my bondmate.

"Not necessary." Ione swished his tail.

"Probably not, but it's nonnegotiable."

"We'll build a ward," Xander said. "If my magic is primary, perhaps the Kraken won't notice it."

I didn't agree. Werewolf enchantment would stick out like

boxes of ammo in a candy store. Rather than alienate Xander, I replied, "Wards aren't all that effective in the sea. If we merge with a pod of Nereids, their energy can serve as a shield to confuse the Kraken."

A series of images of a deserted beach surrounded by sandstone cliffs spilled through my mind. "What are these?" I asked my bondmate.

"Where I used to meet him. I will go there and catch fish."

"What makes you think he'll show up?" Xander rumbled in his deep voice.

"He always has."

I drew my brows together. "This fish project of yours. It extended long after the time he tormented you?"

Ione purred. I took it as an affirmative and asked, "Why?"

"He turned into a friend."

Crouching next to him, I murmured, "What if he followed Poseidon's path?"

The purr turned to a snarl. "Then I shall help you end him."

My travel spell was winding down, the transition abrupt as the walls of my living room took shape around us. I took a moment to ensure the rest of my team could enter easily, and then we left for the beach where Ione fed the Kraken. Ione teleported, but Xander and I covered the distance on foot. Even if the Kraken showed up right away, Ione would have a window before things turned to shit. He'd be catching fish and sharing them with his buddy.

Grigori had obviously been onto something when he'd said Ione missed having a connection with other magical animals. Him glomming onto the Kraken, who'd made his life miserable, was significant.

Xander unzipped his jacket, removed it, and hung it off his shoulders. "Warm here."

"Compared to northern Russia," I said.

People flowed around us in a constantly moving stream. The Adriatic seaside was busy year-round, and the crowds grated on me. We moved past the market square, and I motioned Xander to follow me into a space between two buildings so I could build a ward. Passersby would see us vanish into the darkness and not think twice about it, probably assuming we were enjoying one another.

Once we were concealed, I moved quicker. The street started up a steep hill. At the top, I scaled a cliff. Xander took to his wolf form, and I envied his four legs. After a thousand-foot climb, we reached the top, and I snugged up my warding. It was looking as if we wouldn't need help from the Nereids after all.

Our vantage point yielded a view of the deserted beach far below. Ione left the sea with a respectable fish in his mouth. He dropped it next to a pile of others just like it and sat on his haunches, waiting for the Kraken.

"Where is Ione's pack?" Xander asked.

"He doesn't have one."

"Impossible. He rose from somewhere."

I'd always suspected Mother created him, but I'd never asked for details.

A disturbance in the waves snapped my attention forward. A scaly head emerged, followed by the Kraken's top set of arms. Ione might trust him, but I didn't. Trying for stealth, I picked my way down the cliff. If anything, it was steeper than the other side had been. Xander chose a path to my right. We stopped a few feet above the beach.

The Kraken was fully out of the water and slithering to his bounty. About the size of a dragon, his scales were the circumference of meat platters. Once they'd been shiny black, but they'd developed a grayish hue. Many were riddled with holes. Three sets of arms sprouted from his upper body. Acres of tail coiled behind him. Spines protruded from his neck and shoulders. Poseidon and the sea witch had made others like him, but the Kraken killed each and every one.

Guess the specter of competition didn't sit well.

Ione's tail swished back and forth. He got to his feet to greet his friend. The Kraken hissed at him. Ione batted his side with a paw.

"So far, so good." Still in wolf form, Xander settled next to me.

"Until Ione starts asking questions."

Tension pulsed through me; I judged the distance between us and Ione. We should have hatched up a script, but we hadn't. I had to trust my bondmate to pick the right words.

The Kraken inhaled the fish, not bothering to engage his triple rows of teeth. The last one moved from claws to gullet in record time. He growled the word, "More," at Ione. It pissed me off he was treating my bondmate like a servant.

"No more for right now," Ione said firmly. "We must talk."

"Talk?" The Kraken sounded mystified. "About what? We never talk."

I edged nearer, needing to hedge my bets in case this ran off the rails. Xander shadowed me. The werewolf knew it was showtime. No need to risk discovery employing the quick burst of magic more telepathy would eat up.

❦   4   ❦

I one swished his tail back and forth before asking, "Who do you trust?"

A simple enough question, but it seemed to throw the Kraken off-guard. He looked around for more fish, but then remembered he'd eaten them all. "More," he bellowed.

Ione shook his shaggy head and repeated, "Who do you trust?"

The Kraken's small, beady red eyes shifted from side to side. Finally, he grumbled, "No one. I trust no one."

Ione feigned surprise with a muted roar. Maybe it hadn't been the answer he was expecting. Hard to tell about these things.

"What about your master?" Ione asked pointblank.

The Kraken lowered his head until his neck was crimped into a U-shape and he stared right at Ione. "He sent you. That's what this is about."

The snow leopard brayed feline laughter. Annoyed at

being laughed at, the Kraken raised scaly lips, displaying rows of yellowed teeth. Ione snarled, showing with his own set of fangs.

"No one sends me anywhere." Ione inserted spaces between each word for emphasis. "Besides, your master loathes me, blames me for Kylian leaving the seas."

"He was gone long before you showed up," the Kraken observed.

"You know that, and I know that," Ione agreed. "Poseidon's never been especially fond of the truth when it gets in the way of his version of reality. Besides, he has to blame someone when people desert him."

A long, low growl issued from the Kraken. Turning, he lumbered toward the sea.

"Wait." Ione called, but the Kraken kept moving, so Ione ran after him. Just before the Kraken reached the breaker line, Ione added, "I am your friend."

I'd never have guessed the impact of those four words, but the Kraken ground to a halt. "You shouldn't be," he pronounced. "I have not treated you well."

"We got off to a rocky start," Ione agreed, "but we figured things out."

The Kraken slithered his snakelike lower body back and forth until he faced Ione. "I know what you want, and I cannot do it. No matter how much I resent my master, I will not raise scales and talons against him."

"He's tried to replace you." Ione reminded him of other Krakens born of Poseidon and the sea witch's magic.

"I killed them all."

"Someday, he will discover a way to create one you cannot kill."

The Kraken lashed his head back and forth. "Unlikely."

Ione padded in a circle around the Kraken. "Poseidon has joined his power with Satan's."

I was watching closely. Ione's message hit the Kraken with all the force of a freight train. No beast, magical or otherwise, could fake that level of astonishment.

"You're wrong. He did not." The Kraken straightened the kinks in his neck, drawing himself up tall.

"Looks like you called this one," Xander said softly.

The Kraken's head whipped around. "Who else is here?" he bugled. "Show yourselves."

The time for hiding had passed. I dropped the few feet separating us from the beach and loped toward Ione and the Kraken. Xander paced me.

"I expected you." The Kraken jerked his scaled chin my way. "Where does a werewolf fit in?"

Intrigued, I tilted my head. Had the Kraken purposely projected a dumber-than-dirt persona? He didn't appear the least bit slow-witted at the moment.

Xander shimmered into his human form and bowed his head. "I am here seeking allies on behalf of the Circle of Assassins. Grigori is an old associate of mine."

A tongue of power blasted from the Kraken, circling Xander. "More than an associate, you two are from the same pack," he announced and withdrew his probe.

"I do not deny it," the werewolf said.

To defuse the situation, I added, "We're all here on behalf of the Circle. War is upon us. We are gathering support where it will aid us most."

"The Circle is but one of my reasons," Ione piped up. "The Kraken and I are friends."

Interesting. The snow leopard kept harping on that tidbit even after the Kraken had all but admitted he'd done nothing to nurture the relationship. Was it because he understood the Kraken was truly alone? Like all cats, Ione has keen intuition about everyone around him.

An odd, keening note burst from the Kraken. He muttered, "Leave me out of this," and beat a path into the sea.

I started to follow him, but Xander said, "Let him go."

"It's a beginning," Ione murmured around a muted purr. "He thinks about things, that one."

"We gave him grist for the mill." I patted my bondmate's shoulder. "You did well."

"How did you know he doesn't trust Poseidon?" Xander asked.

"He said we never talk, but it's not accurate," Ione replied. "He's regaled me with stories about killing baby Krakens. How could he have faith in someone who's been working on a more compliant version of himself?"

"Is that what he said?" I sought clarification. Poseidon had created more Krakens, but this was the first I'd heard it was to improve on the current one's faults.

"Reading between the lines, yes," Ione replied and settled on his haunches. "Everyone views him as stupid. He's not, but it takes him a while to get from point A to point B. Sometimes, when he thinks he can get away with it, he ignores Poseidon's orders."

"It works to his advantage when others view him as thick-headed," Xander muttered.

I'd discovered more about the Kraken in the last half hour than in the past several centuries. Still, predicting his next move was a crapshoot. "Will he find us?" I asked Ione.

The snow leopard rotated his shoulders in a shrugging motion. "Hard to say. But if we engage Poseidon in battle, his Kraken might not answer a call to arms."

"No one else will, either," I pointed out.

"Surely, it can't be that simple," Xander said. "His people may hate him, but many rulers have been in that position. Underlings support their liege out of fear of retribution if he somehow comes out on top."

I offered Xander points for stating the obvious. I'd never viewed Poseidon in quite that light before, but then I'd never envisioned him embracing Satan as a partner, either.

"How did you know the Kraken wouldn't light into you when you told him about his master?" I asked Ione.

"Because I'm the closest thing he has to a friend. Today, I reminded him of that. No need to bring up how one-sided things have been. He already knows. It will go a long way toward bringing him around to our camp."

"You're a sly one," Xander said approvingly.

"You just described every cat who ever walked." Ione stalked near the werewolf and announced. "You may pet me."

Xander cracked a broad grin and buried his fingers in Ione's fuzzy pelt.

We'd done all we could here. Time to return to the villa and wait for Quinn, Ciara, Rhiana, and their bond animals. To avoid the cliff and a ward to conceal Ione, I swathed us all in a quickie transport spell.

Between all of us, we might have enough magic to immobilize Poseidon and ferry him to one of his infamous dungeons. I turned the idea end over end poking it for holes in my reasoning.

The villa was the same as we'd left it: empty.

Ione strode into the kitchen and batted at a large magic-powered freezer. Before he opened it and started dragging its contents onto the floor, I beat him to it. "Do you really want anything from in there?" I asked. "The meat all has freezer burn."

The cat and I peered inside. Because I ran appliances with constantly perpetuating spells, the inside temperature fluctuated enough everything was coated with a thick layer of ice.

Ione sank onto his haunches. "I can make do with the tourists," he said in a deadpan tone that could have meant anything.

"Bold." Xander had come up behind us and stroked Ione's fur, earning a long, low rumble of a purr.

I mucked around in the lower section of the freezer and came up with what might have been half a goat—or a sheep—and handed it to Ione. One chomp sent ice chips flying, but he sank to his belly intent on his meal. To be on the safe side, I dropped the other half in front of him.

"Looks good," Xander commented.

"If you're serious, help yourself. Or you can join me."

The werewolf furled his silver brows. "What's on the menu?"

"Nothing fancy. Cheese. Flatbread. Maybe olives if I didn't eat them all last time."

"I'll split the difference," Xander said and filched a side of meaty rib bones from the freezer before pushing it shut. A fast burst of enchantment flipped him back to werewolf form, and he took up residence on the floor next to Ione.

The crunch of strong teeth against bone filled the kitchen as I made up a generous plate in case Xander was still hungry. By the time I carried it out to the veranda, along with a bottle of mead, he'd settled into a chair.

"Best of both worlds," he commented and picked up a goblet I'd filled for him.

I clinked my glass against his. "To success."

"Success," he agreed, and drank. When he set the cut-crystal goblet down, he said, "You have a plan. What is it?"

"I do, but it's very rough," I admitted.

He made come-along motions with one hand, and I answered his question with one of my own. "Do you think we have enough power between us to capture Poseidon and dump him in a dungeon?"

The werewolf's eyebrows shot up. "Ione isn't the only bold one."

Perhaps in response to his name, the leopard padded out to the veranda, what was left of his bounty clutched in his jaws.

"That wasn't exactly an answer," I observed.

"He commands the sea," Xander replied. "It puts us at a disadvantage."

"I command it as well," I reminded him. "But it would be simpler if we lured him to land, first."

Xander popped a bit of flatbread covered with cheese into his mouth. When he was done chewing and swallowing, he said, "His power diminishes when he's not in the sea, right?"

I nodded. "Yes, and we have the perfect bait."

A slow, wicked grin formed on the werewolf's even features. "He wants to get his hands on Ciara."

"Don't forget Rhiana and Dorcha."

Ione dropped the haunch he was working on. "Someone should make certain we have an easy way into the dungeons. They used to be sealed."

"Sealed, how?" Xander asked.

I trolled through my memories. "If nothing has changed, only Poseidon or the Kraken could open the gates into the complex. I can mimic Poseidon's enchantment well enough to bypass that problem."

"What happens once you're inside?" Xander pressed for additional information.

"Individual cells not in use stand open. Shutting them activates a locking mechanism..."

"Only Poseidon can defeat it," Ione chimed in.

I'd known that but had conveniently forgotten. Not much reason to dump dear old Dad into a cell and have him stroll out thirty seconds later.

"Bet I can reset the locks," I muttered. "My power is close enough to his, I should be able to tweak things."

I drained my glass and stood. "Tell the others where I've gone."

"You're not going by yourself," Xander said firmly.

I cast a pointed look his way. "You're certainly not coming. Werewolf power will stick out like a flashing beacon in the ocean no matter how well you ward yourself."

"Ciara should go." Ione was on his feet too.

"For once, my timing is impeccable. I just heard my name," Ciara murmured as she, Quinn, and the eagles waltzed through a gash in the ether.

In a decent imitation of his bondmate, Quinn swooped down on the plate of food and inhaled half of it. "Where is Ciara going?" Quinn asked around a mouthful of cheese.

I reiterated the bones of my plan, finishing with, "We have to ensure the dungeons are open and ready."

"And not keyed to Poseidon's magic any longer," Ciara tossed out. "I can indeed help with that project."

Quinn left the food and threaded an arm around her. "I don't like it. I should come too."

I shook my head. "Too many of us will complicate matters. We need to sneak in, get the job done, and leave."

"Is anyone in the prison?" Xander asked.

"There used to be," Ciara replied.

Rhiana and Dorcha materialized on the veranda. Apparently, they'd traveled separately. "Been listening," Rhiana said. "I can help."

"For a mage who prefers working alone—" I began.

"We all do," Rhiana snapped.

"Testy, testy," I said to her. "You didn't let me finish."

"Didn't need to," she pointed out. "I know you well enough to predict your words. Something along the lines of thanks so much, but I'll take care of this on my own." She stopped to take a breath before adding, "How do I know? Because I'd have said the same thing."

"Let's think about this." Xander's statement was laced with a calming incantation. "Kylian is the only one who can rekey the cell doors. He'll need sufficient support to both keep watch and command the sea if it rises against him."

"It won't," I said. "Water recognizes me as its master."

"Are you certain?" Xander angled his head to one side and

eyed me. "What if you tell the water to do something, and Poseidon instructs it differently? Who wins?"

"Touché," I said. He'd posed a good question, and I didn't have an answer for it.

"I'm the logical one to go," Ciara spoke up. "My sea mage powers can tip the equation in our favor. Plus, I've been to the dungeons. Have you?" she asked Rhiana.

"Nope. Never wanted the grand tour. Poseidon offered it. He's damned proud of them."

"Bastard," Ciara mumbled under her breath. Turning to her eagle, she said, "It pains me to do this, but you shall remain here with Gwaihir and Quinn."

The bird squawked disagreement but fluttered to Dorcha's back. The unicorn neighed something that might have been consolation.

"I'll manage the ward. You get us there," Ciara told me.

Snapping off a salute, I went to work on a subtle teleport spell. Nothing would reveal we'd passed through the seas. I hoped. Poseidon might be arrogant, but he was far from stupid.

The salt smell of the sea curved around me from Ciara's ward. Ione brushed against my legs, intending to come too. Crouching next to him, I shook my head. "Not this time, old friend. The sea isn't your native element."

"I can breathe underwater," he reminded me.

"I need you here as an anchor," I told him. "A touchstone to draw us back if we get into trouble."

He nodded solemnly. Tory, Ciara's eagle switched from the unicorn's back to his. "I will amplify his signal," she assured me.

My teleport spell was ready, the ward in place.

We launched, trading the sunny veranda for the black of a travel channel. "Smart of you to soothe Ione," Ciara said. "I need more palatable words."

"I wasn't mollycoddling him." My stark words hung between us.

"Did you scry this?" she asked.

"I did not. No time. But if Poseidon finds us, he'll know what we're up to."

"Not necessarily," she retorted. "He'll recognize we're messing with the dungeons, but in no universe would he ever suspect we plan to chuck him inside."

"Don't be so sure of that. We're almost there. No talking. No mind speech. If things go well, we should be done in fifteen minutes."

"And if they don't?"

"Don't wait too long to activate the link with your eagle. Poseidon can trap us in the dungeons and cut off our ability to project magic beyond its walls. Once he does that, we'll have a much harder go of things escaping. And no one will be able to reach us."

"Brocca can. May I alert her?"

"Whose side is the sea witch on?" I asked remembering a desperately unpleasant hag with seaweed mixed in her long black hair.

"Her own," Ciara said succinctly. "No love lost between her and Poseidon. She made me blades to kill him, but I left the sea instead. I figured she'd hate me. Instead, she created a diversion so I could make good on my escape."

"Aye. Alert her," I said and winced. Some of my split-second decisions have come back to haunt me.

A different type of power flitted around Ciara. When it settled, she said, "It is done."

"What'd she say?"

"Nothing. I didn't want to risk opening a two-way channel, but she knows where we'll be. Curiosity will drive her to show up."

I placed a finger over my mouth in the universal sign for silence. The teleport channel frittered to nothing leaving us so deep in the sea it appeared black. The dungeon walls rose before us. Crafted of stone and black coral mortared together with barnacles and magic, the structure had been here for hundreds of years.

No pods of curious fish in these waters. We were too deep for their taste.

Ciara shadowed me as I tested the power circling the dungeon. It had Poseidon's stamp all over it. Did it hold a link to alert him if anyone tampered with it?

Probably. It's how I'd have designed things.

Matching my magic as closely to my sire's as I could manage, we oozed through the walls. I risked a scan to make certain we hadn't been discovered. So far, so good. Jeopardizing myself was one thing, but I was responsible for Ciara too. She wouldn't agree with my assessment, but then she'd never know about it.

A few sorry souls stared at us from their watery cells.

I considered freeing them, but if I did Poseidon would know I'd been here. I hoped to keep that little part secret until he was secured. Once the deed was done, I'd spring everyone else.

Even though it would take longer, I lined things up, got everything ready. Rather than resetting the lock one step at a time, I'd do it all at once, but I had to have the pieces in place. We'd breached the outer wall, but it didn't mean the cells weren't booby trapped to let Poseidon know they'd been tampered with. I was still surprised he hadn't bothered to set an alert system for the wall we'd just transited. Guess he didn't expect anyone would break into the place.

I HUNCHED OVER AN OPEN CELL DOOR AND PROBED THE lock with unraveling magic. Everything Poseidon crafted utilized water. He didn't control the other three elements. The mechanism yielded to my inspection. If I weren't invested in silence, I'd have cursed up a storm. The lock contained elements of the Kraken's power too.

All I had to do was tamper with one lock, but I couldn't reinstitute the Kraken's portion. Eh, perhaps I didn't have to. Aware of minutes ticking by, I rebuilt the whole thing, borrowing heavily from fire and air. The important thing was it held, kept him from escaping. He'd never be able to dismantle the intricate braided power I poured into the lock.

Pleased to have found a solution, I was closing on finishing the reset when Ciara's magic brushed across my mind.

Fuck. So close, but not heeding her warning could be deadly. I pushed through water that was thickening around me and came face to face with Brocca. She shook a misshapen finger in my face and pointed to my left.

Poseidon and the Kraken swam into view. An idea raced through my mind. I raised a hand in greeting. "Well met, Sire. I brought you someone you requested. I was just preparing a cell for her."

"Bloody, fucking bastard," Ciara screeched from behind me. "You're supposed to be on my side."

"Blood's thicker than whatever you have to offer him," Poseidon sneered and aimed his next words at me. "Finally came to your senses, eh?"

"You might say that." Revulsion crept down my spine. How in bloody hell could I be related to that piece of trash?

❄ 5 ❄

The die was cast. No going back now. I'd been afraid Ciara would never forgive me for using her like that—until I caught sight of her huddled in the cell I'd been working on. She must have teleported inside. The lock wasn't functional, but Poseidon didn't know.

Brocca had something up her filmy sleeves. I'd have given a lot to know what.

Poseidon swam near enough to stare at Ciara through the cell door. "It's about time," he snarled. "You've led me on quite the merry chase."

Raising her upper lip, she sneered.

I edged next to the sea god and continued tinkering with the lock. I'd been close to being done. Maybe I could pull this off right in front of him. Maybe.

"What are you doing?" He reached with magic, but I erected a hasty barrier around my work.

"Making certain she can't escape. You promised me the Nereids. I don't want an unfortunate mishap to intervene."

"I can take it from here," he informed me haughtily.

"No need, my liege," Brocca cut in smoothly. "Enjoy the labor others do on your behalf." She slid between him and me —and the lock. The diversion gave me what I needed, and I sealed my work with a few layers of obfuscation, to hide what I'd done.

One of Brocca's hands was busy beneath Poseidon's robe. They'd been lovers; it was where the baby Krakens came from. I risked a sidelong glance at the Kraken. He stared at me and nodded slightly. Or perhaps he didn't nod at all, and it was wishful thinking on my part.

If he helped, we could finesse this. Moving Ciara out of the cell would be simple. Pushing Poseidon into it and holding him there long enough for me to spring the lock was the hard part. Now was when I could have used Quinn and Rhiana. Dorcha's horn would have been a plus too.

Brocca had edged Poseidon off to one side so they were partially hidden by shadows. She'd also opened a path between Poseidon and the cell door. Should I do this? I'd never get a better chance. He was a handful of steps from what I hoped would be his for-a-while prison. No need to knock him out and transport him, hoping to hell he wouldn't wake up and break every travel channel in the region.

Ciara had been huddled toward the rear of the cell; she moved next to the door. The Kraken closed the distance between us breathing fetid breath down my neck. For once, I welcomed his foul, rotten-fish stench. He was telling me he was with me on this one. Watching the sea god and the sea witch going at it must really piss him off. When Poseidon was close to release, she'd take his seed into her mouth and make more Krakens from it.

I'd researched how they managed it a long while back, and the process disgusted me since it perverted the stuff I was made of. Brocca was on her knees in front of Poseidon. I hoped she'd bite off his dick.

A breathy sigh from Ciara told me it was time. With the Kraken right behind me, I swung the cell door open. Ciara sprang out. She, I, and the Kraken surrounded Brocca and Poseidon, except the sea witch was done with her blow job. She hit him dead in the balls with a visible jolt of power. While he was squealing in outrage, the rest of us shoved him into the cell and slammed the door.

Maybe because he'd been sunk in rut, it took far longer than I'd expected for him to begin yelling at us and tinkering with the lock. He expected he'd spring himself in short order.

With a self-satisfied grin on her face, Brocca tapped the other locks, freeing the few dungeon occupants. "Come, my pretties," she crooned. "Let Momma Brocca take care of you."

"Don't eat them," Ciara said sternly.

"You misjudge me, my dear. They've suffered enough." Herding her charges before her, she vanished from the dungeon.

I looked for the Kraken to thank him, but he, too, was gone.

Poseidon was muttering to himself. Power swirled around him. Before he called the sea down on us—if he even could from within the dungeon's walls—I reached for my link with Ione. It pulsed weakly because the dungeon's innate power was in the way. Or maybe Poseidon retained more in the way of his magic than I believed he would.

Regardless, it took considerably more effort than I anticipated before we transited the stone-and-coral walls and swam in the sea again. Ciara set the bones of a transport spell in place. The sooner we returned, the better. Ione would have felt me reaching for him, and the others were probably plotting a rescue. I was too far away for telepathy to reach, so speed was our friend.

"Sorry to use you as bait," I told Ciara.

She laughed. "Never apologize for success. I came up with the same idea once I understood Brocca brought him to us."

Surprise flooded me. I'd assumed he showed up because he'd felt me mucking around with the lock.

"She's hated him for a long while," Ciara explained. "She might have lacked details, but she's canny enough to know this was a prime opportunity to rid herself of him forever."

"Probably not forever. Sex was a good diversion, though," I said. "It must have cost the Kraken to turn on his master."

"Maybe not so much," Ciara replied thoughtfully. "This way, he'll remain the only Kraken with no fears of a newer model taking over his turf." She turned a speculative glance my way. "Will you be taking his place?"

It took me a moment to catch her meaning. She'd asked if I had designs on being the new god of the seas. "Not just no, but hell no," I sputtered. "The sea creatures don't need a god. They've been getting along fine dodging the one they had."

She smiled warmly. "Right answer, Kylian. I never knew you well, and I'm relieved you're not viewing Poseidon's demise as a vacancy waiting to be filled."

"I value my freedom. And my bondmate. And the Circle. Not much room for picking up a trident." Breath rustled from me. We'd solved one problem; others faced us.

"Brocca was inspired. I'll have to thank her," Ciara murmured.

"And I owe the Kraken."

"We all do," she said. "Victories create unlikely bedfellows."

Her spell developed translucent edges, and we emerged in the villa's great room. Ione jumped on me, licking my face. Ciara's eagle landed on her shoulders and ran its beak alongside her head. Quinn wrapped his arms around her, relief streaming from him in visible waves.

I wasn't used to Circle members having mates. It was a big change from my days with the group.

Rhiana, Dorcha, and Xander peppered us with questions. "We were literally ten seconds from launching a rescue," Xander said.

I grimaced. "My bad. When we left the dungeon, we were too far away for telepathy, but I could have let you know we were en route once we drew nearer. No excuses. Not really. Ciara and I were processing what happened."

"Aye, we'd all like to know," Xander prodded.

The cavalcade of questions that had begun the moment we arrived flew thick and fast. We emptied two bottles of mead, passing them around, before the tale was told.

"I knew he'd help," Ione purred, sounding vindicated as he mentioned his friend, the Kraken.

"It was hard for him," Ciara said, "but he chose rightly. As did Brocca, but her loyalties were never in doubt."

News to me, but I kept my mouth shut. The sea witch's reputation was far from sterling. Ciara hadn't been joking when she'd said not to eat the prisoners.

"Time to leave," I said.

"Aye. We should report in," Xander agreed.

He and Rhianna and Dorcha traveled together, as did Quinn, Ciara, and their eagles. It left Ione and me. I cleared up the food and drink debris and shuttered the house. Even with Poseidon out of the picture, it was unlikely I'd visit more often. Ione hadn't complained about the temperature, but it was warm here. And damp.

Not exactly tropical, but not far from it.

I gathered us into a spell and set a path for the guild house.

"I should have been there," Ione insisted. "I would have helped the Kraken."

I ruffled his fur. "If I'd known how things would pan out, I'd have brought you."

"Will the cell hold him?" Ione leaned into me, purring.

"I'm not certain," I admitted. "For a while, but maybe not forever. If he harnesses the power of the sea to destroy the dungeon, the cell will become an anachronism."

"What does that mean?" the snow leopard asked.

"If the walls and roof and floor are no more, he can float out the top of his enclosure, but he will be diminished in the eyes of his people. No one will come to his aid. Even if he manages to escape, embarrassment and humiliation will drive him away."

"This really was a win. I wasn't certain."

"Neither was I. Not until the cell door clanged shut and stayed that way."

"I want to return to the villa before our next assignment," Ione said.

"But you hate it there," I reminded him.

He nodded his shaggy head. "I do, but I want to bring the Kraken fish and thank him. He has no one."

The snow leopard wasn't normally compassionate. "What is it about him that touches you?" I asked.

"He wasn't always Poseidon's lackey. Once he was free to cruise the seas."

I made a snorting sound. I remembered those days. "He terrorized ships and sailors," I pointed out.

"So?" Ione rumbled. "He was his own man. Feared. Respected. Poseidon turned him into a sad joke."

It appeared he'd chatted about far more than fish with the Kraken. Or listened. Cats have patience in abundance. The courtyard shimmered around us, glistening with the dawn of a new day. The rest of my team would have beaten us back, which meant Grigori had all the information.

How had the other teams fared?

I started for the house, Ione by my side, when Grigori bolted down the steps, a satisfied smile on his face. "I heard the news. Congratulations."

"Thanks. We had help."

"From unlikely quadrants. Xander covered that as well. We're having a breakfast meeting. Everyone else returned yesterday or last night."

I considered asking for a rollup, but I'd hear soon enough. I settled for, "Are we gaining ground?"

"Most definitely." Grigori clapped me across the back. "I've missed you."

I angled a glance his way. "Curious since I was never here long enough to do much."

"Your opinion, not mine."

We mounted the steps into the guild house. "Do I have time to clean up?"

"Aye. Be quick about it."

Ione head-butted me. "I'm going hunting. Meet you inside in a while."

After bidding Grigori goodbye, I hustled to the guild house wardrobe room to grab fresh trousers, a shirt, and a vest. Probably should have showered and changed at the villa, but I'd been anxious to return. This worked too. All the guild houses had clothing collections from every era starting around 1600. Sometimes I had to scrounge to find my size, but not often.

Joss, the faun who manages the laundry and clothing stocks was nowhere in sight. I've always liked him. He has an easy way, friendly but not overbearing. I could have walked, but it was quicker to teleport to my corner room. I stood in the shower until I'd washed off the Kraken's drool, hurried into my clothes, and beat a track for the dining room.

Even without all the delectable food smells, the clink of silver against china would have told me breakfast was in full swing. Dishes were lined on a back table. I grabbed a plate and helped myself. Ione joined me in the buffet line grabbing this and that. He didn't require dishes or flatware.

"Thought you went hunting," I murmured.

"All I found were mice. Still hungry," he said around a mouthful of smoked salmon.

Xander motioned us to a table he shared with Rhianna and Shira. I rustled up tea to go with my breakfast and ate while the five other teams reported their progress. We'd done well. Only two casualties, and they were expected to survive.

When it was our turn, I walked to the front and hit the high points of our assignment.

"You imprisoned your Da?" a voice cried from the center of the room.

"Who said that?" I shaded my eyes and peered at the assemblage.

"Me." Joss got to his feet. "I am so sorry. It must have cost you."

Families were important for fauns. "The worst part was fearing we'd fail," I told him. "If you're imagining family dinners and cozy outings, they never existed. Mother raised me. Poseidon never bothered to visit."

"Just another deadbeat dad," Quinn joked.

"Maybe we should drop by and taunt him," Rhiana suggested brightly.

I held up a hand. "Levity aside, it's a mistake to assume the dungeon will hold him forever. We probably bought a few months, maybe even years if we get lucky, but eventually he will tear down the dungeon and escape. My best bet is he'll drop out of sight, but by then he may be so eaten up with revenge fantasies, he'll find me."

"The Kraken will be his first stop," Xander said.

"That won't go well," Grigori tossed out, adding, "We have more important items to strategize. We've done well, made progress, but we are far from finished." He blew out a breath. "We may never be done, but it's not productive to think that way."

The elemental mage who'd tutored me in warfare had always told me to fight the battle in front of me. Sound advice since it was the only one I had any direct control over.

"We will take a break for the next three days," Grigori

was saying. "Refresh yourselves during that time. You'll stick with your team assignments since they seem to be working well. Our next logical move is to bring whoever remains of the elemental mages back and incorporate them into the Circle."

"They'll never agree," Rhiana said firmly. "We killed off over half of them. Why would they want to fight on our behalf?"

"Conquered people frequently join forces with those who defeated them," Grigori pointed out.

"Might work for mortals." Rhiana sounded doubtful.

"Any idea where they went?" I asked.

Xander shook his head. "We ordered them to be gone from the world they'd stolen from the dinosaur shifters."

"I can locate Mother," I said slowly. "If she's not one of the ones you ended."

"Give it a try." Grigori nodded briskly. "Be subtle if you can. I don't want them to know we're looking for them until we show up."

"Of course not. They'd assume we rethought our strategy and are coming back to finish off the rest of them," Rhiana muttered.

Something about her tone snagged my attention. "Are you all right?" I asked.

"How would you be if you'd been instrumental in wiping out a big chunk of your remaining kinfolk?" Shira demanded. She'd been quiet during our meal, but she jumped to Rhiana's defense.

I held her clear blue gaze. "We're batting for the same team."

She made a face. "Sorry. I can come off pretty strong, but

no one knows more about how important family is than me since I didn't have one."

"How'd you end up Aidyrth's bondmate?"

Shira shook her head. "It's not important. Speaking of the dragon, it's time for me to find her."

I watched her walk out of the room. Tall and slender with a ramrod straight spine, she exuded a "don't fuck with me" air. "Did I say something wrong?" I asked Xander and Rhiana.

Rhiana shook her head. "She's young, still finding her way. She covers with bluster and bravado, but underneath it all, she's wonderfully competent."

I retreated to my original query. "Are you okay with what happened to the other elemental mages?"

"Never any love lost between us. I fought the Celts. They ran. No one backed me. Dorcha believes the others blamed me for their predicament."

I snorted, working to muffle a laugh.

"I fail to see what's funny," Rhiana said stiffly.

I thumped my chest. "I'm the reason the Celts turned into a pack of cowards. I'm stronger than most of them, and it made them very nervous. What if more gods created offspring with an elemental mage? It wouldn't take too many like me for them to get kicked off their pedestal."

She thumped the flat of her hand down on the table, making the plates and silverware rattle. "Goddammit. I knew there had to be a reason."

"You can see why they were closemouthed about it," Xander said.

"Pfft. Made them look like a pack of cowards," Rhiana ground out.

"First time I've admitted it out loud," I said. "I argued

with the Celts, but their minds were made up. Poseidon was a tangential part of their group, so I was limited in what I could do. Then. Today, I'd make different choices."

I pushed to my feet. "I'm going to do some spade work on hunting for Mother. See you in the morning. Thanks for including me at your table."

Xander stood too. "No thanks needed. I like you." He held out a hand.

I shook it. "The feeling is mutual."

After stopping by the dais to tell Grigori good night, I raised my mind voice hunting for Ione and set a path to intercept him. We'd travel to the last borderworld where the elemental mages had been. Tracking their energy from there should be simple.

Should be.

Every time I underestimate a task, it rears up and bites me in the ass.

"Did you get enough to eat?" I asked Ione.

"I did. Where are we going?"

"Hunting." Grigori had said to take a break for a few days, but if I managed to locate the elemental mages and co-opt them to our side, we'd be ahead of the curve.

The big cat's tail swished; his whiskers quivered with anticipation. He lived to hunt, but then so did I.

<h1 style="text-align:center">❧ 6 ❧</h1>

had a fair idea which world I was aiming for, but I didn't get it right the first time. An infinite number of worlds beyond Earth spanned several universes. Quinn had set out to map them once, but the task overwhelmed him after a few years. My second try dumped us on a rolling plain in the middle of the night. Prairie grass rustled, heavy with fragrant dew.

"This is the right place," Ione announced.

It was. I smelled the blood of my people. Worse, I felt their anguish as death claimed them. Immortality may get old, but the alternative is a million times worse. We bitch about unending life. Still, it's our birthright, and we guard it jealously.

No one was near, but I swathed us in invisibility anyway. No reason to upset the dinosaurs. Following a scent track, we located the killing ground easily. I was tempted to scry what had happened. Reconstructing the past is simple, especially when you're right on top of where the events in question occurred.

My curiosity wasn't why we were here.

I latched onto Ione's power, and we crafted a tracking spell. Mostly, I wanted a trajectory, a direction. Grigori had said to be subtle about things, and Rhiana had raised the best of points. If the few remaining mages sensed we were looking for them, they truly would vanish.

One last task remained. I sorted the dead, all men and women I'd known. To do it, I walked the field, sectioning it into overlapping segments to make certain I didn't miss anyone. Ione stuck by my side. He knew what I was doing.

Necromancy isn't part of my skillset, but the dead do yield their secrets to a seer. I kept count, added names to a list in my head. After I was done, I repeated my wandering track through the field. The second time went far quicker.

Relief coursed through me making my skin prickle and the odd tight place leave my midsection. Mother was still alive. Either she'd never been here, or she'd escaped. I'd seized one parent, imprisoned him. It felt important to not lose the other one too. Not at the same time. And then I cursed myself for caring.

But I did. Not about Poseidon, but about Mother.

A high, keening shriek cut into my thoughts. Wings with sharp-edged feathers made the air come alive; a flock of pterodactyls surrounded Ione and me shifting as soon as their webbed feet hit the ground.

"We know you're here," one snarled. "You may as well dispense with your warding."

"You must leave. Now," another said firmly.

Since my ward was apparently useless, I let it go. "I'm not who you fear," I told them.

"We fear no one," the first shifter informed me.

"Fine. Poor choice of words. I'm part of the Circle of Assassins. Ione is my bondmate. We are here to track the elemental mages who left."

Ione curved his neck into a stretch and yawned.

"Should have killed them all when you had a chance," the shifter muttered.

"Would you condemn your kin to genocide?" I asked.

"Perhaps not," he admitted after a lengthy pause.

"Are you done here?" a third shifter piped up. From the higher cant to the voice, I assumed it was a woman. When she stepped into view, I saw I'd been correct.

"Aye. We are. Thank you for your hospitality." I turned in a slow circle, eying the group ringed around us. Would they allow us to leave without fanfare?

"What were you doing walking this way and that?" the woman asked.

"Cataloging the dead."

"Why?" she pressed.

"To see if my mother was among them."

Her dark eyes widened. Power pummeled me as several shifters assessed my makeup. "You spoke truth," she said.

"Why would I not?" I rolled my shoulders back. "Apologies for disturbing you, but we need to get on with things."

I seeded my words with compulsion. They could have fought it and remained, but they didn't. Back in feathered form, they spread their huge wings and rose into the night sky, blending with its darkness.

"They must post sentries," Ione said.

I still had no idea how they'd sensed us through my warding, but I filed it away. This wasn't a place I could sneak up on. Not easily. No matter. It was unlikely I'd ever return.

After casting a couple of simple tracking spells—and getting nowhere—I understood locating the mages who'd fled wouldn't be straightforward. Why should it be? They were fleeing for their lives, although to hear Rhiana's version, her team had backed off to spare those who remained.

"Any leads?" I asked Ione.

A low growl told me he hadn't had any better luck than me. I turned in a full circle, willing clues to spring to the fore. Something I'd missed that would yield a ballpark direction. Whole lot of universes out there. I could blow through half a century searching and find nothing.

"Search for your blood," Ione advised.

I shook my head. "No percentage. Wherever she is, it's probably too far away."

"Do it anyway," he pressed.

I didn't have any better ideas, so I wove strands of the four elements into a seeking spell, leaving the sea god's contribution to my power out of the equation. Surprise streamed through me like a kaleidoscopic light show.

"I'll be damned," I muttered, resorting to telepathy in case someone was listening to us. *"She never left here."*

"Means the others probably didn't, either." Ione punctuated his words with an I-told-you-so purr.

I didn't get it. If the dinosaur shifters could drill through my ward with apparent ease, why hadn't they picked up on elemental mages holed up beneath their feet? This world must have cave systems. For all I knew, it was where my kinsmen had set up shop, although they wouldn't have returned to their original home. Surely, the dinosaurs were aware of its location.

Perhaps they'd manipulated the earth element and persuaded this world to shield them from discovery. If it were true, the only reason I'd located their hidey-hole was because of my blood bond with Mother.

"Why are we still standing here?" Ione demanded. No need for mind speech. Any dinosaurs hanging about were no doubt wondering precisely the same thing.

He had a point. I laid better than even odds the dinosaur shifters were watching us to make damn sure we left. They'd be outraged if we did anything other than craft a teleport spell and exit immediately.

A funny mortal saying crossed my mind: Do not pass go, do not collect 200 dollars. It was another way of saying get the hell out of Dodge.

I draped a spell around us and kindled it. Once we rocked gently in a teleport channel, the snow leopard hissed, "What are we doing? The ones we seek are behind us."

"They are," I agreed. "So are the dinosaurs."

"But they left."

"Did they?" I countered. "If I were them, and I was protecting my world, I'd have stuck around until we made good on our commitment to leave." I paused for a beat. "My plan is to circle round and aim for the underground spot I sensed Mother. We'll have to stop somewhere first and cobble another journey spell together."

Ione relaxed against me, content I was still on top of our assignment. I swear, he's more invested in follow-through than I am. We reached my interim goal, a nearby world.

Unlike the one we'd left, this one was desolate, deserted, with thin dry air that made my nose and throat burn.

We wouldn't be here long enough for it to matter.

I built a trajectory, fine-tuned it, and redirected the spell I'd never dismissed. If it ran true, we'd come out far beneath the surface of the previous world. The elemental mages would sense us. No help for it. Earth-linked power was ultra-sensitive to alterations in magic.

If I was correct about the remaining mages cutting a deal with the Earth to conceal them, that same Earth would warn them company was about to arrive. My only fix was a simple one. When the edges of my spell lightened signifying we were nearly there, I called for Mother with reassurances I only wished to talk.

I had no expectations. They're pointless, particularly when they don't pan out. My only hope was I'd judged correctly and wouldn't bring us out in the middle of a solid clump of rock and dirt. A cave flared to life around us, setting that concern to rest. Judging from the proliferation of footprints in the sandy dirt, the place saw a lot of traffic. Clean, earthy scents soothed my abraded nasal passages and dry throat.

My spell settled around us. I stood still, waiting. Someone was bound to know we were here, and I didn't want to do anything to project aggression. Ione lay on his belly, head resting on his paws, the picture of feline contentment with purrs rumbling from him.

Perhaps a quarter of an hour slid past before Mother glided into the room. Hair like spun gold fluffed around her, falling to knee level. Her face held hints of Elven beauty despite her not having any Elven blood that I knew of. High, sweeping cheekbones, a well-formed chin, and a noble forehead framed her copper eyes. A cream-colored robe swathed her six-foot frame. She's always been substantial, broad-shouldered, and stocky. A jaunty red sash held the robe together. As usual, her feet were bare.

She stopped about ten feet away and leveled her gaze my way. "Come to finish us off?" she inquired.

I shook my head. "Quite the opposite. I've come to offer inducements to work with the Circle of Assassins to defeat our common enemies."

"You are our primary adversary," she informed me tartly. "No one else brought unicorns to kill us."

I sidled past her statement. I couldn't refute it; neither would I apologize. Very little to gain by shifting blame for the deaths to them. The "if you hadn't done X" defense was a bitter pill, one that choked going down.

"We could use your magic," I said pointblank. "Grigori has offered all who are left asylum."

"Why would he bother?" Her tone was bitter. "His henchmen killed over half of us."

I bit my tongue to avoid pointing out the obvious: They'd started it; we'd fought back. If they hadn't gone after us, no one would have died. "It's a generous offer," I persisted. "You're not welcome here, but you already know as much. It's why you're hiding down here, counting on Earth's protection to keep you from discovery.

"It won't work," I went on. "Not over the long haul. The shifters will find you sooner or later, and, when they do, they'll be furious."

"We can pull it off," she insisted.

"Maybe. Maybe not. The Circle is a sure thing."

"What about the bond animal part?" Mother narrowed her eyes in Ione's direction. He raised his head, his upper lip showing a rack of teeth.

Grigori and I hadn't fleshed it out, so I trod carefully and said, "For those of you who wish to stay, the bond is required. It's not a decision you have to make right this minute. You can fight on our side as you are, unbonded, for a time."

The snow leopard pushed to his feet and walked deliberately toward Mother. She widened her stance and held her ground. He yawned, arched his back, swished his tail. Next, he curled at her feet and began to purr.

Mother's serious expression vanished, traded for a reluctant smile. "You don't fool me with your innocent housecat act," she told my bondmate.

The purr turned into a snarl. "Is that better?" Ione asked.

"Are they all like this?" she asked me.

"If you're asking if the bond animals have a sense of humor, some of them do, but most don't. Besides, you're who found him for me."

I'd delivered my message. I should wrap it up, tell her where to find me—not that she required help in that department—and leave. But I didn't want to. "It's good to see you," I ventured.

"You as well," she said. "How is Poseidon?"

"Moldering in his dungeon."

She grinned. "Did you perchance have aught to do with that?"

Her regression to archaic language amused me. "I might have."

"But you'll never tell."

"Nope. I'm not the kiss-and-tell type."

"That's my boy." She closed the distance between us and hugged me.

I hugged her back, quick and hard, before letting go. "Please. Talk with the others. We would welcome your expertise in the Circle. The only elemental mage is Rhiana, and of course me, but I haven't been there enough to count."

"Why not?"

I shrugged. "Been figuring things out."

She bit her lower lip, frowning. "Next time we talk, I want to hear more about what you found."

"Not much, I'm afraid. For now, the Circle is where Ione and I belong."

"Oooh, you have a name," she said to the leopard. "When I found you, you'd never reveal it."

"Oooh, so do you," he shot back.

"True. Do you know what it is?"

The cat trawled through my head. Because he was in a hurry, he wasn't especially gentle. Finding what he sought, he said, "Your name is Auralie."

"You cheated." She shook a finger his way.

He purred and rubbed against her legs, laying on the charm.

I wanted to stay longer, break out a teapot or a bottle of mead and catch up, but socializing wasn't why Grigori had sent us. "Talk with the others," I repeated. "The main guild house is at—"

"I know where it is." She waved a hand my way.

"Of course, you do." I motioned Ione to my side and built a transport spell. "Hope I see you soon," I told Mother and launched my casting.

"You will," Ione said, sounding certain.

"I will what?" Focused on my spell, I had no idea what he was talking about.

"See her soon. How could they refuse to come?"

"Easily," I muttered. My kin from Mother's side of the family were a stiff-necked crew.

"You're wrong," Ione said with conviction. "No one would choose to live underground forever."

He had a point. Why had they sealed themselves into a living crypt when they could have settled anywhere? Maybe we'd saved Grigori some time. I'd delivered our message. Time would tell if I'd been an effective messenger.

We passed the rest of the journey in silence. I was tired. Seeing Mother had rammed home just how alone I was. Until she and the others had left, I'd nurtured the illusion of family. Illusion because of how rapidly it crumpled when the Celts issued their ultimatum.

Should we search them out? If we were looking for firepower, they'd be welcome allies. Eh, one thing at a time, I told myself. First off, I'd sort of jumped the gun on Grigori's idea to include the elemental mages. All I'd been supposed to do was locate them.

If my gambit worked, all would be well. If it didn't, Grigori would have every right to be annoyed. Nothing worse than underlings who blow off orders. My room tucked under the eaves formed around us. A moon and stars reflected through the windows. Nighttime, perhaps a bit past midnight.

"Going hunting." Ione walked through the open door, on his way out into the night.

I pulled it shut behind him and stripped off my clothes. When I returned from a blistering hot shower intent on lying on the bed and zoning out, Grigori sat in the room's only chair waiting for me. I grabbed a robe off a hook next to the bathroom door and slipped into its soft terrycloth folds.

"Ione told me you found your mother," he said, an expectant look on his face. I waited, but he didn't dun me for bumping my reconnaissance up a notch.

"Aye, we did. It was good to see her," I replied.

The werewolf spun one hand in a come-along motion. He'd probably already pumped Ione for everything relevant, so I hit the high points of what had transpired.

"Do you believe they'll accept the offer you proffered on my behalf? The one you and I didn't exactly discuss?" Grigori asked.

I tried to read his tone and failed. Rather than apologize for overstepping my limits, I said, "I have no idea. I didn't plan things out. They just fell into place. We were about to leave after I catalogued the dead when Ione told me to test my link with Mother. I figured it for a fool's errand, but it wasn't."

"Ione believes they'll join us," Grigori pressed, seeking corroboration from me.

"Ione is an optimist. It's one of the things I love about him."

"He's a cat. They have solid instincts." Grigori pushed to his feet. "Get some rest, Kylian. You look beat."

"I am. See you tomorrow."

After Grigori let himself out I flopped face down on the bed, more emotionally drained than anything. I do best when I'm in action mode, kicking ass and solving problems. Waiting has never suited me.

I thought about Grigori. He didn't miss a lick. Staying on top of multiple issues and mages with divergent abilities was what made him such a competent leader. As I drifted into a trance that passes for sleep, I felt Mother's touch brush across my mind.

I could have imagined it. She'd have to be close to finesse contact. The more I turned it over, the surer I was it represented wishful thinking on my part.

When I woke from my trance, light streamed through the windows. Was it the next day? Or the one after that. Tough to tell. After another quick shower, I made my way to the wardrobe room. Joss handed me my original clothes with a smile.

"Return the others," he said. "I'll take care of them too."

"You're wonderfully efficient."

His smile widened. "I know, but I have the easy job."

True enough. For now, he did, but I bet we'd all be pressed into service before this was done. After thanking him, I made a quick trip back to my room, bundled my discarded clothes into a vector spell, and sent them his way. I'd done everything for myself for so long, being coddled felt incredibly decadent.

The guild house was quiet as I walked down several sets of stairs intent on the kitchen. It wasn't mealtime or I'd have heard the buzz of conversation and the clink of flatware. Preparations for the evening meal spanned several counters. I made myself a sandwich, layering slices of cheese atop fresh baked bread, as a stopgap.

I was halfway through eating it before it struck me that the lack of mages wandering in and out was unusual. Joss had been at his post, but where was everyone else? Activating my link with Ione, I left the kitchen, sandwich in hand, to locate him.

The snow leopard met me in the courtyard, casting covetous eyes at my sandwich. He wasn't serious. While he liked cheese, bread wasn't on his favorite food list.

"Where is everyone?" I asked.

"Grigori dispatched reconnaissance teams."

Surprise flooded me. "How long did I sleep?"

"Two days."

"Crap. You should have woken me."

"Not my decision."

"Mmph," I grunted. "Reconnaissance for what?"

"When the elemental mages didn't show up right away, Grigori sent teams to Hell. Each one had a unicorn."

I winced. "He's afraid my blood kin will reestablish their alliance with Satan."

Ione didn't bother to answer, but I could put two and two together. Any mages consorting with the wicked one would be executed via unicorn impalement. Ione had said unicorns, as in plural. From what I knew, Dorcha was the only one.

"How many unicorns are we talking about?"

"Three. Dorcha enticed two others to join the Circle. They're not bonded, so they may not remain."

I stuffed the last bite of sandwich into my mouth. When I was done chewing and swallowing, I said, "We should go after them."

"No need. They're expected back by dinner."

The supper preparations I'd seen in the kitchen rolled through my mind. "Did everyone go?"

Ione shook his head. "I believe several mages are sparring in the basement, experimenting with battle tactics."

It was as good a place as any to lose myself for a few hours and renew old acquaintances. "See you later," I told Ione.

"Not so fast. Have you heard from your mother?"

I started to say no, but then remembered her scuttling across my mind. "Maybe."

"What does that mean?"

"As I was drifting into trance, I thought I felt her, but I could have imagined it. Why'd you ask?"

"Because I can't see her joining ranks with evil."

"But you don't know her well," I protested.

"No, but I know you."

I sank a hand into his thick neck ruff. "Thanks for the vote of confidence, but one of my dick parents is moldering in a dungeon."

"He's not who raised you." Ione ducked from beneath my hand and loped off, tail pluming behind him.

I wasn't quite ready to test my link with Mother again, so I headed for the guild house basement. Grigori had constructed something like *Star Trek's* holodeck. Cunningly woven magic allowed an infinite variety of battle scenarios. Eerily real, they challenged the best of us.

Not that I'm arrogant, but I'd pit my skills against anyone's and trust I'd come out on top. I've never actually lost a battle, but I have had to leave and regroup a time or two. When I entered the arena, several groups of mages were engaged in a variety of situations, some with magic and others with weapons.

Because I was in the mood for physical pursuits, I snagged a broadsword off a wall rack and joined a mixed group of Fae and Sidhe working on technique. All men, the ones who knew me shouted a greeting. I'd figure out who the others were later.

For the next two hours, I swung and ducked and feinted, enjoying the heft of the blade in my hands. The stage the group had chosen featured lighted panels in the floor and a sultry female voice announcing victories—and defeats. Because they were six before I showed up, I alternated working with different mages. We'd spar until the killing blow, and then switch things up.

"Damn it, Kylian," a Fae shouted after I removed the edge of my blade from where it rested on his neck. "Do you ever lose?"

"Occasionally," I lied.

A Sidhe I remembered from years back thwacked me across the shoulder blades. "Good to have you aboard," he said.

"Grigori called all the old ones back," the Fae who'd remarked on my winning streak commented.

"Never heard it," I admitted, "but then I've been in some pretty remote locations."

"Doing what?" the Fae asked.

Everyone formed a circle. Apparently, we were taking a break.

"This and that," I hedged. "I've done a lot of mercenary work—with, erm, mortals."

"You and Quinn make quite the pair," the Sidhe said.

"I'm surprised your paths haven't crossed outside the guild house," the Fae tossed out.

"I'm not," I told him. "Mortals thrive on chaos. Lot of soldiers of fortune milling about."

"Will you stay with the Circle this time?" the Fae asked.

"Going to try."

"Good," another Sidhe said. "My hawk is quite fond of your leopard."

Interesting. If Ione had been making friends, he hadn't told me, but then we hadn't had much of a chance to talk about anything beyond the important stuff. Even on the best of days, we rarely engaged in small talk.

The Fae's head swiveled around. "Everyone's either back or close to it," he announced.

I mock swatted him. "I may come out on top in swordplay, but you're better than me picking up on subtle magical emanations."

He grinned, lighting his even features with mischief. "Want to trade?"

The question was rhetorical. I didn't bother answering. Swapping the broadsword for a towel, I wiped sweat from my face. The other groups had wrapped up long since. I'd been so intent on fighting—and winning—I'd never noticed their departures.

When I spread my power in an arc, I did sense a critical mass of mages already here with others on their way. Doing what I should have earlier, I tested my link with Mother.

Son of a bitch. She was in the grove. How long had she been there?

I left the arena with the others and smelled dinner as soon

as we reached steps leading to the main floor. Food could wait. I peeled off, aiming for the front door.

"Dinner's this way," someone called.

"Back soon," I replied and opened the elaborate front door with a shot of power. Once through it and down the steps I broke into a run. The grove wasn't far. Mother would have felt me reach for her. Had she assumed I'd finally get around to looking? Was it why she'd touched my thoughts days ago?

I tried to keep an open mind, but the way this was rolling out pissed me off. Like some sort of game of who blinks first. Not in the best of moods, I burst into the grove. Mother sat at the far end, her back balanced against a tree. I skidded to a stop a couple of feet away.

"You could have told me you were here."

"I did." She locked gazes with me.

"Pretty damned subtle if you ask me. I was falling asleep and figured I'd imagined it."

She got to her feet and dusted her hands together. "I failed. No one believed me about Grigori, so I am the only one here."

"And probably the only one left," I said sourly.

"What do you mean?"

"When elemental mages didn't show up, Grigori went looking in Hell. He sent teams armed with unicorns." I stopped there. No need to spell out the endgame. She'd already know.

Auralie shook her head sadly. "The Celts would have done us a favor if they'd wiped us out."

I walked near enough to grab her shoulders. "Stop that.

We have bigger problems. Are you here to fight for us? Or did you only stop by to tell me what happened?"

"I am not sure."

Desolation underscored her words; I let go of her. Like I've said, compassion isn't one of my strong suits, but I tried to put myself in her position. It wasn't a good place. Spurned by her companions, she probably assumed she'd sent them to their deaths.

"They made their choices," I reminded her. "Come inside. Join us for a meal."

A breath hissed from between her teeth. I figured she'd demur and teleport out of the grove. Instead, she said, "Thank you. Company that isn't sour and used up would be welcome."

Ione bounded to us between the grove and the house. The set of his tail told me he was pleased to see Mother. It also screamed vindication he'd been right about her. Cats can be real sons of bitches.

Dinner was in full swing, the dining hall noisy with the sounds of victory. Crap. Maybe this wasn't such a good idea after all. They were celebrating the demise of Mother's kinsmen. I bent close to her ear. "If you want to change your mind—" I began.

"I do not," she said in a clear, ringing voice.

It got everyone's attention; the room quieted within seconds. All eyes were trained on Mother and me. Grigori got to his feet and swept lightly from the dais, heading for us.

I held myself ready, unsure what he had in mind. Fresh from a killing field, he might assume Mother was some kind of spy in our midst.

The werewolf halted a few feet away. "Auralie. Why have you come?"

"A fair question," Mother replied. "I remember you from when you seduced Kylian from our ranks."

Grigori's mouth twitched into half of a smile. "I remember you as well, one pissed off mage."

"I suppose I was." She nodded, fair hair dancing around her. "I apologize for my kin. I extended your offer. They declined."

"I gathered as much. I cleaned a few minds before the unicorns delivered death blows."

Sadness spilled from Mother in waves, but she held herself proud. "They deserved what they got," she said in strained tones. "None of us should ever propagate evil."

"Will you fight with us?" Grigori's question was soft.

"Aye, that I will. My family is gone. A bigger question is whether you'll have me after my kinsmen's defection."

A silver unicorn trotted to where we stood and laid a horn on Mother's shoulder. Auralie twisted to look at the beast. I did too. This must be one of the other two Ione had told me about.

"I want this mage as my bondmate," the unicorn told Grigori.

The werewolf raised russet brows, clearly surprised by an unanticipated development. "What do you think?" he asked Mother.

She turned and laid both hands on the unicorn's withers. Power flickered between them, but I didn't listen in. What passed between bondmate and mage was private. The rest of the room were on their feet; they'd formed a rough circle around us, their food forgotten.

Waves of welcoming magic wafted our way, wrapping around us. Newly bonded pairs were always cause for celebration. Mother switched her focus from the unicorn to Grigori and said, "I agree to the bond," in formal tones.

"Excellent news." Grigori extended his hands in front of him, chanting to seal the partnership.

Was this something new. I didn't recall him doing that for Ione and me. Eh, of course he hadn't. I'd arrived already bonded. I traced the bones of his spell and found a purification element. Grigori was no fool, and he wanted Mother and the unicorn to get off to a good start.

When he was done, he said, "I apologize for what happened to the other elemental mages."

"No need," Mother replied. "They brought it on themselves."

The unicorn nudged her shoulder. "Come with me."

Mother vaulted to her new bondmate's back, and they left the room. Food and introductions could wait. What she would do in the next span of time was far more important.

Grigori flapped his hands at the circle of mages. "Finish your meal. This is a good ending to a difficult day."

I didn't ask for details. They weren't important. Moving to the back of the room where food was spread on a long table, I filled a plate and looked for a place to sit. As he'd done before, Xander motioned me over. Tonight, he and Rhiana were at a table with four women: a Fae, a Sidhe, a wolf shifter, and a mage whose origins weren't readily apparent.

Rhiana poured something spicy, smelling of anise, into my goblet. I killed it in one long swallow and held out the glass for more.

"I told Grigori to include you on one of the teams,"

Xander told her, "but he overruled me. Said nothing would be gained by you being party to killing more of your own."

"He was right," Rhiana said firmly. "I still haven't gotten over what I did. And I doubt I ever will."

No wonder Grigori had issued orders not to wake me to join the carnage.

Xander placed a hand over one of hers in a protective gesture. I focused on eating. I've never been much of a foodie, but I was hungry. Any meal I didn't have to prepare was a win.

"Aren't you going to introduce us?" the shifter asked.

"Sorry," Rhiana said. "Kylian, meet Mora, Braen, Sarae, and Tessa."

Assuming she'd listed the women in the order they were seated, I glanced at the one I couldn't figure out. "Are you Tessa?"

"I am, but that's not what you really want to know." A pair of green eyes twinkled merrily. Flame-red hair had been cropped to shoulder length and fluffed into curls. Her fair skin was freckled, and she was dressed in a flowing white linen shirt that wrapped around her tunic style. The swell of breasts pushed against the filmy fabric. Rings adorned every finger, and a series of copper necklaces sported a variety of semi-precious stones.

"What do I really want to know?" I smiled and set my fork next to my plate.

"What I am. No one gets it right the first time." She winked broadly, daring me to guess.

I took a different tack. "If you want me to know, you'll tell me. What animal are you bonded with?"

"A red fox."

"Does she match your hair?"

"Now that you mention it, she does."

The clip-clop of hoofs told me Mother and the unicorn were back. Mother walked next to the creature's side; a soft glow surrounded them. I glanced at Xander and Rhiana. "What's the unicorn's name?"

"Demelza," Rhiana replied. "I'm happy for her. Dorcha was urging her to find a bondmate, but it's not simple. All the mages here are already bonded, which means looking out in the world. Aidyrth managed it by pilfering dreams, but it took her years to find Shira."

Grigori stood and raised his hands, calling for everyone's attention. "Tomorrow, we will move our base of operations to the Nevada guild house. It's not as large as this one, but it has far better access to our next target."

Intriguing since I had no idea where we'd strike next. From the expectant looks on people's faces, neither did anyone else.

Rhea joined Grigori, facing the assemblage. "I am just learning to pluck information from the unwilling," she said. "Grigori is an excellent teacher. He coached me while I drew thoughts from our last, erm, target." She cleared her throat. "One of the things we unearthed was a Vampire alliance spread through the United States. They have close ties to mages who've turned traitor."

"They are our next logical target," Grigori growled. "We will find them, destroy them, and ship their pieces to Hell."

"But they're already dead," Shira pointed out from her seat in the center of the room.

"When we get done with them, they'll be even deader," Grigori assured her with a feral grin.

I catalogued the various methods for killing the Undead. Beheading has always been a personal favorite. Maybe my subconscious knew something when I decided to practice with a broadsword earlier today.

"Decapitation or a stake through the heart," Grigori was saying. "We have the location of several nests, but after we hit the first one, I bet the others will be empty."

"They decompose fast," Rhiana spoke up. "If a Vamp is several hundred years old, they'll turn into a pile of bones within seconds."

Mother walked forward. "I'm new, so perhaps I shouldn't ask questions, but how will this forward our cause?"

"We will strip information about traitorous mages from them," Grigori explained. "If we do a good enough job, they may not surface for centuries. It's happened before in the Old Country. When they feel threatened, and their seethes are destroyed, they drop out of sight."

The whole Vamp gig was coming back. I stood. "They can go into stasis," I added. "Where they slow their already-dead metabolism, so they don't have to feed for as much as a century."

"Aye and they're much harder to find in that state," Grigori said. "We will have to be quick. We'll work in teams and plan simultaneous strikes, but we'll flesh out the details once we're all in Nevada. We leave tomorrow by midday."

"Why not simply wipe out Hell?" Xander asked. "Seems simpler, more straightforward."

"Unfortunately, it provides a balance point," Grigori replied. "My fond hope is that Satan and his twisted princes will go to ground too and behave themselves. If we're a big enough pain in their asses, they might decide the risk-benefit ratio isn't worth it."

He took Rhea's hand, and they left the room. Other mages followed, clearing perhaps half the room. Mother and the unicorn were among those who departed. I wished them well. Being newly bonded is a heady experience.

Mages at my table were standing and bidding one another a good evening. What I did next was totally unplanned, and it happened too quickly for me to modulate my words—or actions.

I walked around the table and caught up with Tessa when she was halfway to the main door. "Care for some company?" I asked.

She stopped dead and twirled to face me, a confused look on her face. "You're serious, aren't you?"

"I am, but if you're tired, I understand."

"Why me?"

"Why not?" I kept my tone light.

A fluffy fox about the size of a coyote bounded across the room. When it reached Tessa, it clawed its way up her side. Now that she was standing, I saw she wore denim trousers. Medium height and slightly built, she projected a waiflike innocence, but she did it to hide her strength.

The fox was perched on her shoulders; it hissed at me.

Tessa laughed. "Don't mind Zoe. She's like an overprotective mother."

"We could sit in the library, or walk a bit," I persisted. Fuck. What was wrong with me? I'd tossed out an invitation. She'd skated around it. That should be the end of things.

"A walk would be nice," she said.

I'd been so certain she was about to send me packing, I stood mired in place, thunderstruck. "What did you say?"

She gave me a look that clearly said men were stupid. "You invited me to go for a walk, right?"

"I did." To avoid further embarrassment, I placed a hand under her elbow and guided us from the room. Selecting a side door, we swapped the guild house for a clear night with a sky peppered by stars.

Clear skies in this spot meant chilly, so I wrapped us in a blanket of warmth.

"Show off," she teased.

"Do you want me to take it away?"

"Sure. Remove your spell."

Not understanding why she'd want to be cold, I reeled in my casting. She sidestepped a short distance away and repositioned herself so she faced me, blocking forward motion. Power swirled around her, and she extended her arms.

Shock seared me. No wonder I didn't recognize what she was. She'd hidden her true nature, but her kind were rarest of the rare.

"Witch shapeshifter," I muttered and watched her morph through a dozen forms before returning to the primary one.

Tessa clasped her hands together. "You've known others like me?"

"Only one, and it was long ago."

The fox chittered displeasure. Maybe she was angry because Tessa had revealed herself. Before I could address her ire, magic split the night, and the two of them were gone. I stared at the spot where they'd been expecting them to pop back into sight. It didn't happen.

Disappointment carved a trail through me. Whoever Tessa was, I wanted to find out a whole lot more about her. If she'd let me.

Big if. This was why I'd avoided women except in cozy groups like the Nereids. Confused why she'd outed herself, and then left, I went in search of Ione. We could hunt. It would kick me in the butt and bring me back to my senses. I did not need Tessa in my life. Approaching her had been a mistake.

Lucky for me, she'd given me an out by leaving.

Whistling an old folk tune, I strode through the night, tracking my bondmate.

❧ 8 ❧

Ione and I hunted through the night, feasting on a variety of small game. I prefer my meat cooked, but I've eaten plenty of it raw too. I gathered a few things, including the broadsword I'd used during my practice session, and the leopard and I were on our way quickly.

Twenty hours later, everyone was assembled at the Nevada guild house. Some of us would sleep in the desert since the place couldn't accommodate our full numbers. I hadn't seen Tessa, but I kept looking for her on the QT. I thought I was being surreptitious, but I didn't fool Ione. He knew something was up.

Maybe she'd be at dinner, I told myself when I hadn't located her. And then I reminded myself of last night's mini self-lecture. The one where I'd made it abundantly clear she was a bad idea.

One I'd regret.

We were here to wipe out enough seethes to deal vampires

out of the equation. They could shapeshift too, much like Tessa... Some could even fly. I shook myself from head to toe and pushed through the guild house door on my way outside. A run in the desert, by myself, was in order. All roads did not lead to Tessa.

What was the matter with me?

Once I'd settled into an easy lope, I ticked off all the reasons I had to forget about her. At the top of the list was her fox. Her bond animal didn't like me. Hell, it might not have been about me. Maybe the creature didn't like anyone getting too close to her bondmate.

Reason two was all about me. For the moment, I'd rejoined the Circle, but Ione and I probably wouldn't remain once the current crisis was over. I didn't see incorporating another mage into my peripatetic mercenary lifestyle. Particularly not a woman. While mages are evenly split gender-wise, very few soldiers of fortune were of the female persuasion.

Dusk was creeping across the sagebrush, turning it violet. From the looks of the sky, a storm was brewing. The desert was pockmarked with washes where water had taken the path of least resistance. When I searched for small animals, they'd mostly gone to ground. A brisk wind blew up kicking sand and pebbles into my hands and face. Sharp little bits that stung when they connected.

Ione dropped out of nowhere and matched his pace to mine once his paws connected with the ground. Guess he'd been looking for me. Instead of his usual laconic greeting, he hissed, "What's wrong with you?"

I stopped running and faced him. "What's wrong with you, mate?"

Every whisker sat at attention; hackles rose the length of his spine. "How can you not feel that?"

I'd been focused inward, dithering about Tessa. In response to Ione's question, I sent power spinning in an arc. Breath whistled from me. "Because I wasn't paying attention, but I am now."

"Everyone else is inside the guild house. A separate group of ghouls has it surrounded. We kept waiting for you. I knew exactly where you were, but you weren't moving any nearer."

"Ghouls? Where the fuck did they come from? Why didn't you reach for me through our link?" Gathering water and earth, I built a ward and tossed it over the two of us. Once I had bare bones protection in place, I turned in a full circle testing, probing.

Not that I'd doubted Ione's assessment, but a slimy batch of Undead circled us. I should be honored I'd rated my very own cadre, separate from the one next to the guild house. How had so many congregated in one spot? There must have been a major battle here long ago, but it didn't explain why the army lurching our way hadn't crossed over.

Mortals die. Reapers come to collect them. End of story. The occasional stubborn soul refuses to leave, but I'd never come across a group nearly this size. Reapers report to Death. Surely, she knew about this recalcitrant pack. The question was why she hadn't intervened.

Quinn used to have a cozy relationship with Death. Maybe he could ask her.

Unlike Vampires, ghouls didn't drink blood or make new ghouls. They did, however, feast on the living, mowing through whatever they found and moving on. We'd never had problems with them before in this spot, but this many of us had never been at the Nevada guild house, either.

I snapped my fingers, pleased to have stumbled onto a reason they'd risen from their final resting places to storm the guild house. Next to me, Ione crafted a teleport spell.

"Good plan," I murmured.

"If it works," the snow leopard growled.

His power swelled around us, various colors ripped this way and that by the wind. Increasing by the moment, it howled like a mad thing. But it wasn't only the wind. Some of the noise was inchoate moaning from the host drawing steadily nearer.

Visible now, they surrounded us. Like all ghosts, they moved through one another, reforming on the other side. The wind shifted; an unholy stench wafted our way. Long-dead flesh somehow renewed itself enough to smell freshly killed. Acrid and sour and rancid all wrapped into a nauseating brew. Where skin had fallen away, bone glistened in what was left of light from the dying day.

It seemed Ione's spell would take. The scene around us faded, but then it snapped back into place.

I tapped into Ione's magic, adding to it. "Try again," I urged.

Confident we could power our way out of this, I laid on the afterburners. With the same results. We edged toward escape for all of a minute before a blast of enchantment ricocheted back at us.

Ione ramped up for another try, but I said, "Nope. Conserve your power. Not going to happen that way." Eying the horde, now maybe a hundred feet away, I switched to telepathy. Ghouls shouldn't be able to intercept it.

Of course, someone was probably behind them, piloting them, but I'd address that once we found an escape hatch.

"We're going to make a run for it," I said.

"But we'll run right into the circle around the guild house," Ione protested.

"We'll break through that one too." I hesitated, and then added, *"Our only other option is sinking into the earth. She'll open channels for us, but it will take a lot more time."*

No more talk. The guild house was a couple of miles away. At top speed, we'd be there in under ten minutes. If things turned to shit, I could implement plan B and lose us in the earth beneath our feet.

I tapped Ione's shoulder and bolted forward, running as fast as I could. We reached the leading edge of the ghouls almost immediately. They weren't as insubstantial as I'd assumed. Rather than cutting through their dead flesh, we ended up weaving in and out while teeth and nails tore at us. Ione's thick fur protected him, but blood flowed down one of my arms where the lower part was torn open.

Ione knocked one loathsome stinking corpse down, leaving bloody claw marks. How in the hell could these abominations still have anything that even approximated blood? Vampires did, but they were different. The transformation mired them in a spot between life and death.

These fuckers should be well and truly deceased.

An eerie twilight formed. My sense of direction, usually cast in stone, wavered. Was I leading us in a straight line? I didn't see how I could be since ghouls stretched on all sides. No matter how far we ran, we never got away from them.

Was their infernal circle moving with us? I couldn't tell.

A long-dead woman with wispy clumps of steel-gray hair

and empty dark eyes chomped into my wrist. Pain flared, running up my arm. I stopped long enough to flatten her permanently with the unmaking spell. She'd lost any chance at the afterlife, but I didn't give a fuck. Even though she was unraveling before my eyes, the pain battering my arm intensified.

I slapped magical patches around the damage, hoping to keep it local. Her bite meted out far more pain than it should have. When I probed my wrist, an unexpected answer pissed me off. The ghoul's saliva contained iron pyrite, a poison specific to magic-wielders. None of this was possible, but it was happening anyway. It circled me back to my theory about someone directing the onslaught.

Determined to get to the guild house while I still could, I hunted for it and established a vector to follow. If Ione and I had been running in circles, my strategy would circumvent that problem.

"What happened to your arm?" Ione sounded worried.

"Run," I shouted and pelted forward, keeping the vector to my left. Night had arrived. It made my shining strand of power easier to hold in view. The snow leopard fell in behind me, keeping ghouls at bay. Despite my best efforts, the iron from my wound was spreading.

I felt hot and then cold. Sweat soaked through my clothing. I didn't understand any of it. I'd never been injured before. By anyone. Forcing my legs to propel myself forward was becoming harder and harder. We'd passed the circle of ghouls, breaking through the last of them. Undaunted, they stuck behind us in pursuit. We were quicker, but it wouldn't last.

My strength was fading, along with my magic.

Ione looped another teleport spell around us. For some unknown reason, this one worked. Maybe we were far enough away from the horde, or perhaps whoever was running the ghoul show needed to replenish their stores of power. Because we circumnavigated the pack of dead around the guild house via Ione's casting, we were inside in short order.

My bondmate's plaintive yowling seemed as if it were coming from a long way away.

Hands lifted me and carried me somewhere with me protesting I could walk. Big words. In my state, crawling was beyond me. Blazing pain did battle with the ripping sounds of fabric as someone cut through my sleeve from shoulder to wrist with a blade that penetrated flesh as well as fabric.

A cloying stench assaulted my nose, so revolting I tried not to breathe. With far more effort than it should have taken, I pried my eyes open long enough to look at my arm. Air whooshed from me; I forgot about not breathing. My right arm was swollen to twice its normal size. The flesh was black except where the White Fae laboring over me had sliced through to bone.

"For fuck's sake. What did that to me?" I wheezed.

"Quiet," someone, perhaps Grigori, ordered.

"What happened?" Damn. Talking was excruciating. I worked at it afraid if I faded beyond where I could find words, there'd be no coming back. I'd run into iron before. It had posed a superficial annoyance, nothing like this.

Ione padded past the phalanx of mages around me and lay next to my injured side. He reached for me with his magic, linking us together and lending me strength.

"It would be simpler if he weren't here," someone murmured.

Ione growled. I felt rather than heard the vibration where his body was plastered against mine.

"Work around him," Grigori said in terse tones.

He of all people understood how critical the bond was when either mage or animal was critically wounded. For him to overrule the White Fae told me how perilous my condition was.

My thoughts fragmented after that. I drifted in and out, sometimes aware of the guild house infirmary, but more often floating in a nether realm with bits and pieces of my past flashing by. I lost track of time, or it lost track of me. Through it all, Ione's presence was an anchor, the only thing holding me on this side of Death's door.

Speaking of Death, she rose out of nowhere, an imposing figure in her heavy black robes. Sickle in hand, she shook a finger at me and told me it wasn't my time, that I had to try harder. With her long black hair shot with silver and penetrating dark eyes, she always looked the same.

Heat poured off me in waves, followed by uncontrollable shivering. When I broke out in a cold sweat, it seemed I'd passed a critical juncture, but I still had no idea if I'd make it or not.

Whinnies assaulted my ears. Crap, my senses were hyper touchy. Horns ran the length of my body, focused on the side where my arm throbbed mercilessly. My mouth was parched. If I'd had any spit, I'd have ordered them away, told them to leave me be. Anything adding to the torment my body had turned into was intolerable.

I grunted but reined it in before I cried out. I'd hold onto what little dignity I retained, for the gods' sake. The infirmary shattered, replaced by my father grinning like a gargoyle.

"Imprison me, will you? Impertinent whelp. I will make your life a living hell. How do you like it so far?" Cackling laughter chilled and infuriated me. Fuck. I should have ended him when I had the chance. I didn't have a way to do that, but I could have had Aidyrth ferry him to Fire Mountain and drop him into a fumarole.

A small satisfaction bloomed in me. I'd been right about a renegade mage powering the ghouls. That it was my father was totally unexpected, but now I knew who I was dealing with, I'd figure things out.

Poseidon faded to streamers of blue light. The dungeons must have hampered his magic, just as I'd hoped they would, but he'd reached through the sea to activate the ghoul army. Someone had to be helping him, or he'd never have known where to find me.

The next time the infirmary shaped up around me, I tried to tell the healers leaning over me about Poseidon. Knowing the iron had been harvested from the sea would help them fight it. My mouth and tongue and lips refused to cooperate. Did I have enough power for telepathy?

No time like right now to find out. I was still losing ground at an alarming rate. *"Ione?"*

"Yes?" His reply was instantaneous and shot full of worry.

"Poseidon's doing. All this." Crap, I was far from articulate, but the snow leopard would understand.

He did. Snatches of his deep rumbly voice faded in and out as he told whoever was in the room about the god of the sea's vendetta against me. Everything fuzzed out after that.

Until I opened my eyes to a circle of anxious faces

ringed around me. Grigori. Rhea. Quinn. Ciara. Xander. Rhiana. Mother. And many White Fae. I wasn't sweating or panting or struggling to breathe. Death was nowhere in sight. She'd done her job—or been a hallucination. When I looked at my arm, it was normal size again. Most of the black had retreated, leaving a long, red scar from shoulder to wrist.

"Thank you," I murmured and flailed around struggling to sit. They knew better than to help me. After battling a wave of dizziness, I managed to cross my legs and straighten my back. Ione moved behind me, giving me something to lean on.

"Knowing it was Poseidon must have helped." I looked from one White Fae to the next until I'd exchanged glances with all ten of them. Whoa. They'd put out a call for reinforcements. Guess Death hadn't been an illusion after all.

"Very much," one of the Fae replied in solemn tones.

"It gave us a firm starting point," another agreed. "Before that, we were trying different combinations, but nothing was especially effective until we latched onto the sea blood in you."

"Part of that is my fault," Mother said. "I was instructing them wrongly because I assumed Poseidon was tucked safely away."

"He might be tucked away, but his reach is still broad." I winced. How could I have made such a monumental error thinking I'd shackled him? I'd expected him to work on freeing himself, but I figured I'd bought myself a century or two of peace.

"What happened to the ghouls around the guild house?" I asked.

"They melted away as soon as you were inside," Grigori replied. "It was when we understood you were their target."

"Why'd they bother with posting ghouls around the house?" I wondered.

"They didn't know where you were," Quinn said. "When Ione went looking for you, the only pack of ghouls was here."

My memory had holes, but before the snow leopard found me, there hadn't been ghoul one. "They followed you," I told Ione. It made sense. Poseidon knew damn good and well who my bondmate was.

A deep growl suggested Ione didn't care for my implication. I twisted to stroke his dense coat. "Not your fault. They'd have located me regardless through my blood link to Poseidon."

"Are you together enough to consider what happens next?" Grigori crouched in front of me and offered a flagon of something alcoholic.

"Of course." I nodded. Grateful to be back in action mode, I took the mug and drained it.

"We still need to implement our original plan," Grigori went on. "While you were being treated, some of us worked on how to deal with the larger seethes in North America."

"Poseidon has to be my problem," I said firmly. No way would I allow my twisted father to get in the way of the Circle's business.

"You can't kill him," Rhiana said.

"No, but I'll come up with something."

"You're not alone in this," Mother said.

Hearing her voice was still a shock after all these years. "I should be," I told her. "If I'd planned better, he wouldn't have leveraged his connection with Satan to loose the ghouls."

Other mages were crowding into the infirmary. The White Fae must have barred it to everyone not essential to my treatment. Not wanting to appear weak, I got my feet under me and glowered at everyone.

"I'm fine," I growled. "Thanks for your concern."

Fine was relative. I was still shockingly weak. If it hadn't been for Ione still being linked with me, I'd have fallen over.

Xander draped an arm around my shoulders. "You need food," he announced. "We can continue our discussion in the dining room."

"Thanks," I mumbled. Food. Rest. Time. Between the three, I'd rise to fight another day. A glimpse of red toward the back of the infirmary drew my attention. Had Tessa come to look in on me?

Why not? I asked myself. *Everyone else is here.*

Except, they weren't. The infirmary was large, but it wouldn't hold much more than twenty-five. I shook my head to clear the layers of fuzz coating my brain. Even if Tessa was here, it didn't mean anything.

She'd revealed what she was and vanished.

Xander supported me as we strode from the infirmary, but he was subtle about it. To casual eyes, he appeared to walk next to me.

Whatever had been in Grigori's brew was working. I felt stronger by the moment. Before we reached the dining room, I was walking on my own. Thank all the gods, I was recovering my strength quickly. I'd need every whit of it before too much longer.

"Good to know who our enemies are," Xander said.

I nodded agreement. Tonight had been rough, but it could

have been worse. "I wonder if the dragons will agree to hold him on Fire Mountain. It's a big favor."

"That's a good question for Aidyrth. I'll find her. You eat something," Xander replied.

I snapped off a mock salute. "You got it."

fter a pleasant dinner where everyone made a point
of stopping by and wishing me well, I made my way
to an isolated circle of Joshua trees and waited for
Aidyrth. Chilly, clear, and lovely, the night surrounded me
with an enchantment all its own. Desert nights are full of
chittering rodents warning one another of predators closing
in. The piercing squeal of night hawks on the prowl mingled
with the odd, piercing noise foxes make. Wolves howled in
the distance.

After an initial period of reticence, the Joshua trees
accepted Ione and me into their midst. They aren't exactly
trees, but large cactuses with their trunks full of water. Both
Grigori and Xander had reached out to Aidyrth, and I choose
the most private meeting spot available. It wasn't magical like
the grove near the main guild house, but it would have to do.

Not wanting to make a total pest out of myself in light of
the enormity of the favor I was about to request, I was

content to wait. Ione alternated pacing with purring. Night was his time; I felt certain he'd rather be hunting.

"Do what you want." I made gentle shooing motions in his direction. "You'll know when she shows up."

He shot me a pointed look and resumed pacing. He hadn't left my side since my stint in the infirmary and, while I appreciated his devotion, it wasn't as if I'd melt into a puddle of goo if he took his eyes off me.

"Go on," I urged.

Mage energy flared nearby. Assuming it was Aidyrth's bondmate, Shira, I didn't examine it closely. A cursory scan of the night sky didn't yield the dragon's unmistakable bulk. Neither did I sense dragon enchantment. Its blend of fire and ash and stones baking under an African sun is impossible to mistake.

I'd been slouched against a tree, sharing its essence, but I shot upright and extended tentacles of seeking magic. No clear answer emerged. "Grigori, is that you?" I asked softly.

"Nope. Me." Tessa glided into the grove.

I stared at her dumbfounded. She'd slipped a fluffy black jacket over her shoulders and a black watch cap over her bright hair.

"Aren't you going to ask why I'm here?" She flashed a mischievous grin my way.

"You'll tell me, regardless." I aimed for nonchalant, but I was delighted to see her. No matter how I damped it down, some of my enthusiasm had to seep through.

She nodded. "I will. First off, I adore Aidyrth. But more importantly, I'd like to sign on for taking Poseidon down."

Her fox raced into the clearing hissing and spitting. "No. No. And no," she squealed. "I will not allow you to—"

Ione planted himself in front of the fox, blocking forward motion with his thick body. "You and Tessa have a working partnership," he reminded her.

"Thanks," Tessa told him. "At least one of you has common sense."

A high keening wail from the fox was followed by, "This is not our fight. Poseidon didn't attack you, and—"

Unfamiliar magic swirled around Tessa rife with the scents of pitch, vanilla, and wet leaves. She morphed into a much larger version of her bondmate and sidled between Ione and the fox.

"Quiet." Tessa infused command into that single word.

"But I want you safe," the fox whined.

Tessa's form sprouted wings, shifting from a giant fox to something more like a griffon.

"We do not make decisions for one another," Tessa reminded her bondmate.

The fox sat still, whiskers twitching. It was as good a time as any for me to ask, "Why do you wish to accompany Ione and me?"

With a shake of her head, Tessa reclaimed her human form. "Poseidon violated me long before the fox and I joined forces." She paused a moment before adding "You don't look surprised."

I muffled a snort. "Because I'm not. What happened?"

Tessa shrugged. "Same shit. Different day. I was young and playing in the sea wearing a Selkie's form. The Kraken swept me up in a dance and—"

"The one where his coils undulate around you and sentient thought takes a powder?" I cut in.

Tessa twisted her mouth into a sour expression. "Ah, so you're familiar with it."

"Aye. My father has used his pet sea serpent to imprison many women. You were far from the first. Neither were you the last."

Ione growled. The fox was rubbing its body along Tessa's ankles. Distress sheeted off the animal at how shabbily her bondmate had been dealt with.

"Go on," I urged. "What happened after this dance?"

"Ensorcellment deprived me of consciousness. When I woke I was in the sea god's dungeon. It took me years to figure a way out."

"Why not take advantage of the times he, erm, visited?" It was my diplomatic way of asking why she hadn't clonked him over the head and escaped during sex. If there's one time men are vulnerable, that's it.

Bitter laughter wafted from her. "It was only once, and he didn't get anywhere. I kept shifting bodies. No magic of his was strong enough to hold me in a fuckable form."

Fierce protectiveness arrowed through me. I was pleased she'd stymied him, overjoyed he'd finally bitten off more than he could chew. "How long before you broke free?"

She set her mouth in a tense line. "Nearly five years. The dungeons hobbled my magic if I projected it beyond the coral walls. I've had nightmares about my time there since it happened, so this is personal for me. Surely, you could use another mage. More hands. Diverse magic. How hard could it be? You've already captured him."

"Harder than you might think," I admitted. It went against the grain not to play the macho card and gloss over difficulties.

Much as I wanted Tessa along, I opted to be practical. What I had in mind required split-second timing. A second mage might well get in the way, and I didn't trust her fox at all. If I got lucky and Aidyrth agreed to help, Tessa and the fox would make three bonded pairs milling about in the depths of the sea.

One task I'd farm out to Ione was warning the Kraken to lie low. Poseidon was vindictive as hell and had a long memory. Hanging onto the sea god once we sprung him would be the dicey part, and the Kraken had to be well out of harm's way in case something went wrong.

The heavy flap of wings from overhead drew my gaze skyward. Aidyrth's red-and-gray bulk hurtled toward me. Dragons throw off both heat and light; what was left of the night retreated around her. Breath rustled from me. I'd been close to moving to plan B.

It still might happen. Dragonkind owed me nothing, and I was asking them to take on a forever burden.

Aidyrth skidded in for a landing, sending sand and small pebbles flying every which way. Shira jumped from her back, breaking her fall with a shot of visible magic. She'd changed her hair again. This time it was black and purple-blue and set off her features better than the pink-and-purple scheme had. On the ground, she trotted this way and that, presumably to sort out stiff muscles. Dressed in black from head to toe, she blended in with the night.

I'd have given anything to be stiff from riding a dragon—or a unicorn. But the unfinished bits on my bucket list weren't relevant.

Fiery ash plumed from the dragon's flared nostrils; she folded leathery red wings behind her back. Tessa's eyes rounded with wonder. Dragons had that effect on most everyone.

"I kept you waiting because I had to confer with our council," Aidyrth announced.

Damn it. Meant Grigori—or maybe Xander—had already posed my dilemma. I'd have preferred to manage it in my own way. Soften the burden with promises to send rotating groups of sea people to watch over their damaged king, so the task didn't fall squarely on the dragons.

I straightened my back, ready for whatever she had to tell me.

"Consensus was a long while coming," Aidyrth went on. Her jaws lolled, displaying double rows of gleaming teeth.

I took a chance and jumped in. "What exactly did Grigori tell you?"

Spinning eyes zeroed in on me. I held her gaze, which was far from an easy task. "Don't you know?" the dragon boomed.

"Nay." I reverted to Gaelic. "My expectation was they'd tell you I wished to confer over an important matter."

"Your sire nearly killed you," Shira ground out. "Important matter is quite the understatement."

Ione left the fox's side and glided to Shira, rubbing his head against her ribcage. She sank her fingers into his lush pelt. Rumbly purrs filled the clearing.

"What he said," Aidyrth went on, sounding like a buzz saw, "was Poseidon partnered with Satan to raise ghouls against you. Since your sire is already imprisoned in his own dungeons—and it's clearly ineffective—something different must happen. In this case, you were hoping my kinsmen would accept the sea god and keep him from further mischief by imprisoning him on Fire Mountain. Is that close?"

"Close, aye. I command the sea people and will ensure assistance watching over Poseidon."

Smoke billowed from the dragon's jaws. "Not exactly a selling point. As you know, dragons rarely concern themselves with non-dragon affairs. We wouldn't welcome a rotating group of sea folk on our world."

I nodded and girded myself for a no. I didn't actually have a Plan B, but I'd come up with something even if it meant ferrying dear old dad to a distant borderworld and permanently hobbling his magic so he couldn't leave. Like I said, my fallback plan needed a whole lot more details to turn into something viable.

"In this case," Aidyrth went on, "we will make an exception because of Poseidon's obvious link with Satan and the underworld."

I culled through the long years of my memories seeking a connection and not finding one. Bowing my head, I said, "Please extend my heartfelt thanks to your council. It's none of my affair, but what did Satan do to offend dragonkind?"

Smoke turned to fire. A nearby Joshua tree started to smolder, but their trunks are full of water, so they're not prone to burning. "Tried to steal Fire Mountain from us," the dragon said through still more flames. "And that is all I shall say about it."

Shock rolled through me. First I'd heard about it, which meant the dragons had kept the attempted coup quiet. I could see Fire Mountain's allure. With its ring of volcanoes, extreme heat, and remote location, the dragons' home world would be attractive to demons. Sort of like an above-ground version of Hell, but so far away from everywhere no one would bother them.

Shira moved to Tessa. "Are you part of this?"

"I'd like to be." Tessa replied. Her fox streaked from the clearing making little hissing noises.

"Do you have a plan?" Aidyrth asked me.

"The bones of one," I told the dragon. "We free him, bind him, and then you transport him to Fire Mountain where I hope you can toss him into a pit so deep there's no escape."

"Why not transport him from the dungeon?" Aidyrth asked.

"Magic doesn't project well from there," Tessa answered.

The dragon shifted her attention to the shapeshifting witch. "Been there, eh?"

"I have."

"Everyone Poseidon imprisons is magical," I explained. "The dungeon would be worthless if people teleported right back out of it."

Aidyrth arched a scaled brow. "No dungeon ever constructed could contain a dragon. Shall we hedge our bets?"

I nodded, waiting to hear what she'd recommend.

"Do you suppose he has a few of Hell's minions on tap?" Shira asked.

"It's likely," I replied. "Satan doesn't do well in the sea."

"Go-betweens?" Tessa furled her red brows.

"Makes sense," Shira muttered. "Demons for whom water is more of a native environment. They're probably who ferried the message to Satan to loose his ghouls."

Aidyrth bugled, scattering fire about. "We missed at least one spy in the Circle. Otherwise, how could anyone have known where you were?"

"Perhaps they didn't have to." I spoke slowly. "The location of the guild houses isn't exactly secret. Satan and his princes could have collected that information from the spies we caught."

"Are you thinking they set guards at each location?" Tessa asked.

"Maybe, but they wouldn't have had to be even that fancy," I told her. "A simple beacon system attuned to the presence of magic would do it."

"We're getting off track," Shira spoke up and looked at her bondmate. "Tell them what you told me while we were en route."

"Come close," Aidyrth crooked a talon our way. We formed a semicircle in front of her. Three mages and a snow leopard. The dragon bugled again, and Tessa's fox slunk between two Joshua trees. "You do not get to sit this one out," the dragon said firmly."

I'm not sure what it cost the fox to stand up to the dragon, but she raised her muzzle, whiskers quivering. "I am not in favor of this mission."

"You don't have to go," Tessa said crisply.

"Aye, she does," Aidyrth contradicted her. "Both of you, or neither of you."

Tessa tapped my upper arm. "Will you accept my help?"

"Not if your bondmate is this ambivalent. All she'll do is cause trouble."

The fox twisted long enough to hiss at me.

"Give me a shot at her. I believe I can get through." Tessa screwed her mouth into a frown. "I don't get it. We've never had this kind of disagreement before."

"Maybe you've never presented a task she disagreed with," I said.

"That's not it. Back in five." She morphed into a large

black bird, snatched the fox in her talons, and took off. I still couldn't get over the ease with which she traded forms. Even shifters took far longer to move from one form to another.

Residual magic from her shift permeated the air, leaving it liquid and glittery. "Why do they both have to come?" I asked the dragon.

"What we have set out to do is dangerous. She knows too much to leave behind. Or she will once we've set the steps in stone. Even if she's not here listening, she has a direct line to Tessa's thoughts." Aidyrth hesitated before going on. "The one caveat from my kinsmen was I would do this quietly, not draw attention to us or our destination."

Of course. The dragons wanted to avoid a repeat of demons mobbing Fire Mountain demanding Poseidon's release. Far better for his location to remain a closely guarded secret.

The dragon dropped a sound shield around us. She wasn't trying for stealth, and it clanked and clattered as it locked into place. "My basic idea is this," she said. "I will enter Poseidon's cell and breathe fire down his throat. It will immobilize him, but it may not last long. While I am doing that, the two of you will carve a track from the sea to his cell where you sweep away whatever enchantment circles the dungeon."

"Make a hole so your teleport spell doesn't run into any impediments," I clarified.

"Exactly," Shira said. "The two of us can manage it, but it would go quicker if Tessa helped. She can change into a fish or a Selkie."

"Speed will be our friend," Aidyrth seconded. "The one big unknown is how long I can knock him out. If I have to grapple with him and pilot a transport spell at the same time, he might slip from my grasp."

"I told her she needed one of us along," Shira said. "Maybe both of us. You're the logical choice since you share part of his magic."

"Not necessarily," the dragon broke in. "It cuts both ways. Poseidon will know precisely how to hobble Kylian."

"Half of Kylian," I inserted dryly. "He never did understand the elemental mage portion of things."

"Tessa is back," Ione said and swished his tail. "And Quora."

I hadn't known the fox's name, but it made sense Ione would.

Aidyrth dismantled the sound shield and crossed her forelegs over her scaled chest. The fox scampered to the dragon and touched her chin to the dirt. "Forgive me, oh ancient one. I was being selfish. It would be an honor to be included in this venture."

If I'd been thinking, I'd have tested her words. They represented such a radical shift of position, I hadn't been ready for them. Aidyrth uncrossed her forelegs and extended one. A thin stream of reddish-white power circled the fox, who stood quietly beneath her scrutiny.

Tessa waited until the dragon was done. She'd discarded her bird form but appeared more disheveled than usual. Perhaps many rapid changes drained her. "When do we leave?" she asked.

"After I've fed," Aidyrth said.

"We should eat too," I told everyone. Dinner had been hours ago, and our magic had to be in tiptop shape.

"May I hunt with you?" Ione asked Aidyrth.

"Certainly."

"I want to come." Quora swished her red tail.

No one told her no. The dragon spread her wings and took to the air. Ione left at an easy lope with the fox behind him.

"What'd you say to her?" Shira asked Tessa.

The witch shrugged. "It might be our only opportunity to work with a dragon. And I stressed how important this was to me."

"It worked," I said. Peace in the house was important. For the next span of hours, we'd be responsible for one another. Teams that were beset from within never did well, and we couldn't afford to make any mistakes.

"I'll let Grigori know what we're doing," I said.

"I'll fill Tessa in on the plan," Shira volunteered.

"Meet you in the dining room." Tessa offered a gentle smile. "We'll make you a plate."

"Thanks." I considered a quick journey jump into the guild house, but conserving my power was important. I'd mow through a good big bunch before this was over.

An easy lope brought me to the house in a quarter hour. I passed scuffle marks in the sand from the ghoul infiltration, but it made no sense. They weren't corporeal, so they shouldn't have left evidence of their passing.

Still puzzling through what it meant, I ran up the front steps and beneath the lintel. Mother glided to my side. She'd obviously been waiting for me.

"I know where you're going," she said. "I'm coming too."

"You can't," I said flatly. "Too many of us will ensure failure."

"But I know him," she insisted. "Far better than any of the rest of you, and—"

I held up a hand to stop her flow of words. "Shira, Tessa, and I will be in the dining room. You can sit with us and plead your case but the one you'll have to convince is Aidyrth."

"Fine. I'll begin there." Mother whistled briskly, and Demelza trotted across the parquet floor. Much like the dragon, light swirled around her, changing her silvery-white coat into a prism of colors.

Addressing the unicorn, I said, "I suppose you want to come too."

A brisk whinny could have meant yes. Leaving them to it, I bolted up the stairs, intent on dumping the whole problem of who was included in Grigori's lap.

"You're the team leader," Grigori informed me after I'd asked him about the growing numbers of who wanted to be included. His blue eyes reflected a somber mood. The stakes were high; the fallout from an error could cost the Circle dearly.

Blowing out a breath, I adopted another tack. "If it was your mission, would you include four mages and their bond animals?"

"It's not like you to solicit advice," Grigori pointed out. "What's really going on here?"

His question caught me up short, but the answer wasn't long coming. "My error in judgment created this crisis. I assumed Poseidon's own dungeon would contain his evil; it didn't. I don't want to be forever staying one step ahead of my sire."

"The odds of him escaping once you've removed him from his cell are...significant," Grigori pointed out.

"Even with an infusion of dragon's breath?"

The werewolf nodded. "I'm not sure it will even slow Poseidon down. When you pit different magics against one another, the outcome is never certain. You need a backup in case Poseidon proves intransigent to Aidyrth's magic."

"But she has to be stronger than him," I protested.

"In some ways, she is, but perhaps not in the way you need. Hobbling him so transport doesn't turn into a disaster won't be as simple as dragon's breath. If he regains consciousness, he could blow up the journey channels. It would cripple our ability to use them without extensive repairs, which could take centuries."

I hadn't considered that, but as usual Grigori was correct. Poseidon held the raw ability to scorch the earth and everything around him to bedrock. "We have to put distance between him and the sea." I spoke slowly. "The farther away he is, the weaker he becomes."

"What if he brings it with him? In water droplets or suchlike?" Grigori arched russet brows.

"I don't know."

The werewolf kept his steady gaze on me. He'd never out and out tell me what to do, but he was a master at shaping events. I'd been approaching this task from my initial viewpoint, which had been to take care of it myself. Rather than labeling additional mages as excess baggage, perhaps I'd be better served to take everyone who wanted to come, plus perhaps a couple more.

"You've worked alone for a long time," Grigori reminded me.

I waited for more of a lecture, a rebuke for absenting

myself from the Circle so much of the time. It never happened. The werewolf was never one to hold grudges.

"Thanks." I mimed a salute. "Good chat."

Grigori sent a rare smile my way. "Thanks for hearing me. You'll be taking a decent number, correct?" When I nodded, he went on. "You may not need them, but if Poseidon slips the dragon's noose, only sea-based power will reestablish the control you'll need."

"Noted. I'll report in when we're done," I told him and walked out the door. An idea was forming. Rather than sending the Kraken away, I'd see if Ione couldn't talk him into aiding us. No love lost between the sea serpent and my father, and his magic was derived exclusively from the ocean. I bet Brocca would join us too.

Tessa and Shira met me at the bottom of the stairs. They handed me a cup of steaming coffee and a couple of the nauseating bars that pass for food in the twenty-first century.

"We were on our way to roust you out of Grigori's study. Sorry for the change in plans," Tessa said, "but Aidyrth wants us all in the courtyard."

I ripped a wrapper open with my teeth and pushed part of a bar studded with nuts and raisins into eating position. "It's okay," I said around a mouthful of chemicals that held the healthy parts of the bar together. "By the way, Auralie wants to come too. Grigori thinks the more the merrier, but we can talk about it when we're all in the same spot."

"Your mother, right?" Tessa asked.

"Yeah. We'll need all the sea mage power we can lay our hands on."

"Should we bring Ciara?" Shira asked.

"If she comes, Quinn will too," Tessa replied.

"I'd love to include Jake, but his magic isn't a good fit," Shira murmured.

I'd met him and his wolf, Arrow, and liked them both, but she was right about his mixture of witch, demon, and gypsy power not adding what we needed. Or was she? "He has demon blood, doesn't he?" I asked as we hurried outside.

"Yeah, he sure does," Shira said. "It's from his gypsy side. His mother was a witch."

"Oooh. Like me," Tessa cut in. "No wonder I think he's amazing."

Shira elbowed her. "I found him first."

"Aw come on. Sure you're not up for sharing?" Tessa teased.

"Quite sure," Shira said a bit snippily.

We reached Aidyrth, Mother, and the unicorn. Ione and Quora were chasing one another and screeching uproariously. "She can come," Aidyrth told me. "Demelza will be a great boon since she can end Poseidon, a fact he'll understand all too well."

The unicorn factor. How many other critical elements had skated past without me giving them a second glance? I aimed for diplomatic wording but didn't find any. "Grigori's not certain your breath will knock Poseidon out."

"It may not," Aidyrth agreed.

Whew. I hadn't offended her.

"We need to make certain before we drill that hole through whatever's wound around the dungeon," Tessa noted. "Otherwise, he'll scoot through the breach we created."

"Or have another strategy to deploy if the first one fails." Demelza stamped a hoof.

"Why drag him all the way to Fire Mountain if the unicorn can end him on the spot?" Shira asked.

At the time I'd hatched up my plan, we hadn't had a unicorn in the lineup. It altered things. A lot. "What do you think?" I asked Aidyrth, not wanting to step on any toes.

"Saves a whole lot of effort," the dragon replied. "Even if I got him to Fire Mountain without him spewing destruction, there's still the problem of hanging onto him."

It answered my question. The dragons had only agreed because of their antipathy for Satan. This got them off the hook. It fell into the realm of a win-win—for everyone except Poseidon, and he scarcely counted. Jake and Arrow chose that moment to join us. Shira must have alerted them. Or perhaps Aidyrth had.

Jake sported the dark, dangerous looks I've always associated with mercenaries or career military. Tall and broad shouldered, he had black hair that fell untidily past shoulder level and a shrewd set of brown eyes. Like the rest of us, he was dressed casually in soldier-of-fortune garb. Khaki pants with many pockets hung off his hips, and a vest with cutouts for bullets and grenades covered his torso. Arrow had thick sable fur and glittery amber eyes to go with his lean, long-legged body.

I made a decision I hoped wouldn't cost us. "I vote for the unicorn solution."

Demelza neighed loudly, clearly entranced by the idea of sinking her horn into the god of the seas. An unscrupulous bastard who'd run roughshod over anyone who got in his way, his absolute lack of compassion was about to kick him to the curb.

I voiced my next executive decision. "Since we're no

longer moving Poseidon out of his cell, there's no need for more of us than are standing here."

"Agreed," emerged from several throats.

"He's not going to stand still while I gore him," Demelza pointed out.

"He might if he's on fire," the dragon replied dryly.

"We'll be in the sea," I reminded her.

"Makes no difference," she retorted. "Dragonfire burns anywhere."

I addressed my next question to Ione. "Will the Kraken help?"

The snow leopard stopped batting at the fox. "I thought my job was to warn him to lie low."

"Changed my mind. If he's willing to help, he can wind his coils around Poseidon."

"I won't need long," Demelza whinnied.

"I'll leave now to talk with him," Ione said.

After shuffling logistics, I replied, "We'll be at the villa. Let us know as soon as you've kicked this around with the Kraken, and we'll launch."

The snow leopard swished his tail. "The best part about this endeavor is we'll never have to spend time there again." With a final swish, he vanished in a spray of magic unique to bond animals. It left a trail of stardust in the clear desert air.

"Why doesn't he like the villa?" Tessa asked. The fox had crawled onto her shoulders and draped its body around her neck.

"Not the villa, but the climate. It's too hot for his taste." I sent coordinates to everyone and asked, "Do any of you have feelings one way or the other about including Brocca?"

"The sea witch?" Aidyrth arched a scaled brow. When I nodded, she exchanged a pointed look with Demelza. "What do you think?"

"What can she do?" the unicorn asked me.

"Quite a bit if it fits her self-interest. She helped us imprison Poseidon by sucking him into public sex to divert his attention." Breath whooshed from me as I weighed my next words. I didn't fancy overlooking a potential ally, but neither did I want her fierce independence to hogtie us.

"You may as well spit out whatever you're thinking." Mother spun one hand in a come-along motion.

I nodded. "Ciara is the one with ties to Brocca. The witch is...unpredictable. She made herself useful last time, but she's just as likely to show up and help Poseidon escape if it meshes with plans she hasn't bothered to tell anyone. She's shrewd, that one. And Poseidon will be justifiably furious with her."

"So if she helps him now, it digs her out of negative territory," Shira growled.

"Aye. Exactly what I mean about her hedging her bets. By now she's figured out Poseidon's not as helpless as we expected."

"So she's probably pedaling as fast as she can to redeem herself," Jake muttered.

"I'd say this topic is closed," Mother spoke up. The old version of her would have rebuked me for bringing it up in the first place. Perhaps both of us had mellowed.

"Agreed," I replied. "I don't want to miss a potential source with strong sea-based power, but she brings more risks than benefits."

Tessa walked to my side. "Mind if we travel together?" Her

scents changed with her form, or maybe her mood. This time, evergreen mixed with wild mint filled my nostrils. For once, the fox wasn't hissing.

"Not at all." I tried for gallant but did a shit job hiding my enthusiasm for her request.

Mother cocked a knowing brow my way. "The rest of us will travel as a group too," she said.

Tessa built a spell. Like all her magic, it was quick and efficient. "This whole thing just got easier," she said once we were underway.

"Perhaps."

"What do you mean?" She was close enough for heat from her body to sear me.

"Underestimating Poseidon would be a mistake. He's wily and resourceful."

"But he's imprisoned."

"It didn't stop him from pulling strings to mobilize the ghoul army. For all I know, we'll drop into the middle of a pack of demons."

She pounded a fist into the flat of her other hand. "I want him dead."

Her intensity surprised me since he hadn't violated her. "Why?"

"I already told you."

I touched her mind lightly, probing as I skittered from one spot to another. A barrier dropped between me and her. "What?" she said stiffly. "You didn't believe me?"

"There has to be more to it than that. He humiliated you and stole five years, but he didn't harm you beyond that."

"Not for lack of trying. He wanted to strip me of magic and bestow my ability on others."

Hmmm. She'd neglected to mention that part. "What was it about your power that intrigued him?"

"It's different. Ancient. Strong." Her eyes had shaded from green to burnished bronze.

Truth slammed into my guts. Not a shapeshifting witch after all, but a goddess masquerading as one. When I tried to zero in on which goddess, my efforts blew up in my face. It felt as if I'd been slapped with a set of brass knuckles.

"You will never tell anyone." Her voice roared through my head.

"Agreed." Questions buffeted me from all sides. I pushed them away. We had an offensive to plan. The personal could wait—maybe forever since I'd blundered into something that was none of my affair.

"You got that right," she snarled. "Not your business." With her witch glamour gone, she was a few inches taller and no longer shielding her ability. Power eddied around her, brilliant with color and the smells of an autumn forest. The fox cuddled closer, soaking in her bondmate's enchantment.

I pointed at the fox. "She knows."

"Of course. She is Kitsune."

My eyebrows shot up. Far more than a magical fox, this one could take human form. "May I ask one last question?"

"Aye, but I might not answer it."

My lips twitched into half a grin. "Does Grigori know?"

"What do you think?"

I shrugged. "No idea, which is why I asked."

Tessa offered a Mona Lisa smile, but no words. She couldn't have been with the Circle for more than a hundred years or so because I didn't remember her from my last sojourn through its ranks.

"How'd Poseidon overpower you?"

"You said one question," she pointed out.

I offered what I hoped was an engaging smile. "I lied."

She glared at me. "He was a colleague. I had no reason to distrust him. I didn't suspect the Kraken was engaged in other than play—until I was trapped."

"But your magic would have been a match for his," I protested.

"On an equal playing field, aye," she said with bitter undertones. The colors swirling around her took on a reddish hue.

"I'm sorry," I murmured.

"Why? This wasn't of your making."

"Nay, but my sire always enjoyed slinging power about. He probably saw you as a challenge."

Tessa laughed long and loud. "He assumed I'd sign on with the program and play along with his captured-sex-slave game plan. Kept assuring me I'd enjoy it."

"A reasonable assumption," I mumbled. "You weren't his first rodeo."

"After Demelza is done with him, there won't be any more rodeos. It serves him right." Tessa's glamour slid back into place. Because it was her transport spell, she recognized we were nearly at my villa. I'd have known if I'd been paying attention to anything other than her.

If she'd fascinated me before, now I was smitten. Sucker for lost causes could have been stenciled across my forehead.

Aidyrth was outside on my deck swathed in concealment. The others had gathered in my kitchen. Having rifled through the cupboards and gone shopping—judging from bags with logos from nearby markets—they'd laid out an assortment of edibles. Cheese, crackers, bread, and olives go well at any time of day.

"You made good time," I commented and sliced myself some bread.

"We were beginning to wonder what happened to you." Mother angled a speculative glance my way. She's never missed much, but was my infatuation with Tessa all that obvious?

"We were talking. You can't have been here long," Tessa said by way of explanation.

Her fox unwound herself from its position on her shoulders and leapt through the air, landing next to the cheese. After fluffing her tail around her haunches, she selected a slice and stuffed it into her mouth. I've run into the occasional Kitsune in Faery, but never out in the world. It made Quora quite the anomaly. I wanted to know more about her.

"Maybe fifteen minutes," Shira offered in response to Tessa's question about how long they'd been at the villa. "We'd have been quicker if we hadn't stopped for a few groceries."

"He's in," rumbled through my mind from Ione.

"Where shall we meet you?" I sent back.

"Same beach where I fed him fish."

"I heard that," Jake said.

It surprised me since I'd pegged his power as weak. "I'll inform Aidyrth where we're going," I told the others. "Is everyone good to leave in ten minutes?" Seeing nods all around, I walked through the house to patio doors leading to the deck.

"How are you doing?" the dragon asked. Before I sorted

through what she was getting at, she added, *"He may be a rotter and an opportunist, but he's still your sire."*

"Eh. I got over that years ago. He's had ample time to clean up his act. He never bothered. Playing the god card only gets you so far."

"Not exactly an answer." Aidyrth's pinwheel eyes skewered me. Bronze with deep-green centers, they were beautiful—and deadly. Nothing can withstand their hypnotic pull, not even me.

"It's the only one you're going to get," I told the dragon, grateful we were on the same side. *"Nothing about any of this has been easy. Rhiana killed her kinsmen. Many of them. Ridding all worlds of my father will be a boon. No one will mourn for him. Least of all me."*

I dug deep, testing my words for honesty. Hunting for anything is a two-edged sword. I wanted truth. What zinged back at me was the knowledge I should be the one to kill him. My sire. My job.

"Eh-eh." A plume of smoke arced skyward. While the mortals scattered along the beach couldn't see her, they'd surely see the smoke and struggle to determine its source.

"Eh-eh, what?" I asked pointedly.

"Let Demelza do her job. She has the tools. You do not."

"Stay out of my mind," I growled.

"Work on your team skills," she shot back.

I winced. *"Touché. Ready to leave? It's why I came out here. To share the location where Ione and the Kraken are."*

Dragon enchantment brushed against my mind, plucking coordinates and probably a whole lot more. Bending, she placed her heavy spiny chin on my shoulder. *"The Circle needs you, Kylian, but you need it too. All your years alone haven't improved...anything."*

I bristled and started to catalog all the battles I'd fought solo. Before my thoughts coalesced into telepathy, I chopped them off. She was right in so many ways. Poseidon's long years as a one-man show had turned him into a monster. Not a path I wished to tread.

"I'll send Shira out to you," I murmured.

Aidyrth lifted her head. *"Jake too,"* she said.

I patted her scaly hide. *"Thanks for reminding me I can jam my head so far up my ass it feels normal."*

She snorted dragon laughter. *"Anytime."*

I turned and walked back inside.

"Is everything all right?" Tessa asked.

"Aye. Aidyrth just gave me a dose of dragon wisdom."

"Oooh, she must like you," Shira noted. "Or she'd never have bothered."

Unwilling to delve too far into touchy-feely land, I said, "She asked for you and Jake. We're ready to leave."

Shira, Jake, and Arrow walked out of the kitchen. Demelza pawed the polished floor with a hoof and said, "Come close. I will transport us to the Kraken."

I'd planned on taking over the teleport aspect, but I remembered Aidyrth's team pep-talk and sidled next to the unicorn with Mother, Tessa, and Quora. "Thanks," I told Demelza.

She touched my shoulder lightly with her horn. "No one will recognize my magic," she explained, "or if they do, it will be so unexpected, they'll chalk it up to stray enchantment mucking up the ether."

With zero warning, the whitewashed walls of my kitchen dropped away, replaced by craggy cliffs overlooking the beach.

The whole transport spell was over with so quickly, it startled me. I've never spent much time cataloguing various magics, but the unicorn's was on a par with any dragon.

At the water's edge sat Ione and the Kraken, leaning into one another and gazing out to sea.

Seeing Ione and the Kraken like that warmed me. Once the Kraken had been respected and feared. If I had anything to say about it, he'd roam the seas again as a free monster, not anyone's lackey. Aidyrth scudded in for a landing. She'd barely quit moving when Jake, Shira, and Arrow jumped from her back. We all converged on the Kraken and my bondmate.

Ione stretched out all four paws in the way cats do and sauntered toward me. "Demons have been making his life miserable," he announced.

Scarcely surprising news, but my ears perked up at the opportunity to gain information. "How many? And what manner of demon operates freely underwater?"

"Beisht Kione, Charybdis, Leviathans." Ione grimaced and shook himself. Not much unnerves him, but letting wicked names roll off your tongue has that effect.

Those weren't demons in that they didn't answer to Satan

in any universe I was aware of, but they were definitely monsters. I strode to the Kraken. He'd craned his neck around, keeping both red eyes trained on all of us. He trusted Ione but had no reason to extend that fragile confidence to our group.

I met the creature's direct gaze. "All sea monsters pass through here from time to time. What is different now?"

The Kraken opened his enormous mouth and roared. The noise stopped the rush of the incoming surf for a moment. "What's different you ask?" He mimicked my inflection. "They're after me is what's different. I was on my way to the Arctic Ocean when Ione found me."

"Why is it safer there?" Aidyrth joined the conversation.

"Too cold for them."

"But not for you?" she persisted.

"I don't like it, either, but I like being pursued even less."

I narrowed my eyes in thought. "If Poseidon is dead, will they leave you alone?"

His scales rattled against each other as he shrugged. I tried to make sense of what I knew. Poseidon had never been chummy with anyone except the Kraken, and that relationship had only survived because of its one-sided nature. None of the abominations Ione had listed would bow and scrape to anyone. So Poseidon had no use for them.

Why were they doing his bidding now?

"What?" Mother jabbed me in the side.

"None of this makes sense." I added my quick-and-dirty assessment of hierarchies in the sea, the one I'd just sketched out in my mind.

Aidyrth positioned herself so she was in front of the

Kraken. He unkinked his neck to eye her as she asked, "Will Charybdis and the others be near the dungeons?"

A quick head shake with more rattling scales.

"Any idea why they're after you?"

"Because of Poseidon."

"They never liked him," I cut in. "No one did, so why would they be stalking you, the one who moved his game piece off the table?"

"Let me see what I can do," Tessa said. She'd moved next to me without me noticing. When I glanced her way, her eyes shaded to bronze for a brief moment.

"You're not going alone," I told her.

"Aye, I am." She started for the sea.

Aidyrth grabbed her forearm with a talon. "Bring Kylian, or do not go. We are a team, not a bunch of independent consultants." Her brisk bugle probably scared the crap out of anyone close enough to hear it. "Why do I have to keep reminding everyone of that?"

Did the dragon know what Tessa was? My bet was yes. Dragons are wise and canny. I circled back to our problem. One more question for the Kraken, and then we'd kick this can down the road. "Where are the ones who are after you?" I asked him.

"I don't know. They only show up when I'm in the sea."

"But they weren't shadowing you on your journey north."

"No."

"My read is they wanted to make your life miserable, not kill you."

He thumped his chest with one of his upper set of arms. "No one can kill me."

I didn't bother to point out the unicorn could. Assuming

he opened his mouth to invite her horn. He'd already made that mistake once. I doubted he would again.

"Give us ten minutes, fifteen tops," I told everyone. "Tessa and I will do a reconnaissance."

"I'm coming," Ione announced.

"Me too," Quora yipped. She was draped around Tessa's neck again with no intention of leaving.

"Bad idea." Demelza pawed the damp sand. "No one knows we're here. Once you enter the sea, they will."

She had a point. For a fleeting moment, I missed working with humans. They expressed divergent opinions too, but in the end they obeyed orders. This bunch, not so much.

"But—" Tessa began before snapping her mouth shut.

Yeah. She'd been about to tell them she could play the god card and maybe get rid of Charybdis. I wasn't at all certain about the others. The Leviathans would thumb their noses at her. The beisht kione could go either way. A literal translation was black beast, and they answered to no one but their own. I'd assumed they died out—or left Earth. I hadn't laid eyes on one in close to a thousand years.

Grigori had to remind me I was team leader, and now I reminded myself. "Unless anyone has strenuous objections, we'll teleport from here to the dungeon and remain warded until we see who we have for company. We have one objective. Enter the dungeon and immobilize Poseidon long enough for Demelza to gore him. If things go our way—"

"They won't," Aidyrth interrupted, "so we must be ready for anything."

"I still think I could do some good in a short time," Tessa argued.

I didn't answer her. Instead, I said, "If anyone sees

problems with my approach, speak up. If not, we're out of here as soon as I can build a transport spell." Without waiting, I drew power from the sea, shaping it into a dual purpose spell. Both ward and transport, it would spit us out inside the dungeon. Poseidon should be the only resident since Brocca had freed everyone else our last trip through.

Mother added a stream of sea power to my working, weaving it in with mine.

"I will get there in my own way," the Kraken announced and lumbered into the sea. At least his presence wouldn't alert anyone, although they might wonder why he'd returned.

"He should have remained with us," Ione mumbled.

My opinion too, but the beast didn't answer to me. Besides, he was gone. I spread my casting to encompass everyone and ignited it. My spells aren't nearly as fast as Demelza's, but we traded cream-colored sand for the ocean's depths as I ferried everyone to the stone-and-black-coral prison. I felt my way as I went, fine-tuning our exit point.

The smaller the target, the tougher it is to hit precisely, and the interior of the dungeon was damned small. I wasn't at all certain Aidyrth would fit, but she was resourceful and could shrink her bulk to some extent.

"Well, well, well, I knew you wouldn't be able to stay away after the ghouls." Poseidon's rich baritone had scratchy places, probably from where he'd shouted until his throat was raw. It surrounded me even before the magic powering my spell cleared.

The water was murky. I could scarcely see Aidyrth and Demelza, let alone everybody else. I batted at it with a hand, willing it to clear, but nothing changed.

"For the fucking love of Danu," Tessa sputtered and

chanted in a very old form of Gaelic. Whatever was occluding the water settled immediately. Her spell earned her a penetrating look from Aidyrth. It answered my earlier question. The dragon hadn't known the shapeshifter witch had another magical affiliation—until now.

The dungeon looked the same as when I'd left it. All the cell doors stood open except for Poseidon's. Footprints in the sand in front of his door suggested he'd had a hell of a lot of company. Did any of them belong to Brocca?

It didn't matter. This was showtime. Where was the Kraken? If he didn't materialize on his own, I sure as fuck wasn't about to track him down. The unicorn stamped impatiently. We'd counted on the Kraken to wrap its coils around Poseidon. Without him, we'd retreat to dragon's breath—and fire.

My sire was on his feet, long-fingered hands curved around the bars. He looked worse than I'd ever seen him, but some of it could be illusion. His gaze swept through who stood before him, and he cackled. "I'm honored. My estranged wife decided to drop in. And Andraste. My dear. Does this mean you've finally forgiven me?"

It took longer than it should have to connect the dots. I'd sought Tessa's identity. Dad had just handed it to me on a platter.

Tessa jettisoned her glamour and drew her features into a sneer. "Nay. It means I've come to rejoice in your suffering. No one shanghais me."

"I did," he reminded her.

With a feral cry, she sent a beam of red light racing through the water. It sliced through the fingers curved around the cell door's bars. After an initial grunt of pain, Poseidon laughed.

"He's stalling," I cried. Kraken or no Kraken, we had to do this now. Before his slimy reinforcements showed up and we had to split the fight on two fronts.

Aidyrth grabbed hold of the cell door with her powerful jaws and yanked it aside. She was ready for Poseidon's rush to freedom and doused him in dragonfire. I grabbed his chin and held his mouth open for her to breathe fire down his throat. I'd expected at least a minute when he wasn't thrashing and projecting magic this way and that. Never happened.

Tessa wedged herself in between him and the broken door, golden cords draped from her hands. Quicker than I could follow, she wound them around him, cinching them tight. Ione dove for a calf and clamped it in his jaws hard enough to break both lower leg bones.

An unfamiliar female form with brilliant red hair ran long claws down Poseidon's chest, shredding his ratty robe in the process. The fox was gone; she had to be its human form. Jake started for her, but I shouted, "No. She's Tessa's bond animal in another body."

"What the fuck?" he snarled.

"Let him have her. She's Kitsune." Mother gritted the word as if it meant something. Did bad blood flow between them and elemental mages? If so, I'd never heard about it. The fox Fae growled, showing far too many teeth for anything remotely human. The only way she pulled off her guise had to be by keeping her mouth shut.

Tessa's bonds snapped one by one as Poseidon levied power against her. Water churned around us, turbulent and brimming with a mix of magics. Poseidon was still jammed between Tessa and Aidyrth, so close the fire burning his hair had jumped the gap and ran through Tessa's hair in blazing streaks.

The Kitsune gave up on clawing tracks down Poseidon's flesh long enough to douse Tessa's head with a cooling flow that put out the flames. I'd planted myself dead in front of my sire. With the cell to his back, a dragon on one side, and Tessa on the other, he was hemmed in.

An intense cracking boomed so low I felt the vibration in the pit of my stomach. The wall behind us thudded to the sea floor; behind its demise, the water turned black as if a giant squid had emptied sacs of dye.

Demelza shoved me aside. We'd reached a now-or-never point. Reinforcements were upon us. Poseidon thrashed from one side to the other, understanding the unicorn's intentions full well. I felt my sire reach for a teleport spell. Now that a wall had been breached, nothing remained to hold him within the dungeon.

I scrambled. Working by feel, I stayed one step ahead of his magic. It would have been harder if he commanded other than the sea. Aidyrth still poured fire down his throat. Reflecting through the translucent skin of his throat, it added an eerie glow to the blackness around us.

Mother raised mage lights until half a dozen floated around us. I'd heard Jake screeching and bellowing. Now I saw him slashing and burning his way through misshapen creatures attacking from where the wall had disintegrated. Looking like a mad scientist's genetic experiment gone bad: serpentine bodies were glued to fish heads, human heads, gnome heads. Scissory legs split the ends of their tails, suggesting they could walk as well as swim.

No wonder Satan had formed an alliance with Daddy-O. Together they were building a strike force, one that appeared to be able to operate on land or water. Fuck. Were they somehow in cahoots with the Russians and their clandestine lab in the Arctic?

Dark magic wrapped Jake like a shroud. I'd pegged him as weak. What a miscalculation. He carried demonic power, but he'd tamed it, forced it to do his bidding, and now he raised it against the same. Sparks flew, turning the water murkier still.

Shira stood by his side hurling insults and magic at a rapidly growing force. Mother joined them, holding the warped army at bay.

Ione finished chewing through Poseidon's right calf and moved higher once the first bits dropped to the sea floor. With a mighty heave, the sea god almost eluded my efforts to contain him. My attention had wavered; no more.

No more was right. Pain blazed from the crown of my head to my fingertips on both sides. Burning, stinging, it reminded me of walking into a wasp's nest. I swore up a storm. That old bastard had done his best to hit me with the unmaking spell.

Demelza tossed her head this way and that, seeking precision. She had to skewer Poseidon's magical center, or her kill strike would merely maim him. No second chances.

Moving more silently through the water than I'd have thought possible, the Kraken slithered around the mass genetic experiment, killing anything that stood in his way.

"You came!" Poseidon crowed. "All is forgiven, old friend. Help me out of this mess, and I'll see you richly rewarded. It'll be like the old days. You'll see."

Would the Kraken fall for it? I started to tell him not to

listen, but didn't. He had to come to that conclusion on his own. Tessa angled her hands at the Kraken's chest. I shook my head.

"We can't let him undo our work," she said into my mind.

"Maybe he won't," I countered, drawing more power from the sea and holding it at the ready. It wouldn't be a match for Poseidon and the Kraken working in concert, but I prepared it just the same.

Ione let go of Dad's leg and gestured the Kraken forward. He trusted his friend to do the right thing. I saw it in every sinew of his body, and I hoped to hell it would tip the scales in our favor.

Tessa glided next to me, making space for the Kraken. The Kitsune jumped aside. With lightning speed, the Kraken slithered into the opening and wove its coils around Poseidon. The sea god trusted him and relaxed into the undulating coils expecting instant transport out of the hell his dungeon had turned into.

It was the opportunity Demelza had been waiting for.

Even quicker than the Kraken had been, she lunged and drove her horn dead center into Poseidon's abraded chest. A shining river of magic poured from him, pushing back the black sludge the sea had degenerated into. He sagged in the Kraken's coils, and the beast loosed his lifeless corpse.

I studied his face, but then looked away. No matter how miserable Poseidon had made him, today's actions had cost the Kraken. I wanted to help, but no magic in any world could stuff the genie of patricide back into the bottle. In the early days, when Poseidon had courted the monster, he'd been a lot like a benevolent father. It was only later once he was certain of the Kraken's affections that he'd dispensed with any illusion of caring.

Why hadn't the Kraken left? He could have.

Tessa dragged Poseidon out from under the unicorn's feet. A shot of magic jettisoned what was left of him into the hungry horde. Not unlike the ghouls, they weren't picky. My sire's body vanished in a churning mass of teeth, mouths, and scales.

The spillage from Poseidon's magical center still shimmered near where he'd fallen. Loose magic can be diverted by evil, so I funneled what I could into me. It didn't look or feel tainted. How had he turned from a narcissistic jerk into one of Satan's henchmen?

The magical stream bifurcated as the Kraken scooped up some for himself. If I'd known he wanted it, I wouldn't have taken so much. Ione stood by his friend's side. The Kraken bent and touched his forehead with a hand before vanishing as quickly as he'd arrived.

The Kitsune was back in fox form, fighting from Tessa's shoulders.

I joined Shira, Jake, Mother, and Tessa. Aidyrth lumbered close and took up a position at the end of our line. It was time to leave. Our task was completed, but we couldn't let this batch of twisted protoplasm run free. My head still throbbed from Poseidon's attempt to end me with the unmaking spell.

I opened a link to the others. *"Shall we drop a net over them and be done with it?"*

After fielding a chorus of ayes and yesses, I grabbed a stray water current and rode it until I was past the weird mix of soldiers. Landing lightly on the other side, I told the others

I was ready. We'd needed an end point for our spell, impossible to gauge without actually seeing it.

Power wafted toward me, I encouraged the water to move it quicker, before any of the enemy noticed what was happening. It wasn't likely. Someone had to be behind this. Father had been part of it, but not all. If he had been, the ragtag group would have dispersed once he was dead.

Enchantment rolled from me, snagged the layer of mixed magics hovering above the unsuspecting soldiers, and formed a canopy. Once it was complete, I barked a power word. It echoed from Mother, Tessa, Shira, Demelza, and Aidyrth. The canopy plopped down on the serpentine soldiers, tightening until we had a nice, neat package.

The unicorn whinnied. I felt the zing of the unmaking spell brush past, and the clump of unnatural beings folded in on itself until nothing remained. Even in the sea, the sharp tang of expended magic burned my nose and mouth. I stroked back to where everyone was.

Everyone except Ione. *"Where are you?"* I raised my mind voice.

"I will join you later. At the guild house."

My bet was he'd chased the Kraken down.

"I will take us back," Tessa announced.

Aidyrth dropped a foreleg onto her shoulder. "And then you will march into Grigori's office and tell him what you are. Pfft." A plume of fire rose in the water. No longer black, it had begun to clear. "I should have recognized you."

"Maybe not. My glamour was foolproof."

"I'm a dragon," Aidyrth huffed. "Nothing is foolproof, but I saw what I expected to see and never had reason to look past it."

The Kitsune chittered in what might have been laughter. Mother shook a finger at it. "I will see you're reported to whatever passes for a government in Faery."

The chittering turned to a snarl. "For what?" the not-a-fox asked.

"Impersonating a bond animal."

"We are bonded," Quora said huffily, "but not in the same way as the others."

A corner of Tessa's mouth twitched into a smile. "Not much choice on the Grigori front, is there?"

"None," the dragon said firmly.

"If you don't tell him, we will," Shira chimed in.

I needed to close up the villa, but it could wait for a long while, months if not years. "Strong work, everyone," I said and boosted Tessa's power with some of my newly augmented magic. The sea might be primary for me, the closest thing I have to a native element, but I was glad when it dropped away.

No matter what came next, it couldn't be any tougher than today had been. Poseidon had been a shitty father, but I wish there'd been another way. He'd sealed his doom with his actions, but that didn't make Demelza goring him any more palatable.

Watch it, one of my inner nags cautioned.

No kidding. Watch it, indeed. Feeling anything except relief over Poseidon's death was stupid. If one lesson has sunk in over the years, it's that things can always, always get worse.

Ione was waiting when we tumbled out not far from the guild house. From the looks of the sky, it was around midnight. Perhaps Tessa had thought not landing right in the courtyard would offer an escape route. Not so. Mother took one arm, Shira the other. The dragon and unicorn walked behind them as they headed for the house.

The Kitsune was nowhere in sight. After her show of temper with Mother, perhaps she'd decided lying low was in her best interest.

They didn't need me. Jake had already decided the same. After a jaunty wave in my direction, he and Arrow sprinted into the sagebrush to run off residual tension from our mission.

"Did you know about the Kitsune?" I asked Ione.

He shook his shaggy head. "If I had, I'd have told you. In my defense, I've never seen one before."

"Didn't her scent tip you off she was...different?"

Another head shake. "Mostly, she smelled like Tessa." He angled his head to one side. "Maybe it's why she always stuck so close."

"Could be." Switching topics, I asked, "You went after the Kraken, didn't you?"

He purred an affirmative.

"How is he?"

"Still leaving for colder waters but doing okay after we talked."

I waited to see if Ione would add details. He didn't seem inclined. "Probably no reason for him to leave now," I ventured. "With Poseidon gone, whoever was bothering him will probably go away."

"He wants a fresh start," Ione explained. "Somewhere he hasn't been for a long while."

"We pass through Arctic waters from time to time. Maybe you'll see him again."

"I told him to find me if he needed anything," Ione said.

"It was kind of you," I replied as we turned and walked toward the house.

"Not kind. Through all this I discovered I respect him." Ione nudged my side with his shoulder. "You and me. We have each other. He has no one, and he never did. Poseidon enslaved him and called it a partnership. It took centuries before the Kraken determined he'd been duped. By then, he was in too deep to dig himself out."

I could easily envision Poseidon doing just that. Playing the heavy and then backing off when the Kraken was furious with him. He'd probably offered promises much like the ones in the dungeon where he extended forgiveness like an olive branch.

I dug my fingers into Ione's thick pelt, and we covered the remaining distance to the steps leading to the front door. "Coming in?" I asked.

"Nah. I'll see you in the morning."

"Good hunting."

"Always." He faded into shadows, moving with his trademark grace.

I stood next to the steps considering what to do. I could teleport to my room. I could eat something—and I was hungry. Or I could join the party in Grigori's study. I dredged up what I knew about Andraste. She wasn't one I'd ever run across, and when the Celts left, I had assumed it meant all of them.

Had she gone and returned? Or had she never left at all?

A fourth option presented itself: the library. I could eat later. Grigori didn't have too many rules, but he made it clear no one ate or drank in the libraries. Without thinking things to death, I ran up the steps, through the door, and across a broad hall to the guild house library. Not as complete as the one at the main house, still this one would have basic information about every deity.

To save time, I fashioned seeking magic and asked it to dump materials into my lap. After the third scroll, I cut the flow. I didn't need to know everything, just the basics. Unrolling crumbling vellum scrolls and skimming their contents filled in some of the blanks. Andraste was similar to the Morrigan, but without a three-fold presence. Goddess of warriors and victories, ravens, and battles, she was rarely seen without her helm, armor, and a long spear. She also possessed powers of divination and was frequently summoned to predict the outcome of a skirmish.

I rerolled the scrolls and sent them back to their places with gentle air currents. She and I had common interests, but it wouldn't matter since I might never see her again. Grigori would be furious. If I were a betting man, I'd wager he'd order her out of the Circle because of her duplicity.

It would be shortsighted of him since we were embroiled in total chaos. Her magic was welcome, particularly now that she didn't have to bury half of it to conceal her identity. Another thought rocked me. Maybe she could call in a few chips and summon another god or two.

With enough firepower, we'd win this war. Not have it drag on forever with no clear gains on either side.

Armed with what I hoped was a selling point for keeping Tessa around—never mind I wasn't exactly an uninterested party—I left the library intent on locating Grigori. It had been a while since the bunch of them had marched into the guild house, and it was damned quiet from upstairs.

Was I too late?

A quick shot of seeking magic told me everyone was in the grove of Joshua trees where I'd met Aidyrth. It seemed as if our conversation had happened ages ago, but it hadn't been more than a couple of days. Determined to be part of any decisions where Tessa was concerned, I left the guild house.

The air had stilled and possessed a crystalline quality that said morning wasn't far off. Ione fell into step with me when I was a hundred yards from the grove. Dried blood dotted his muzzle, so I knew he'd had a good night.

"Were you waiting for me?" I asked.

"Aye. What took you so long?"

"Reading up on Andraste."

Grigori must have draped a sound shield around the grove

because I didn't hear a thing until I stepped through it. "Why'd you pick the Circle?" Grigori was asking. "Third and final chance. If you decline to answer again, you and your Kitsune pal are finished here." Dressed in field gear, he wore dark trousers and a black shirt and jacket. His wolf was near the surface, its outline merging and flowing behind him.

She glanced my way before focusing on Grigori. "I needed to blend in somewhere no one knew me."

"But many of us did know you—if you'd been truthful," he pointed out in stern tones.

She twisted her neck from side to side amid the cracking of small bones. "My kinsmen understood Poseidon had kidnapped me. They did nothing to free me. From what I was able to gather after I freed myself, I was quite the laughingstock. Mages who were supposed to be my friends placed bets on how long it would take me to get out of my predicament.

"I complained to Danu. She laughed at me, told me I was being juvenile."

Breath hissed through Tessa's clenched teeth. "I set a few traps. Stole a voice here, eyesight there. Blinded one particularly dickish fellow. Not permanently. None of the damage I meted out would have lasted, and they knew it. But they had no sense of humor when the tables were turned, and the joke was on them."

Interesting. So much for my working theory she could ask the other deities to aid us. She'd probably rather die, and even if she asked, no one would respond.

"Disgusted with them all," she went on, "I left determined to find a place for myself. It took years to perfect a glamour that hid who I was. Once I had it down pat, I took stock of all the groups of magic-wielders. The elemental mages were closed to any not like them. No matter what I did, my glamour wouldn't pass for long in Faery. Too much loose magic there.

"I set up shop in Northern Scotland as a witchy woman. It worked for a few years, but then the world changed. No one believed in charms and magic any longer."

"So the Circle won by default?" Grigori asked dryly.

"Something like that," Tessa mumbled. "Remember, I had Quora to explain too. During my witch-for-hire days, mortals thought my pet fox was adorable. We faked her death a few times, and she picked a smaller form to make it believable I'd adopted a new familiar."

Grigori folded his arms across his chest. "Were you ever going to tell me?"

Tessa tipped her chin upward. "Not if I didn't have to."

"Why?"

"Nothing to do with you, or the Circle. I wished to remain hidden from sight."

"But the other gods are long gone," he persisted.

"Are they?" She offered a ghost of a smile.

"You tell me," Grigori shot back.

"Some are. Some are not. Much like me, they don't wish to be found. Their time has passed. Poseidon was the only one who didn't believe that, who kept right on ruling as if his presence—and his power—meant something."

Ione head butted my thigh as if to say, *see. I knew what a bastard he was.*

"The others aside," Tessa went on, "a good working rule is the more people who know something, the less likely it is to remain a secret. The Circle is large, and as we've discovered lately, not all the mages trustworthy. If the truth about my identity had leaked—and it would have—someone would have found a way to take advantage of it, and the blowback could have been damaging to you and your Circle of Assassins."

"So you kept quiet out of consideration for me?" Grigori arched a brow.

"That was part of it. Safeguarding myself and the Kitsune another."

"What do you want to do now?" he asked.

She narrowed her eyes. "Does it mean I have choices? I've wronged you. You have every right to banish Quora and me."

"Is that what you want me to do?" Grigori asked the same question with a slightly different spin.

A small rustling alerted me the Kitsune had arrived. In fox form, she crawled up Tessa's side and settled across her shoulders, licking her whiskers nervously. If the gavel was going to fall, she'd overcome her fear to be by Tessa's side. I wondered how they'd partnered up in the first place. Other deities had their animals, like Athena and her owl and the Morrigan and her crows, but none of them could take human form.

Tessa rolled her shoulders straighter. "I would like to stay, but I would also prefer it if my identity remained amongst us."

"And Jake," I reminded her.

She nodded. "And Jake."

"It would be highly unusual," Grigori told her. "We're a family. No secrets."

"Did anyone bother to hunt for you after you vanished?" Mother asked.

Tessa huffed out a couple of breaths. "Of course."

"What would they have done if they'd found you?" Grigori arched a russet brow.

"Probably nothing, but I was done with them. I still am."

"Then how could them locating you here have negative consequences for the Circle?" Grigori persisted. "I'm not seeing it. Not as if we've been holding you against your will. Even the most stiff-necked of the Celts understand how I built my group of paranormal assassins."

Color stained her fair cheeks, and she glanced at her clasped hands. "Maybe it was just an excuse I made up—so I'd appear more altruistic than selfish."

He took a step toward her. "You may remain as part of the Circle. Goddess knows we need your magic more than ever, particularly the true extent of it. There is one condition, however."

She unclasped her hands; her arms fell to her sides. "I have to come clean, right?"

"You do," he agreed. "We have a dragon and unicorns in the Circle. Kylian carries the blood of the gods, and Xander is as close to a god as we have in werewolf society."

"May I think about it?"

"Nay. You will decide before we leave this grove."

Light flickered between her and the fox. I assumed they were talking and edged to Grigori's side with Ione pacing me. The werewolf held out a hand; I clasped it. "You did well under the seas," he said.

"If the Kraken hadn't shown up at the eleventh hour..."

"Aye, but he did. I've always believed when people's backs are up against the wall, they make the right choices."

"How'd it go with the vampires?"

He rolled his shoulders in a shrug. "Progress. Another couple of nights and we'll have knocked out enough of them to spook the rest. I'd forgotten how much I hate them."

"Yeah. They're not much good to anyone. Did anyone tell you about the unusual band of warriors we faced?"

"Not exactly. Only that there were a lot of them."

I glanced at Tessa. She and the Kitsune were still deep in a discussion. I described what had looked like gene-splicing to me and followed it by saying, "This was too close for comfort to a mission I was engaged in before coming to the main guild house."

"What do you mean?"

"I was part of a strike team dispatched to take down an installation in the Arctic run by Russians. Turned out it was a front for a gene farm where someone was merging humans and animals into warriors. I destroyed it, but I'm certain it's not the only such operation."

Grigori frowned. "What makes you believe they're connected?"

"The one pulling the puppet strings in the Arctic was a dark Fae."

The werewolf's eyebrows shot up. "Mortals aren't in the habit of employing those with magic."

"Maybe we only think they aren't. It would have taken human scientists far longer to accomplish what I found in that lab."

"I'll ask Rhea. She used to work as a scientist."

Shira had sidled closer. "Plenty of humans used to hire me. In fact, they were all human. I found jobs on the dark web. Those who posted them didn't care how I accomplished my tasks, only that they were carried out discreetly and not in a manner that would ever be traceable to who'd hired me."

"More crossover than I'd expected," Grigori murmured.

"Except they had no idea I was employing paranormal elements." Shira nudged him. "Until now, I assumed many of your assignments came from mortals—before the current mess, that is."

He shook his head. "Hundreds of years ago, when most of us were repurposed court assassins, sure. Our focus of late has been keeping dark magic from tainting the human realm."

Intriguing. Perhaps if I'd stuck around more, I'd have figured that part out. Most mortals had no idea magic existed. They'd lost ground with their insistence science had answers for everything. I waited to see if Shira had anything to add, but she remained silent. She'd done the same thing I had, worked side by side with mortals without revealing what she was.

"Back to not believing in coincidences," I went on. "I've had a chance to think about this. Creating new life forms is in a class by itself. Somewhere, there's bound to be a link. Maybe the same dark minds at work, chucking power about."

"Heh. Maybe they wanted the humans to experiment on before they started in with mages," Grigori muttered. "Sort of a collateral damage subset."

Motion caught my eye. Tessa was scribing a small circle as she looked at all of us in turn. Mother. Demelza. Shira. Aidyrth. Grigori, Ione, and me. "What about the rest of you?" she asked in a clear, ringing voice as her gaze settled on the dragon. "Do you have preferences about me leaving or staying?"

Aidyrth puffed steam. It circled Tessa. "You forget," the

dragon chided. "I know you well. We've stood together through many battles, you and me."

"Aye, but I never kept things from you in those days."

"I never gave you cause to not trust me," Aidyrth said.

Tessa winced. "True, but I couldn't pick and choose whom I told. It was all of you—or none of you."

"I knew you too," Mother said softly.

"Aye, I haven't forgotten."

Something passed between them, but I couldn't decipher what it was.

She shut her eyes for a moment. When she opened them, she focused their burnished bronze on Grigori and bowed her head. "I apologize for deluding you. I never planned to remain long, but every time I told myself it was time to leave I came up with an excuse. And then, another."

Breath whistled from her. "Quora told me time and again we should leave, that if we didn't we never would. Turns out her prescience outshone mine. This is the first family I've had in so very long I didn't want to abandon it. I know what it's like out in the world. Borderworlds too. I've traveled to many of them but never remained long.

"The Circle has given me a sense of purpose, something that had eluded me since mankind quit believing in those like us."

Grigori opened his mouth, but Tessa waved him to silence. "Let me finish, please. I've never divulged any of this. One of the times I told you I was researching something, I showed up in Southeast Asia. War was in full bloom. They needed me, except no one paid any attention to anything I said. The generals I located treated me as if I were a mortal woman who'd gone mad. They'd never heard of Andraste."

She shook her head sadly.

"Even if they had," I muttered, "they'd have relegated you to the sphere of myths and fables."

She went on. "A few years passed. Undaunted, I tried again in the Middle East with even worse results. They tossed me into a prison cell for interfering in top secret matters. I'm sure they're still wondering how I escaped.

"After that, when I returned to the Circle, I'd decided to remain. Indefinitely. I understood the risks when I asked to be included in the mission to end Poseidon, but I figured I could pull it off."

"I didn't," the Kitsune said clearly and sent a pointed glance my way.

So that was why the fox had been so frantic to keep Tessa out of things.

Tessa reached up to pat her bondmate. "Kylian figured out what I was, but not exactly who."

"When was that?" Grigori cut in.

"Just before we left," I replied.

"Why didn't you say something?"

Oh-oh.

Nothing but the unvarnished truth would do. "Several reasons." I ticked them off on my fingers. "I was preoccupied with the mission. No love lost between Poseidon and me, but I was setting out to murder my sire. Not much room for missteps. If I'd failed, my own existence could have been forfeit, and I would have been looking over my shoulder for the rest of my days.

"Beyond that, I wasn't certain which of the goddesses she was. I did ask her if you knew. She didn't answer."

Tessa nodded agreement. "Aye, he asked me. It wasn't the time to go into it."

"How'd he home in on your identity?" Grigori asked.

"Poseidon outed me." She made a face. "I did time in that dungeon, thanks to him, but the old fucker actually believed I'd free him."

"He was delusional about a lot of things," Mother muttered. "Worst mistake of my life was the day I married him."

I schooled my features to neutrality. After all this time, Mother still sounded quite bitter, but spending more than a few minutes with the erstwhile sea god had that effect on people.

"Enough talk. What are you doing?" Grigori asked Tessa pointblank.

She rolled her shoulders back and stood tall. "Staying. I will reveal myself whenever you wish."

Dawn was breaking, adding pinks and purples to the lightening sky. One of Grigori's fingers spiked a talon. He sliced into the ball of his thumb and walked to Tessa. "Blood oath."

She held out a hand. When he opened a gash, they joined the cuts. Blood flowed onto the ground. Where it landed, lush red and white blossoms shot out of the dry desert soil. Bending, she gathered them and handed half to Grigori. "These shall serve as a reminder of my commitment to full honesty within the Circle. If it's all the same to you, I would prefer to retain my current name."

"Why?" he asked.

"Andraste is dead. I see no reason to revive her."

He folded the blossoms into a pocket. "Good enough for

me. Breakfast is at eight. It's as good a place as any to begin unraveling your deception." In a flash of blue light, he shifted to his wolf form and loped out of the grove.

"Just like that." Tessa stared after him.

"Just like that," Aidyrth said. "He's not one to hold grudges."

Tessa smiled. It transformed her face into something softer, more approachable. "Thank Danu for small favors, eh?"

For some reason it seemed funny, and we started to laugh. We were still chuckling as all of us made our way toward the guild house to start the new day. "You made the right choice," I told Tessa.

Mirth falling away, she trained her hammered-metal gaze on me. "Time will tell," she murmured. "Time will tell."

❧ 13 ❧

I started to say I totally understood, given my own ambivalence about the Circle, but wisdom prevailed. My situation was nothing like hers, and with Poseidon finally out of the picture, it was no situation at all. He'd been the only one who'd ever given me a hard time about Grigori.

A staunch bugle was followed by the swoosh of Aidryth's leathery wings as she soared skyward.

"She's heading to Fire Mountain," Shira explained. "The dragons are awaiting Poseidon, and she needs to let them know they won't be hosting him as a prisoner."

"Must be a relief," I said.

"Yeah, it is. She told me they imprisoned the Morrigan centuries ago. It went so badly, they ended up crafting a deal with Satan where she spent half her time in Hell."

"Must have been before Satan tried to commandeer Fire Mountain," Mother commented.

"It was." Shira pressed her lips into a thin line. "The

dragons suspected the Morrigan was hip-deep in the plot, but they could never prove anything."

"What'd they do?" I asked.

"Moved her cell to a spot where it's surrounded by fire on all sides and suspended her visits to Hell." Shira gave a little shrug. "I've never been to Fire Mountain. It's difficult to describe something I haven't seen."

Interesting. So at least one more of the deities hadn't left with the rest. What had the Morrigan done to so thoroughly alienate her kin? I was curious, but the question would keep. Demelza whinnied and cantered off. Ione ran after her.

"Do you want to hunt with the others?" Tessa asked the fox.

"Will you tell them about me too?" Quora's whiskers quivered.

"I pretty much have to."

"Then I will remain with you," the fox-that-wasn't-one announced.

We reached the steps. Mother and Shira continued inside. Tessa started after them, but I placed a hand on her arm. "A moment, please."

She didn't turn around. "Can whatever this is wait?"

"Sure. Mostly, I wanted to thank you for your help with Poseidon."

"You already did that." She twisted to face me. "Nothing you can say will make the next couple of hours easier. And then, I'll have to repeat everything at the other guild houses."

"What are you most concerned about?" I extended a hand. She ignored it.

"I've broken our laws, the gods' covenant. Twice. My role in Poseidon's demise was forbidden, as is my affiliation with the Circle. By the pledge binding the gods, my existence should be snuffed out."

"No one minded while you freelanced as a witch?"

"It fell into the barely acceptable category but wasn't expressly prohibited, so long as no one knew who I really was."

"Mmph. I can see why the others would be upset about Poseidon—at least on the surface. Behind the scenes, they'd be planning to pin a medal on you. But what's wrong with the Circle of Assassins? It's not as if you hooked your star to a bunch of humans." I stopped for a moment before adding, "Poseidon gave me a raft of shit about my Circle affiliation, but he never told me I had to sever my ties."

"Don't take this wrong, but your 50 percent blood doesn't make you part of the in-crowd. Last time I studied the covenant, the lowest percentage for inclusion hovered around eighty."

"Whew." I mimed wiping sweat off my forehead. My fingers came away streaked with dried blood.

She smiled. "You have no idea how many times I've wished to be anything other than a full-blooded goddess."

"But why would they prohibit your inclusion in the Circle?" I persisted.

"Most mages are decent mind readers. Like all the other deities, I carry our history—and our secrets—within my mind. Sooner or later, someone could unearth what must remain hidden. It's why any type of paranormal group is expressly forbidden."

"I see. Knowing that, you picked the Circle, anyway. Why?"

Her direct gaze skittered to the side. "I was tired of being alone."

"You had me," Quora piped up.

She raised a hand and patted the fox. "Aye, sweetling, that I did."

"The rest of us thought those like you left long ago," I ventured.

"It's what we wanted you to think. After burning through several borderworlds, my kin took up residence in a separate realm. Not unlike Faery, it's divided from Earth by a series of veils. A particular combination of repeated sounds parts them. Any divergence will bring someone running to do away with the miscreant skulking around the entrance."

"Have you been there?"

She nodded. "I have. Snuck through a couple of times to verify my suspicions."

"Are you certain they wouldn't be allies to our cause?"

She snorted laughter. "Quite sure. The Morrigan was one of our own. Ergo, our problem. They'd paint me with the same brush: a problem requiring resolution."

"Do you actually believe they'll spring into action if news of you resurfacing reaches them?"

"Hard to say." She narrowed her eyes in thought. "By now, they'll be aware of Poseidon's death. Not that they'd link me to it, but they will remember my stint in his dungeon. Some of the smarter ones will wonder if I had anything to do with it. Beyond their shared world, each god and goddess has their own, individual one."

She shook her head as if to clear unpleasant thoughts. "We should go. Grigori was generous. I don't want to give him reason to believe I'm hedging on my side of our blood oath." She started back up the steps, the swing of her hips alluring.

I followed her. "I'll make certain nothing goes wrong," I murmured as we entered the guild house.

"How will you manage that?" Her caustic tone stung.

"Give me a little credit," I muttered and hustled up the stairs.

"Aren't you coming to breakfast?" she called after me.

"After I clean up."

I kept moving, taking the stairs three and four at a clip. I was all the way to my room with my clothes in a heap on the floor and the shower running full tilt when it occurred to me her question about me and breakfast had been more than small talk. She'd taken my support for granted. Too proud to ask me not to leave her side, she'd turned her worry into a question.

Was there hope for us as a couple? It had seemed damned remote when I'd believed her to be a witch, and even more so now. She'd fascinated me from the moment I laid eyes on her. It didn't appear the attraction was mutual, but she'd never chased me away.

And she could have.

Out of the shower and dry, I bent over my discarded garments. Even though I'd been in the sea, they still stank of blood and expended magic. I belted a thick terry robe around myself and teleported to the wardrobe room, dirty clothes tucked beneath one arm.

Not as elaborate as the clothing locker in the main house, still I found khaki slacks, a red woolen shirt, and a black leather vest. After donning clean socks, I stuffed my feet into the boots I'd carried with me. I could take additional time to comb out my tangled hair, but that task would be simpler once it had dried.

Anxious to support Tessa, I trooped out of the wardrobe room and along a corridor leading to the dining area. The buzz of conversation, clink of silverware, and rich smells of food met me long before I arrived. After pouring coffee and filling a plate with eggs and toast and a slice of ham, I looked for empty seats. I also looked for Tessa, but didn't see her.

Xander motioned me over to a table with him, Rhiana, Shira, and Jake. "Congratulations." He thwacked me across the back once I'd set my food down.

"Thanks."

"What were all those weird monsters?" Jake asked. "We were just discussing them."

I settled into my chair and drained half my coffee, wishing the mug was bigger. "We should have brought one with us to make certain, but they looked like lab experiments to me."

"Huh?" Xander arched a silver brow.

"Beings that were created, not born," Rhiana clarified.

I told them about the Russian installation in the Arctic with the Dark Fae incubating his own set of unnatural creatures. "In that instance," I went on, "the mix was humans with various animals. I assumed they were breeding warriors who'd grow to usefulness in perhaps a decade."

"Those things we fought near the dungeon didn't have anything human about them." Jake stabbed his fork in the air for emphasis.

"No, but gene-splicing experiments have many common elements. Maybe we should rustle Rhea up. She used to work as a biochemist or something."

"Do you believe there's a relationship between the unntural manifestations in both spots?" Xander asked.

I nodded. "Don't ask me for reasons. I don't have any. Not yet, but how many projects of that nature can there be? It's kind of an arcane wing of the biological sciences."

"People have been mucking around with genetics for years," Rhiana said. "Cloning babies. That kind of thing."

"Sure," I replied, "but not mixing and matching across species to make something far different from what they started with."

"They do that with fruit and vegetables," Jake spoke up, "but I can see where this would be different."

"The question is whether we need to do something about it," Xander said thoughtfully.

"There's space on my dance card once we're done with the vampires," Rhiana joked. Xander laced his fingers with hers.

"You're having far too good a time with the Undead," he told her.

"But they're so pretty," she teased.

"If only they didn't smell so bad," Xander shot back.

Rhiana made a face. "They are pretty awful in that regard. I always wondered how they shut off the stench long enough to lure mortals near enough to feed."

Grigori glided to the front of the room and clapped his hands to get everyone's attention. "First order of business," he said after the room had quieted, "is getting to know one of our own better."

Probably responding to a prearranged cue, Tessa walked spryly through the double doors in the back of the room. Quora was in her usual spot, curved around Tessa's neck.

She'd dispensed with her glamour. The woman who crossed the room walked like a queen.

A few muted gasps were followed by bits of magic to determine what the hell had happened to the Tessa they knew.

When she reached Grigori's side, she turned and faced everyone. "I'll keep this brief," she said, her voice surprisingly even given her insecurity about what was unfolding.

"For reasons of my own, I have kept my true identity hidden. Those of you who are old may recognize me. My previous name was Andraste, but I went to a lot of trouble to stage her demise. It wasn't easy, and I plan to keep her off everyone's radar. I will still be Tessa, but a Tessa with greatly enhanced abilities."

Every side conversation in the room died away.

She scanned the crowd, probably gauging reactions. "Apologies for deceiving you. My choices were always about me, not about you, and my duplicity has harmed no one." She narrowed her eyes. "What could harm the Circle and those within its folds is if my secret becomes common knowledge. Were that to happen, the gods could storm the guild houses, end me, and strip minds so no memory of me remains.

"Me being part of the Circle as a witch was barely tolerated. It is possible no one would care that I've revealed myself, but we shouldn't take that chance."

The fox jumped down from her shoulders. Power shimmered around her as she took her Fae form. Slightly built with hair the same shade as Tessa's that fell to her feet, she looked the part with pointed ears, gossamer wings, and the translucence I've always associated with the Fae.

Perhaps five feet tall, stars and moonbeams swirled around

her in lieu of clothing. "I am Kitsune," she announced. "I, too, am sorry for deceiving you and your bond animals. I would appreciate it very much if nothing changed. I love you and all your animals. They've generously included me within their midst."

After placing a ringed index finger over her chin, she turned to Tessa. "Is that enough?"

"Aye. Nicely done."

Trails of greenish faery dust hovered around the enchanted fox. When they cleared, she was back on Tessa's shoulders.

Grigori inclined his head. "Thank you."

Tessa returned his bow. "Nay, it's you who deserves thanks for not summarily booting me from the Circle." Back straight and standing tall, she walked toward the collection of tables.

"But I have questions," someone shouted.

"You only think you do," Grigori corrected him. "Our next topic will be the remaining seethes. We will take up that discussion in about half an hour once everyone is done eating."

I stood and hurried to Tessa, hooking an arm under her elbow. "Join us," I invited.

A mix of emotions played out on her expressive face. Before the part that wanted to hide won out, I said, "Bet you haven't eaten. Come on." I let go of her and led the way to the platters ranged on a table next to the back wall. I wasn't sure she'd follow me, but she did.

"Coffee or tea?" I asked.

"Tea. I there's any mead, you might spike it."

I grinned at her. "That's the spirit."

"Enough for me too," the fox said.

I glanced at her. Were we going to be friends now that she didn't have to guard her partner's secrets—and her own? Leaving Tessa to work out what she wanted to eat, I headed for the kitchen and brewed a pot of tea rich with mead, mint, and anise. It smelled wonderful, so I made enough for all of us.

Back at the table, Rhiana reached across and gripped Tessa's hand. "That took guts, woman. Glad you're part of us."

"This is way cool," Shira chimed in. "You can teach me about the pantheon. Books never went far enough."

Tessa finished chewing, swallowed, and said, "Now why would I want to do that? I've spent a long while trying to forget all about them."

"Consider it a favor to me," Shira said. "I was a street kid. Never went to school. I always knew I was different, but the whole magic pill was huge to swallow. I denied my powers for so long, it became second nature."

"As did I," Jake chimed in.

I sipped my spiked tea, quietly pleased by everyone's ready acceptance. Magic was magic, and Tessa had a lot of it. I'd assumed her revelation wouldn't run into much resistance.

Quora jumped onto the table and stuck her muzzle into Tessa's cup, slurping loudly. From time to time, she lifted her head and licked tea off her whiskers.

Grigori returned to the dais at the front of the room and synopsized progress the various strike teams had made against the Undead.

"We're three seethes down," he went on. "Perhaps three more should drive them into stasis."

I got to my feet. "What makes you think we'll be able to

find the others? Word will have filtered down, and they're masters at concealing themselves."

"Our power is stronger than theirs," he countered. "I have faith in you. Three more teams will leave within the hour. Feel like heading one up?" he asked me.

"Sure." At least it would divert my attention away from what I really wanted to do, which was to sweep Tessa into my arms and carry her up the stairs in a terribly bad rendition of Rhett and Scarlett in *Gone With the Wind*.

"Excellent." Grigori rubbed his hands together. "Xander will lead the second team and Auralie the third. Select three or four mages to accompany you. Rough locations are Vermont, Oklahoma, and Oregon."

I didn't care which straw I drew and waited while Xander claimed Vermont and Mother, Oklahoma. "Where in Oregon?" I asked.

"Last know location was in the Pendleton area," Grigori replied.

I returned to my table. "Want to come with me?" I asked Tessa and Quora.

Xander waved a hand in my direction. "I was trying to recruit her."

Tessa smiled. "I'll go with Kylian on this assignment but look forward to working with you in the future."

Xander grinned back. "Diplomatic, my dear."

"How do you think I got along with the other deities for so long?"

"By biting your tongue. Try running a werewolf pack," he tossed out and rose to his feet, scanning the group for additions to his team.

"Any preferences for who will come with us?" I asked Tessa. "We need at least one more."

"We'll sign on," Shira said and gestured at Jake.

"Before I hooked up with you," Jake growled, "I'd never met a vampire. Or a demon."

"Au contraire, sweetie. You'd met demons. You just didn't realize what they were. What can I say?—she offered a wicked smile—"I'm a shit magnet."

"Hey, that was my excuse. You kiped it," he teased.

"Do you really want to ride shotgun?" I asked both of them and considered how their power would slot in with ours. The mix had been dynamite near Poseidon's dungeon.

Shira exchanged glances with Jake. "Yeah," she said, "we do."

"We missed the last vampire hunt because we were with you," Jake explained.

I started to tell him there'd be other opportunities—unfortunately. Instead, I said, "Love your enthusiasm. I'll rustle up Ione. Meet me in front in ten minutes."

After pushing to my feet, I hurried from the dining room. The day was young. We needed to locate the seethe before nightfall. It would be well-guarded. No one understood better than the Undead how vulnerable they were when the sun shone. I'd run across the occasional daywalker, but they were scarce. Finding an entire seethe of them was unlikely.

Famous last words...

I raised my mind voice, told Ione we were wheels up in ten, and stopped by the alchemy room to collect a few choice items. Glass tubes with stoppers for dead-man's blood and silver stakes. My next stop was the armory where I grabbed a likely looking broadsword and a matching scabbard. It was clunky, but nothing quite like a blade with heft for decapitation.

We'd need to raid a graveyard for dead-man's blood, but it shouldn't take too long. Tessa met me in the hall as I was on my way outside. For once, Quora was nowhere in sight. "If you want a sword, the armory's that way." I hooked my thumb behind me. "I collected everything else we'll need."

Power settled around us, thick as honey and redolent with the scents of the mead we'd drunk. It shielded us from view. "What are you doing?" I asked her, not wary but wondering if I should be.

"This," she said. Closing the small distance between us, she kissed me full on the mouth.

☙ 14 ❧

Shock yielded to lust so fast my head spun and my breath faltered. The press of her body against mine kindled longing so deep and primitive I couldn't have walked away if I tried. She moved closer still; her nipples pushed into my chest, hard as polished stones. The scents of desire—musk and amber—mingled with the lush mix of her magic weaving with my own. We fit together perfectly, almost as if we'd been made for one another.

Without her witch glamour, she was the same height as me. Heat from her core seared my thigh. Visions of ripping out the seat of her trousers and lifting her until I was encased in her body flashed through my mind. Damn, I missed skirts. They'd been so much more convenient.

Her breath was sweet as she deepened our kiss, sweeping her tongue into my mouth. I opened to her, sparring and withdrawing as my entire being came alive. Hot. Intense.

Vibrant. This was nothing like my playtime with the Nereids; the goddess in my arms would demand everything from me.

She bit my lower lip until I tasted blood. I bit back. Fitting since we were going after vampires. She licked a trail down my neck. I plunged my tongue in her ear, and then our mouths found one another again. Her lips were full and firm and sensual. I could have kissed her until the world ended, and still it wouldn't have been enough.

I wrapped my arms around her, delighting in the play of muscles beneath supple skin. Between us, my cock hardened, cradled against her belly. I threaded my fingers into her hair and caressed the lines of her head. A very distant voice in the back of my mind shouted it was past time to get moving, that I had a job to do. I could barely hear it over the roar of blood pounding through my veins.

As quickly as she'd approached, she let go and took a step back, an enigmatic smile on her face. With her flushed skin and masses of russet hair bunched around her, she'd have given Aphrodite serious competition.

"Thank you," she murmured. "For standing by me."

I mimed a low bow and made a grab for my out-of-control desire. If I couldn't rein it in, I'd snatch her up, duck into the nearest room, and continue where we'd left off. "Anytime."

"The swords are that way?" She pointed.

"Second door on the left. See you outside." Other words clamored at the base of my throat. I sat on them. What had just passed between us was real. She was as aroused as me. Maybe she'd planned on a quick thank-you kiss, but it spiraled beyond both our control with the speed of light.

I hustled outside with stern orders directed at my overly enthusiastic member to stand down. Nothing like brisk movement to rearrange the blood. By the time I emerged from the guild house, my trousers weren't tented. The scents of desire wouldn't vanish as quickly, but neither did they require any explanation.

Aidyrth, Arrow, and Ione stood in a circle. From the pitch of the magic hovering around them, my guess was they were talking. Shira and Jake approached from the opposite direction.

"Nice sword," Jake said.

"If you know how to fight with one, there are more in the armory."

"It's on the list," he replied, "but I'm better with daggers, guns, and poison."

"Don't forget bombs," Shira said sweetly.

"How could I? Wasn't building explosives almost our first date?"

I laughed at their lighthearted banter. Tessa walked briskly toward us. Quora trotted by her side and angled to join the other bond animals. An intricately carved blade swung from a wide leather belt cinched around Tessa's hips.

"Found one that suits you?" I asked.

She withdrew it from its sheath. The metal made a whooshing sound as she sliced it through the air a few times. "It will do. I've fought with better."

"Doesn't look too difficult," Jake ventured.

"It's not until something goes wrong," Tessa told him.

"Ready to leave?" I asked everyone.

"How long will we be gone?" Shira raised her brows into twin question marks.

"Hard to say. If we don't locate the seethe by nightfall,

we'll go to ground and give it another go come daybreak," I replied.

"We'll travel in groups of two," I went on. "Tessa and me, and you and Jake. Vampires are sensitive to expended magic. Here's our first meeting spot." I sent coordinates via telepathy. "It's near a graveyard where we'll need to collect dead-man's blood."

"Oooh, does that really work?" Shira asked.

"Like a champ," Tessa told her. "It immobilizes them long enough to stake or behead them. Problem will be all the other vampires racing in to save their kinsmen. If there's one scent etched into vampire brains, it's dead-man's blood."

The bond animals had walked close. "I favor a group approach," Aidyrth said.

I glanced at the dragon. "How? I've always ended them one at a time."

"For a big seethe," the dragon went on, "that won't work. We'll lose a lot of them once they understand we're not mortals to be drained and turned. Simpler to blast the lot of them with fire and let 'em burn."

"So long as we can locate them," I muttered.

First things first. I motioned Ione close and built a spell to take us to the Wallowa Mountains, an isolated spot in northeastern Oregon. We'd start there. Shira and Jake could begin hunting while Tessa and I located a graveyard. Pioneer graves were common, but we needed a working gravesite with fresh corpses. Dead man's blood has grown harder to procure with the advent of modern embalming methods.

Harder, but not impossible.

Quora took up her usual position across her bondmate's shoulders. Ione had been quiet; usually it meant he was thinking about something—or bothered by an occurrence he wasn't quite ready to talk about. It couldn't be the vampire assignment; we'd killed plenty over the years.

Having Tessa so close and not touching her was torture. The kiss had kindled something elemental within me. I wanted to tell her how special she was and that I hoped we could find a path to one another, but everything that popped into my mind sounded hokey, juvenile. As if I were a kid on his first date.

"Do you have a plan?" Tessa asked, her reserved demeanor back in place, the one that didn't invite intimate disclosures.

"I do. Once we have vials of blood in hand, we'll split up and search for the seethe."

"Individually, or in pairs?"

"We can cover more ground individually. Does it matter?"

Her forehead creased in thought. "Maybe. Depends on what type of vampires we're dealing with. They have a unique communication network. It doesn't require telepathy. I've never quite determined how they alert one another, but it seems to be related to scent."

The dragon had made a valid point about them not hanging around for us to slaughter them. "This could take a couple of days," I said. "If we can locate them, all we'll need to do is wait until the sun is up."

"It won't be that simple," Tessa said.

"Why not?"

"They post sentries these days," Quora chittered.

"Not the ones we've come across," Ione rumbled.

I dropped a hand onto his shoulders. "We haven't actually laid eyes on a vampire in a couple of hundred years."

"We have," Quora said. "They're smarter than they used to be."

"The three groups who reported during breakfast managed to destroy their targets," I reminded her.

"Aye, but they had the element of surprise. They all struck about the same time. By now, word has spread far and wide. Vamps in those seethes weren't expecting open warfare, but all the rest of them will have initiated preparations—in case their group is next. If they haven't left outright."

Aidyrth's "blast them with fire" idea was looking better and better. Vampires do burn, and it's a hell of a lot faster than staking all of them, or cutting off heads.

I drew a ward around us moments before we emerged in the middle of a busy street. I'd expected we'd come out in the nearby mountains, and my spells were usually accurate. A group of giggling teenaged girls ran into me. Before they were done squealing with disbelief and batting the air where I'd been standing, I rolled them back in time a couple of minutes. They'd be disoriented, but they'd get over it.

We headed down a side street. It led to a rushing creek—and a graveyard. The odds of finding a fresh corpse weren't great, but I checked anyway. So did Ione. Nose to the ground, he could have passed for a truffle-sniffing pig.

He stopped next to a grave without a headstone and pawed the ground. "Here. He hasn't been dead very long."

Tessa constructed a hasty shelter to shield us from view. No one else was in the graveyard, but that could change. I drew on my link to the earth element and sank into the ground next to a plain pine casket. The characteristic scent of formalin didn't burn my nose, but then Ione knew the difference between blood and chemicals.

The next part was simple. I drilled through the box with a jot of power, reached inside, and coaxed thick, congealed blood out of the young man who'd died, filling my vials. The whole operation didn't eat up more than five minutes. When I surfaced Shira, Jake, and their bond animals had joined Tessa beneath her canopy.

Motioning to everyone, I crossed the graveyard, cleared the fence, and led our group into nearby woods where I handed out vials. Before I could assign a search grid, Aidyrth said, "We should stay together."

"Yeah. We ran into a spot of trouble. It's why we were late getting here," Shira said. "Plus, you weren't exactly where you said you'd be."

"What kind of trouble?" Tessa's forehead creased with concern.

"Not vampires, but demons trying to break into our journey channels. A group nearly made it, but Aidyrth burned them to a crisp with magic—not fire."

Hmmm. Maybe that was why my planned destination had skewed westward by a couple of miles. Good to have a possible explanation since our exit point had been nagging at me.

"I fear part of the tunnel was destroyed in the process," the dragon added. "Couldn't be helped. I started with fire, but demons are impervious to it without added elements."

Great. The vampires must have put out a call for reinforcements. I considered the ramifications. "This might make our job simpler," I said.

"How?" Jake asked.

"Demons aren't exactly mental giants. If they're protecting the vampires, all we'll need to do is locate them.

The vamps will be nearby. We're too close to whatever this town is, though," I went on. Seeking spells ate up a lot of magic, so much, mortals would be certain to sense something was amiss.

"Where did your journey spell spit you out?" I asked Shira.

"To the east in deserted mountains. You weren't there, so we tracked you."

"At least you hit the right spot. We'll return there and cast a net, see what pops up."

Aidyrth took care of moving us all. She was dead serious about our group remaining intact. A quiet glen with rocky crags angling upward to the north and east surrounded me. Snowy patches were visible higher up. Somehow, we'd eaten up half the day already. Not an auspicious beginning, particularly coupled with the failure of my initial journey casting. Eh, maybe not failure, but accurate endpoints can spell the difference between success or ugly surprises.

"What are we looking for?" Jake asked. "Demons or vamps?"

"Both." An idea emerged. "Do you, um, have an affinity for demons?"

Jake tossed his head back and laughed. "Do you mean can I find my own kind?"

"Something like that."

"Yup. Sure can. Only problem is way more demons rove Earth than anyone might suspect. Anything particular about who you want me to look for?"

Since there was no way to assess how newly arrived a demon was I shook my head. We fanned out. Ione and I picked the southwestern corner of the glen, and I deployed seeking magic attuned to vampires. I could have searched for demons at the same time, but my results wouldn't have been as accurate. Tessa and Quora stood to our right, also facing south, but in a more easterly direction. Shira and Jake and their bond animals took the northern quadrant.

I wasn't certain how far anyone else's magic extended, but mine can cover at least a couple of hundred miles with decent precision. I swept power back and forth, up and down, but didn't locate anything magical at all.

"Any luck?" Tessa called.

"Nope. You?"

"Not sure. Come look at this."

I reeled in my spell, but kept it balanced between my hands as I joined Tessa. "Where?" I asked her.

She pointed, and I cast a directed beam of bluish light. It shaded first red and then black before it zapped back at me. I intuited what it was about to do and sidestepped out of its path. Whoa. Unusual.

"Mine did the same," Tessa said. "Almost as if someone grabbed it and redirected it back at me."

I snapped my fingers. "That has to be it. They don't want us getting too close."

"To what?" she countered. "I didn't actually find anything before my spell scudded back my way."

A muted yipe from Shira was followed by a blast of fire from the dragon. Tessa and I came at a dead run. Ione beat us to them, his hackles at full mast. Between him growling, the dragon's fire, and the omnidirectional nature of whatever was focusing our magic back at us, alarm sharpened my senses.

Before I could shout a warning, demons streamed out of red-rimmed portals that grew out of nothing. One moment, the air was clear, the next it held the characteristic sulfur-stench of Hell. Four portals disgorged maybe forty demons. Most had red scales, but some were black. Clumps of whitish hair clung to their heads in patchy spots. Close-set red eyes reflected determination. Clearly, this was a forward guard deployed to make certain we never left the glen.

"Who sent you?" Aidyrth roared.

I didn't expect them to answer, and they didn't. One fellow missing part of a cloven hoof launched himself at Tessa. Power shimmered around her, but she waited until he got close enough to drop a cage over. Once she had him, she levied a blast of power right at his head. He screamed and grabbed his head in his hands, but he couldn't protect his mind from her culling.

The cage vanished, and he slumped to the ground, darts protruding from neck and chest. Neat trick. She'd stripped his mind and killed him, smartly and efficiently.

"Lucifer and Asmodeus are behind this," Tessa shouted.

Two bodies hurtled into me from the side. I let them drive me to the ground. Ione leapt atop the pile. I couldn't see, but from the outraged squawks, I figured the leopard was chomping holes in whatever was in front of him. The weight lessened. Ione rolled in the dirt with a demon. Blood shot into the air when a canine severed a major vessel. Ione's creamy coat turned red-black with demon blood.

Lithe as my bondmate, I twisted beneath the demon punching me. Doubling up a fist, I drove it into the side of his face. Bones cracked beneath scales. Getting physical is so much more rewarding than killing from across a field with magic. I hit him again, and again. He closed his scaled fingers around my throat, pressing on my airway as he did his damnedest to break my trachea.

"Gotta try harder than that," I wheezed.

His eyes were my next target, but I had to hurry. My vision swam from lack of air. Honing both my index fingers into dirks, I drove one into each eye and on through into his brain. The pressure on my throat vanished as he grappled for my fingers still embedded in his eyes.

I tossed him aside and scrambled to my feet. He was still rolling on the ground, yowling in pain when I drew the broadsword and cut off his head. Tessa stood in the middle of a pile of bodies. She'd lure them close, and then drive her blade through their hearts. Something about the metal in it parted scales as if they'd been made of butter.

The air had a singed smell from the carcasses scattered around the dragon. Shira killed by exploding heads. Jake wielded a wicked-looking serrated blade that might have been ten inches long. He shared my passion for the up-close-and-personal touch.

The remaining demons didn't bother with portals. They took off on foot. Probably didn't have enough magic left to teleport. Crap. We'd just blown a couple of hours on nothing, and we still had to package up the corpses and blitz them with the unmaking spell. Leaving them for mortals to stumble over wasn't on the approved list.

"Cowards!" Tessa shook a fist after the last of the fleeing demons.

Aidyrth painted their backs with fire.

Maybe the three seethes we'd taken out would have to be the end of it.

I started dragging the corpses closer together, so we'd only have to cast the unmaking spell once. I'd blown through more power than I wanted to, and we still had the vampire nest to locate.

Tessa pushed and prodded demon leavings with bits of power to get them closer to the stack I'd formed. Just like we'd done under the sea, I packaged them up, and we all contributed to the unmaking spell. It sizzled around the remains before the bodies turned from disgusting collections of hoofs and scales to motes of light floating away in the breeze.

I dusted my hands together. Ione came at a lope, shaking water from his fur. He'd found a creek to wash off the nasty stinking blood.

"What's next?" I asked my team.

Tessa's burnished metal eyes gleamed. "I know where the vampires are. We might have just enough time to pull this off before the sun goes down."

"How'd you figure that out?" Aidyrth asked.

She shrugged. "Got lucky. The one I picked to strip-mine his memories had a hell of a lot of them. It's how I found out which of Satan's princes cooked up this scheme. And the location of the vampire nest."

"What are we waiting for?" Aidyrth shot a plume of fire into the air.

An image with a set of coordinates swam through my head. My eyes widened. Talk about hiding in plain sight. "They're close," I said.

"Aye, that they are," Tessa replied. "Good thing because I have a bone to pick with Asmodeus and Lucifer."

I opened my mouth to tell her no, it was too dangerous, but wisely shut it. If she still wanted to run them down after we were done here, I'd go with her. Or better yet, maybe we'd all go. It would make me look less like an overbearing male.

I cared what she thought about me. More than was wise or prudent, but there wasn't a damned thing I could do about it.

15

The nest was located deeper into the mountains to the north of us. Vampires like caves and graveyards. The best of all worlds for them is to start with an old graveyard and use existing tombs as a launching point to excavate a home. That strategy worked well in the old country, but American graveyards are mostly lines of headstones rather than family crypts.

Because it was still daylight, the vamps might not be up to date on the demise of the demon horde. Or they could know everything. Sunlight burns them, but they're not like Sleeping Beauty, lost in unconsciousness until nightfall. And the older they are, the more resistant to daylight. I've known the occasional very old vampire who could wander about with impunity no matter what time it was.

Tessa managed our journey spell. No wonder she could shuffle through forms like a riverboat gambler spewing cards when she'd been masquerading as a witch. Her power wasn't bottomless—no one's is—but it was damned impressive.

We emerged at the bottom of a shallow ravine and switched the group ward for individual ones. Tessa made shooing motions to our right. A quick check of the coordinates she'd sent juxtaposed against our position indicated we had about half a mile to cover the old-fashioned way.

Aidyrth took to the skies with Shira on her back. I felt their magic but couldn't see them. Ione padded next to me. Jake and Arrow were on my other side. Quora ran lightly along shadowing Tessa. I wondered again how their relationship had begun. I've only known a few Kitsunes. Fiercely independent, they weren't the stuff I usually associate with a lasting bond—to anyone.

Not that Ione wasn't independent, but felines have a pack structure not unlike canids. They're happier when they're not alone.

"Found it," Aidyrth sent in shielded mind speech.

We picked up the pace and scrambled up a heavily wooded hillside, across a rocky patch, and down the other side. The earth was damp and slippery. A few drops of rain pattered from gunmetal skies. From the looks of clouds scudding low across the horizon, a storm was brewing.

The ruins of a town spread beneath us. Heavy equipment well on its way to rusting through was scattered about. My first guess was the settlement had built up around a mining operation. The graveyard I expected was tucked between falling-down buildings and the river. Nothing grand. A few crumbling headstones and slabs of wood where names had been etched. Mortals had obviously abandoned this place decades ago.

Maybe the vamps had hastened their egress. Nothing like a few people you've known all your life turning into the Undead to scare the crap out of you.

Tessa halted, surveying our objective. I risked a quick seeking spell, withdrawing it almost as soon as I'd cast it. Vampires were here all right. A whole lot of them lurked beneath the graveyard. Despite the overcast afternoon, no one had ventured above ground. I took it as a good sign. No daywalkers, and probably no ultra-old vamps, either. If I hadn't checked, I'd have been convinced they'd all left.

"Wonder why they stuck around," I mumbled.

"Good question," Jake whispered back.

"Hard to believe, but they're homebodies at heart," Tessa told us. "I've run into master vampires crying over the destruction of a seethe."

"Crying?" Jake's tone was incredulous.

She nodded. "Aye, but remember the master turns most of his minions. Once they're permanently ended, it's like losing parts of himself. Or herself. Sometimes master vamps are female."

Jake scanned the skies, looking for Shira and the dragon. I wondered where they'd gotten themselves off to myself. I could have searched with magic, but the vamps probably already suspected they had company. No reason to announce ourselves further.

"Now we wait," Tessa announced. "For the dragon."

Her approach was to fry the seethe with fire. It meant vamps would race this way and that in their haste to escape immolation. "Ready defensive magic," I told everyone. My words were superfluous. This wasn't anyone's first rodeo. I suspected Jake was far more skilled as a street fighter than I was.

Aidyrth must have been on the ground long enough to set herself up. She and Shira did a bang-up job cloaking their magic since I couldn't sense any leaking through. They became visible about the same time fire shot from her jaws. She'd positioned her snout next to a hole that I'd missed in the rocky earth. Smoke and flames billowed from rents between the graves.

"Over there," Jake shouted, pointing. I'd been fixated on the dragon, but it made sense the vamps would have more than a single entrance to their underground lair.

I ran toward vampires pouring out of multiple cracks in the ground, uncorking a vial of dead-man's blood as I went. When I got close, I tossed it at two fleeing vamps before dropping the vial back into a pocket. Spots coated their backs, but it was enough to slow them down. I didn't hesitate. Blade at the ready, I hacked off both heads with a single swing. They rolled onto the ground, and the bodies they'd been attached to turned from flesh to a pile of moldy bones in an instant.

So much for my theory about none of them being extra old. Why weren't they fighting back?

Tessa grappled with three who'd mobbed her. Fangs extended, they were trying to glom onto her wrists. She'd retreated to her shapeshifter witch trick and was morphing through forms so fast I couldn't follow the transition points.

In her human body, Quora sprinkled dead-man's blood as widely as she could manage. Once a vamp slowed, sluggish from the blood, Ione or Arrow or Jake jumped on them. Ione and the wolf killed with swipes of their powerful jaws. Jake drove silver stakes into their hearts. When I passed him, I handed him a few more.

'Thanks, man," he said without diverting his attention from the creature writhing beneath him.

Taking half a step to one side, I pivoted and brought my blade down squarely on the female vamp's neck. They're alluring—if you can get past the stench. An unholy beauty goes along with the transition to being one of the Undead.

Jake turned toward the next nearest vamp and ran hard to catch him.

I looked in the opposite direction. Tessa's three assailants had turned to piles of bones. We should have made inroads into the seethe, but vamps kept pouring out. And not all from the same places, either.

"Goddamn you nasty stinking punks," Jake shouted.

Spinning, I assessed the problem. Four vamps had waited until he staked a fifth, and then they'd mobbed him. One's fangs hovered over his wrist.

"Think twice, mate," I cried. With a mighty leap, I landed next to the vamp and sliced off his head just as his fangs brushed Jake's arm.

Hands grabbed me from behind. Ione catapulted onto the pile, jaws snapping through flesh and bones with a grisly gnashing. The fingers that had been grappling at my shoulders released.

Christ. Where were all of them coming from? At least a hundred milled about, some running from us, some standing to fight. Tessa ran closer, light on her feet. Her blade flashed, making short work of the vamps still huddled around Jake.

We needed a better strategy. Killing them one by one

wasn't working. And then it occurred to me they were running out the clock. A blood-red sun was sinking toward the horizon. Once it vanished, they'd be ever so much stronger.

"Move aside!" Aidyrth's voice rang through my mind.

I didn't question her wisdom. Ione was munching on long dead bones. I dragged him off a pile and told him to come with me. Fire roared through the remains of the town. Everything that could burn went up like a torch. It had begun to rain in earnest. I hadn't even noticed until the droplets hissed as they contacted dragon fire.

Aidyrth stomped forward, a steady stream of heated death spewing from her open jaws. Even a handful of sparks were enough to turn the fleeing vamps into pyres. Despite our best efforts, some got away. At least they wouldn't be back. In the best of all possible worlds, they'd go to ground and remain in stasis for a good long time.

No reason for stealth now, so I sent power zipping downward. Fuck! For every vamp we'd ended, two more were still beneath our feet. How big had this seethe been? Half the sun was below horizon level. The rest of it would sink out of sight fast.

Shira and the dragon returned to where we stood in the middle of stacks of ancient bones. When vamps die, their bodies revert to what they'd have been if they'd died when they should have. So a two-hundred-year-old vamp left bones of the same age.

"There are more of them," I said tersely. "Lots more."

"The underground cavern must have partitions," Aidyrth said, "or my fire would have made short work of everyone left down there."

"What are we going to do about it?" Shira snarled.

"Smoke them out," the dragon said grimly. Moving quicker than I'd thought she was capable of on land, she puffed ashy smoke down every hole the vamps had run out of.

I readied more dead-man's blood, but not a single vamp emerged. Only one explanation made sense. "They must have an underground route." I added a few choice words in Gaelic to my conclusion.

"We can follow them," Tessa said.

"There aren't enough of us," Aidyrth cautioned. "I agree with Kylian, though. The whole reason we targeted them is their affiliation with demonkind. By now, the ones who remained have left, courtesy of demon magic."

I scanned, taking my time. Damn if she wasn't correct. Where I'd sensed maybe fifty, none remained.

"I didn't necessarily mean following them by the obvious route," Tessa clarified. "I have a bone to pick with Lucifer and Asmodeus. Where we find them, I bet we'll also locate the remains of this seethe."

"I still think we could use reinforcements," Aidyrth said.

"Yeah, we do. Shira and I spent time in Hell," Jake growled. "It's their turf. I almost didn't make it out alive."

"Let's not forget what they did to Grigori," Shira said. "Injected him with something that took a long time to become active, but it would have killed off the virus that made him a werewolf."

"Let's vote," I suggested. I'm all for democratic process with mages. With mortals, it's a pointless exercise since their feeble brains rarely make the correct choice. "Who wants to return for reinforcements?"

Everyone but Tessa said aye. Even Quora didn't back her

up. Tessa fixed her steely gaze on her bondmate. "Not even you?" she spat.

"Not even me." Quora drew herself up to her full five-foot height. "We've passed through Hell a time or two. Not peak experiences."

"We got away," Tessa pointed out.

"Barely."

Breath huffed through Tessa's clenched teeth. "Fine. Let's go back, rustle up a few more of us, and get moving. Otherwise the trail will grow cold, and we'll never find them."

What we did next was Grigori's call, but I didn't point that out.

Aidyrth draped a transport spell around us. Before I could lean into her magic, we tumbled out in front of the Nevada guild house. The transition to night was complete, but it wasn't raining here.

Grigori loped down the steps. "Well?" He surveyed our group.

"We ended many of them, but probably missed the master vamp," I said.

Tessa planted herself next to me, hands on her hips. "They escaped through underground tunnels. I'd have gone after them, but Kylian said we needed more than the eight of us. We're here to gather reinforcements, and then we'll be off."

"Will you?" Grigori arched a russet brow.

"Why wouldn't we?" she shot back. Apparently, outing herself as a goddess also outed a tendency to place herself in control.

"Tell me exactly what happened," Grigori instructed.

"But that will take too long," she protested. "What if we

can't find them? Lucifer and Asmodeus were behind the demons who attacked us. I want them gone."

"Demon attack?" Grigori's brows edged higher. "Like I said, start at the beginning. I need a better picture of what's occurred since the bunch of you left."

I filled in the blanks. Next to me, I felt Tessa's agitation. It rolled off her in waves. Back in fox form, Quora had been around her neck, but she jumped down and went to stand next to Ione and Arrow.

"No wonder you were gone so long," Grigori said after I was finished.

"Now can we leave?" Tessa demanded.

Grigori turned his blue eyes on her. "You are welcome to leave, but you will not be taking any Circle mages with you. Neither is this a sanctioned assignment."

She'd begun tapping one booted foot. "Why not?"

"It's too dangerous. Our odds of success are thin. Demons opened pathways for the remaining vampires. By now, they're ensconced in Hell, or they've been moved beyond our reach. Your group did well. Wiping out all those demons was a huge plus. Even though you didn't capture the master vampire, I bet the seethe won't cause further trouble, which was the whole point of this mission."

"What about Lucifer and Asmodeus?" she pressed.

"What about them?" Grigori countered. "They're two of Satan's princes. They'll be well guarded and exceedingly difficult to kill."

"But I can go if I want."

"Aye, I don't advise it, but I cannot stop you." Grigori turned and trudged up the front steps. When I looked around, only Ione and Quora remained with Tessa and me.

The others had slithered into the night, not wanting to deal with Tessa's ire.

"What will you do?" I asked Tessa.

Her agitation had shifted to anger; she stomped off without answering.

"I'm going hunting," Ione announced and loped toward the west.

Probably a good idea, except my hunting would be through the guild house kitchen. Or perhaps in the dining room. It was dinnertime. The clink of silverware and buzz of conversation greeted me as soon as I was inside. I considered cleaning myself up, but this was a warrior's hall. It wouldn't be the first time a mage stinking of the battlefield had helped himself to victuals, nor would it be the last.

Xander and Rhiana motioned me over. Rhea sat at the table too. The empty spot next to her suggested Grigori hadn't yet returned from his chat with us. Had he gone after Tessa? I'd considered it but had wanted to offer her a cooling down period.

"We were getting worried about you," Rhea said.

"Aye, the rest of us have been back for hours," Xander seconded.

"Grigori had been checking and checking. When he jumped up and ran out of here, I knew it had to be you returning," Rhea went on.

"Tell us what happened," Rhiana urged. Her dark hair was damp from a recent shower, and it was just starting to curl around her sharp-boned face.

In between shoveling dinner in as quickly as I could and generous slurps of a robust red wine, I filled them in on our adventures.

"Whoa." Rhea tipped more wine into my goblet. "No wonder you weren't back the same time as the rest of us."

"Will Tessa go after Satan's princes by herself?" Rhiana sounded alarmed. "I know she's actually Andraste and all that, but still there's only one of her."

"Yup, and from the sound of it outside, Quora might even sit this one out." I set my fork down, eyed my empty plate, and motioned to one of the servers to please bring me more. A fresh plate plopped in front of me. I devoured it too. Magic burns a path through you, leaves empty places only food and rest can repair.

"Why aren't we going with her?" Xander asked.

"Grigori said it's too dangerous," I replied. "And he's right. We wouldn't gain all that much, and we could lose a lot." I rolled my shoulders into a shrug. "I'm the original risk taker, and I had my doubts about this one."

"Grigori saw way too much of Hell," Rhea murmured. "It's why he's taking a prudent course. To make certain we annihilate as much of the netherworld as we can."

"Sounds as if you've talked about it." Rhiana offered an indulgent smile.

"Eh, more like I've dragged it out of him." The corners of Rhea's mouth twitched downward. "He's still in rah-rah werewolf mode with me, encouraging me to see all the upsides."

Grigori hurried across the room and slid into his seat, an unreadable expression on his face. I waited, but he didn't seem inclined to be forthcoming, so I angled a pointed look his way.

"If you're asking what she's doing," he said, "I have no idea. She's one stubborn woman."

I drained my goblet and pushed to my feet. "Where'd you leave her?"

He narrowed his eyes my way. "You are not going with her. I won't lose you both."

"All I'm going to do is talk. Promise," I said.

"She was near the Joshua tree grove," he said after a short pause.

I could have located her on my own, but wanted to hang around long enough to make certain Grigori trusted me.

"Want company?" Rhiana asked. "I know her as well as anyone here."

I shook my head. "Thanks, but I'm better off alone with this one. She probably won't listen to me, either. Hell, she may have already left."

"Not yet," Grigori said. "When I gave up and left, she was arguing with Quora."

I sprinted out of the dining room, clapping a few friends across the back as I passed by. Once I was outside, I called for Ione and asked him to meet me near the Joshua trees.

A ward was partially formed before I ditched it. I didn't want Tessa to think I was sneaking up on her. She already felt the rest of us had devalued her strategy. Why couldn't she see she was a party of one? No one else thought storming Hell was a good idea. No one.

Or was it that she'd thrown down a gauntlet and was in so deep she couldn't back out without losing face? The sounds of an argument reached me: Quora and Tessa screeching at one another. Ione and I have had our disagreements, but they'd never escalated to that point.

The snow leopard fell into step next to me. *"What are we doing?"* he asked in telepathy.

"Hopefully, offering both of them a tenable path. One that won't end up with them being dragged into Satan's arms."

"Hello," I called once we were only about fifty feet away.

"Go away," Tessa shrilled.

"Why should I?" I covered the remaining distance. Ione shouldered next to Quora. The Kitsune leaned into him, clearly craving his solid support.

Breath huffed through her teeth as Tessa turned toward me. "Grigori sent you, didn't he?"

"Drape a truth net," I invited and waited for it to clank around me before saying, "No. He didn't."

"Then what are you doing here?" She didn't remove the netting.

I extended a hand. She ignored it, but I kept it out anyway. "I care about you. I'm here to keep you from making a mistake."

"Pfft. Very tender, but I got along for years on my own. A whole lot of them."

"Aye, that you did. But you're here now. Part of a society of assassins. And you've stayed. You chose to remain even after your identity was revealed."

"I'm rethinking that."

"Are you?" I tossed the truth net back her way.

It earned me a wry grin. "Not really. Takes a bluffer to know one."

She reached for my hand then, and I drew her against me expecting a sharp slap or a blast of unpleasant magic. Neither happened. Instead, she tucked her head into the hollow between my neck and shoulder blades and murmured. "I have no fucking idea who I am anymore."

16

I knew how that felt all too well. The sense of being a mage without family or country. The experience of being isolated and burying myself in human affairs, although Tessa hadn't gone that route. I could have said those things, but I chose to remain silent. The simplest phrase is, "I know exactly how you feel," but we so rarely do. The ramifications are different for each of us.

I closed my arms around her, holding her. After a hesitation, she hugged me back. "I've been such an ass," she mumbled against my chest.

"Not at all. You believed in something and were willing to pull out all the stops to make it happen."

Tilting her head back, she cracked a rueful smile. "You're being diplomatic."

"No. I'm being honest. Even if I hadn't had Grigori's blessings to go after Poseidon, I'd have gone anyway."

"Aye, but Ione would have come willingly."

"He would have," I agreed, "because he hated Poseidon almost as much as I did."

"More," Ione growled.

Tessa's gaze shifted to Quora. "My bondmate wasn't as accommodating."

"Maybe it's because she wants many more years riding on your shoulders," I murmured.

Tessa rolled her burnished metal eyes. "Pfft. I haven't gotten us killed yet."

I chose my words carefully. "If you'd gone into Hell alone loaded for bear, it wouldn't have been pretty."

"I've been there before."

"Yeah? And I bet you were well warded. How were you planning to fight through a concealment spell?"

She let go of me long enough to flap a hand dismissively. "All right. All right. Not one of my better ideas. Okay? I like to finish what I start, though."

"We all do."

"Awk. How can I face Grigori? I was horrid to him. All he was trying to do was save me from myself."

"He'll understand," I told her. "You're not the first Circle mage who wanted to bite off more than was wise."

"Maybe so, but I'm not going back in there tonight."

"No one expects you to."

"Did he happen to mention what we'll be doing for an encore?"

"He did not, but my guess is we're done here and will be returning to the primary guild house tomorrow."

Twin furrows formed between her brows. "But we barely made a dent in the seethes."

"Doesn't matter," Quora tossed out. "They're ready for us now. Means it will be harder to find them."

"I bet they're all in Hell," Ione rumbled.

"Not going to work very well for them," I said. "Demon blood is poison for them, and—" I snapped my fingers. I'd missed the obvious. "No wonder the partnership was so cozy," I gritted.

"Aye. Satan knew his precious minions wouldn't be vulnerable." Tessa shifted position and leaned her head on my shoulder again. "I'm done with demons and vampires for tonight."

"Are you hungry?" I asked. "You didn't get any dinner."

"I am," Quora said. Guess she was getting comfortable with me since she was talking more.

"Come with me," Ione invited. "I abandoned part of a deer carcass when Kylian called me."

"Lead out. I'll be right next to you," the fox yipped.

"You never answered me about dinner," I reminded Tessa as the leopard and fox loped away.

"Let's walk a little."

I let go of her, but the spot where she'd been pressed against me thrummed with heat and need. She laced her fingers in with mine; we moved slowly, not intent on any particular destination. Being together was the important part, not where we ended up.

At least that was my take. She'd have told me to get lost in a heartbeat if she hadn't wanted me here.

"Thanks for sticking by me," she said after a few minutes of silence.

"Why wouldn't I?"

A small shrug. "No reason. Shira and Jake took off fast."

"Not to get away from you. They were eating when I went to dinner."

"But they didn't offer one word in defense of my plan." She hesitated before adding, "Neither did you."

Sometimes questions are useful, so I asked one. "Why do you suppose that was?"

"Because Grigori said no dice."

"Not all of it," I retorted. "Dig deeper."

"Did you agree with him?"

"I don't always, but in this instance, I did. You're relatively new to the Circle, but in your years here, you've never seen me. Why do you suppose that was?"

She turned the hand that wasn't latched to mine palm up. "Never thought about it. Mages come and go."

"Yup, but I was gone far more than I was present. If I hadn't uncovered my sire's plot against Grigori, I'd be part of a mercenary operation in some hellhole, pretending to be human."

She stopped and turned to face me. "I don't get it. What was the appeal?"

"Being useful. A lot of Grigori's assignments haven't resonated for a long while, plus the idea of having a boss never sat well."

"Why'd you join the Circle in the first place, then?" Her gaze bored into me. She'd no doubt asked herself much the same question.

"After Mother and the other elemental mages left, my only other family was Poseidon. A piss-poor excuse for all the benefits I associate with families. Ione and I winged it for a while. It was how I ran across Grigori. He and a few mages were fighting a herd of Kelpies in northern Scotland. The water horses were gaining the upper hand until Ione and I joined the fray. Afterward, Grigori invited me to join the Circle."

"Interesting." The lines between her eyebrows deepened. "You signed up but didn't stick around."

"I did for a long while, but I've been..." I swallowed hard. Could I reveal my self-indulgent journey to her? It would make me look like a rich, spoiled playboy seeking fresh meat to carve.

"Been what?" she prodded.

"Chasing rainbows." I grinned ruefully. "Shoring up my seer ability. Avoiding dear old Dad as much as I could."

"You and Quinn selected similar paths," she said slowly.

"Not surprising. We elected to make ourselves useful doing what we do best. Killing bad people." As long as we were sharing backgrounds—or at least I was—I asked, "How'd you and Quora find each other?"

Tessa tossed her head back and laughed. "No one's ever asked me that. I was in Faery visiting Titania. She and Oberon had uncovered a nasty plot to overthrow their monarchy. I had no idea perfidy existed within such a peaceful land. I'd dropped by to catch up, revisit old times. If I'd known about the brewing tempest, I'd have picked another time.

"A group of mixed mages were lined up for questioning. Titania was delighted when I popped in because I can sort through lies far quicker than her."

"So you were conscripted as a judge?" I asked.

"Something like that. Long story short, Quora insisted she

was innocent. Turned out she was, and she begged me to take her with me. I did. It was the beginning of our partnership."

"Were any of the others innocent?"

After a sad little shake of her head, Tessa replied, "Nay, and one of them was Quora's brother. I expected her to beg Titania for clemency. She didn't. I'd been on the fence about taking her with me; that decided things."

"Not so much a bond animal as a colleague," I mused.

"Aren't all the bond animals?" Tessa angled her head to one side. "I've always thought calling them bond animals did them a great disservice."

"I suppose it does, except they know how deeply we value them."

A soft smile transformed her austere features into something softer, more vulnerable. "It's why I joined the Circle," she murmured. "The bond animal aspect appealed to me. And I already had one. No need for Grigori to know our bond wasn't traditional."

"He does now."

Her smile broadened. "It's a relief in many ways. War suits me, subterfuge not so much. The others didn't label me the goddess of victories for nothing."

I loved hearing her voice. Rich and fluid, it washed through me like a Siren song. Except I didn't understand what she'd just said. "Which victory are you gloating over?" I teased.

Her gaze sharpened into a speculative look, and she took off running, long hair streaming behind her like a sheet of dragon's fire. Without questioning my actions—a rare event for me—I bolted after her. Her long legs and lithe build lent her speed. I'd almost catch her, and then she was gone again in a different direction.

"No fair using magic," I called after her.

"Who says I am?"

"I can see it."

Breath burned my lungs all the way to the bottom as I urged my legs to pump faster and faster still, Redolent with sage, the clean, the dry desert air also held hints of her scents. Tonight, jasmine and vanilla tantalized me. If I hadn't been running so fast, my cock would have swelled to fullness. It was trying, but not getting very far.

We passed more Joshua trees before she turned hard left into a grotto. Someone—likely a long-ago miner—had piled stones to make a rough dwelling. Most of the walls remained, but the roof was long gone. Probably sod, it had succumbed to weather and neglect.

Tessa wasn't running any longer. Chest heaving, hair tumbling around her, she looked every bit a Celtic goddess. The cant of her cheekbones was reflected in light from a half moon. Her nipples were outlined beneath her tunic. Reaching down, she yanked the tunic over her head.

My heart had been thudding against my chest before and my lungs on fire, but it grew even harder to breathe. Dumbstruck by her beauty, I was glued in place as I drank in her full breasts with copper nipples the size of silver dollars. They sat high atop a sculpted ribcage that led to the band of her trousers riding snugly on flared hips.

Sinking to one knee, she unlaced both boots before standing and toeing them off. "I never figured you for a prude," she said in a throaty rasp.

Her words broke through the paralysis that had gripped

me. Since my leg muscles no longer needed most of my blood, my cock snapped up the slack. But then, he's always been an opportunistic fellow.

"No one has a right to be so lovely," I choked out, working around a tongue that had forgotten how to cooperate. Or maybe it was that my mouth had suddenly gone dry.

I took a step toward her, and then I rushed forward filling my hands were her lush flesh. Nipples quivered beneath my onslaught, lengthening to rigid peaks and pressing into my palms. Moaning, she leaned into my touch and captured my mouth with her own.

This kiss was different than our last one. Nothing tentative about it. Desire thickened the air, full of the scents of lust and promise. I sank my tongue inside her willing mouth. She sparred with it, bit, and sucked. My erect member jammed into her belly wishing the mouth in question was fastened around it. My lips trailed across her sculpted cheekbone; I kissed the bud of her ear before moving downward.

Shoulder, collarbone, breastbone. Finally, I took a nipple into my mouth rolling it this way and that as I bit gently. A muted gasp from her, an arched back, revealed her arousal. Fingers busy, she peeled off my vest before yanking my top over my head. For a moment, it tangled between where I was making love to her breasts. I hated to leave off even for the moment it took to separate me from my shirt.

I suppose it joined my vest on the rock-strewn ground, but I was too busy to look. Tessa trailed her fingertips across my shoulders and down my back. Her nails left little trails of heat where she dug them in. Grabbing my head between her hands, she kissed me again and hugged me close.

Skin-on-skin was electrifying. Hers was all silk and fire and delight where she rubbed and pressed against me. The feel of her magic surrounded me. In the depths of my mind, I recognized a journey spell.

Where was she taking us?

I started to ask, but I'd have had to stop kissing her, and it didn't matter. Caught up by her spell, mesmerized, I'd have followed her anywhere. The pattern and cadence of the air currents shifted enough I understood we'd left Earth. A chamber shaped around us, one wall nothing but a bank of windows looking out onto a shifting shimmering light show.

The colors merging into one another, forming shapes that broke apart and reformed was beautiful, hypnotic. The chamber smelled like her. Had she taken me to a secret castle? A bed with old-fashioned silk curtains backed against another wall. Pillows and blankets, including a rich fur throw, were scattered over it. A desk and chair sat in the far corner. A basin and ewer in another. Nothing electronic in this place.

Tessa let go of me long enough to unfasten her trousers. They slipped down her long legs, and she stepped out of them. Next she undid my pants. My boots were a problem. I attacked the laces with magic and pushed them out of the way so my pants could rustle to the floor.

A quick intake of breath coupled with the intensity of her gaze pleased me. I wanted to steal her breath, wrap her in the same heat and intensity ratcheting through me. Scooping her into my arms, I carried her across the room and laid her on the bed. We were both still filthy from the field. I didn't care. Bedding could be washed.

She curved her fingers around my wildly out-of-control member. Shock radiated from my core to every cell in my body. Liquid fire hummed through my veins as she explored my shaft from base to tip and back again.

I batted her hand away and knelt between her legs. Bending, I strung kisses down her flat belly to the welter of spiky glowing curls guarding the path to her sex. The musk of her arousal drove me higher still as I licked circles around the halo of hair. Moving ever lower, I breathed heat into her core.

Her hips bucked, straining upward. When that didn't work, she threaded her fingers into my tangled hair trying to force my head downward. Liquid slicked her thighs. Almost as an afterthought, I touched the tip of her distended nub with my tongue. She shrieked and bucked. I licked her nub again before closing my mouth around it and sucking, first gently and then harder.

Beneath me, her hips thrashed from side to side. I buried fingers inside her, touching teasing, delighted as she clamped around me. My cock throbbed. He only had one message. It was his turn. I told him we'd get there, not to be greedy. I've never known the day he didn't want a turn, several, actually.

I ran my tongue up and down her nub before swirling it around the tip. I'd been trying to draw things out, but I felt the beginnings of her climax in the tension in her vault. Sucking harder, I muted my own arousal—this wasn't how I wanted to come—while urging hers to peak.

Waves of desire rolled through us as she melted beneath my hands and tongue. The river of lust crested, retreated, and crested again. Her nectar was sweet in my mouth and dripping down my chin. Before I could prime her for another release, my cock made it abundantly clear he'd spurt on the sheets if I didn't include him.

So much for my efforts to muzzle him. I lifted my face

from her lush flesh. Kneeling between her legs, I seated the head of my oversexed appendage at the entrance to her body. Her eyes had been closed, her head tossed back neck corded with passion.

She opened her eyes. They'd shaded from copper to burnished gold. Her lips were swollen from passion and our kisses. When they parted, she murmured, "A prize worth waiting for," and jackknifed her body around until she was on her knees. The globes of her ass showcased her sex.

Already on the top floor, my arousal shot through the roof. Promises I'd made to myself to be a slow, considerate lover vanished, and I drove into her, not stopping until I was fully encased in her body. Withdrawing, I plumbed her again and again until my entire universe was movement and sensation, the feel of her burning vault gripping me as pussy and cock crashed together, withdrew, and connected again.

The growls and howls coming from me were unrecognizable; I sounded more like Ione than myself. Tessa ground her hips in a circular motion before slamming back against me. Reaching around, I cradled a breast in each hand, rubbing the erect nipples into even firmer peaks. In between pants, a high keening squeal told me she was riding the crest of another release.

I couldn't wait any longer. My balls had been pasted against my body forever. Semen juddered from them, painting her with burst after burst of my seed. The concentric grip and release of her muscles told me she'd joined my passion, adding magic to the mix to heighten our pleasure.

Time stopped as we strained against one another, our mingled breath harsh and ragged in the still air of this world.

Finally, we fell onto the bed, and I turned her so we faced one another.

"See?" She smiled lazily. "Victory."

A victory indeed but I didn't want to talk. It would ruin the purity of what we'd just shared. Gathering her close, I held her as we drifted into a shared trance.

I've never shared a dream trance with anyone before. Never trusted another with the intimate parts of my psyche. Imagery flickered around us as she showed me scenes from her past with her and the other gods cavorting all through the old country. At first, they were happy, but it changed. Once smiles and joy had ceded to harsh words, Tessa left, covering her tracks well.

I shared bits and pieces of my past. Of growing up with elemental mages. Of the day Mother brought Ione home. The parts with Poseidon bore skipping. Not many would mourn his passing, certainly not me.

When we woke, the bank of windows reflected sunlight bouncing off the light show. "Where are we?" I asked.

"Does it matter?"

"Nay, but I am curious."

"This is my world. We all have them, but most are private."

I trailed a hand down the silk of her skin stretched over shoulder blades and spine. "Do you mean like Caer Sidi?"

Tessa nodded. "Aye, Arianrhod's world. Except she told everyone about it, which annoyed the rest of us no end."

"Does this world—your world—have a name?"

"It does, and if it becomes our world, I will tell you what it is and how to find it again."

Good enough. Names hold power, and sometimes my curiosity gets the better of me. "The pile of stones near the guild house," I went on. "Is it a gateway?"

"Intuitive of you."

"Did you build them next to all the guild houses?"

A small shrug. "I may have. They allow me to travel unnoticed without leaving a trail of enchantment."

A bloody smudge on the sheets drew my attention; I winced. "We were both dirty. Sorry about your bed."

"No need. My rooms are self-cleaning."

I kissed her forehead and then both cheeks. "We should get back."

"We should," she agreed, "but I don't want to."

Neither did I, except we were knee-deep in an unfinished war. I rubbed my thumb over her full lower lip. "I can't wait until next time."

Extricating herself from my arms, she rolled to a sit and finger combed her hair. Anticipating she wanted to talk, I sat across from her.

"I want there to be a next time too," she said, "but I'm not into flings. Making love once was...an experiment. If we come together a second time, and a third, it will mean something."

My chest tightened as emotion rolled through me. The knowledge she considered me more than a fling delighted me.

"This meant something to me," I told her. "A lot, actually. And not only because I've been imagining you naked since the day we met."

"Something," she murmured, "but will it be enough?"

I've always been one to hide my deep emotions. So much so, even Ione has complained from time to time. Poised on the edge of a high dive, I leapt off the edge. "I want you in my life forever." My words came out harsher than I'd meant. "It won't be easy. You're as bullheaded as I am. There will be times we hate one another, but the making up will be all the sweeter."

"We will think about this," she announced and got to her feet so she could pick through the piles of dirty clothes littering the wooden floor.

"I have thought about it." I joined her and pulled on clothing as I came across it. Some of my garments were back at the stone hut.

"We will think on this," she repeated. "If we are certain, we will find Danu to bless our union."

My heartbeat sped up. If Danu presided over our mating, it would be permanent. Stability has never been my stock in trade. Would wanting to change be enough to alter patterns I'd honed over my long life?

What? Was I searching for a backdoor, already?

Tessa was looking at me, an enigmatic smile on her face. "I play for keeps," she said. "It's why I've kept to myself since the dawning of time."

"It's none of my business," I asked, "but has anyone else ever been here?"

A smile wreathed her face. At first, I assumed she wouldn't answer me, but she replied. "Sure. Quora. Danu.

A few of the other gods. But no one for a very long while."

Scenes of my romps with the Nereids cruised through my mind, followed by shame. I'd never considered a permanent mate. My life wasn't conducive to it. *My old life*, I corrected.

She walked to me and placed a hand over my mouth. "No need for decisions this moment. I could easily love you."

"I'm already half in love with you." The words tore out of me.

She swept a hand downward. The sumptuous chamber was replaced by stone walls in the northern Nevada desert. We gathered our remaining clothes and walked into the fresh morning. Dawn had broken at least an hour before. Tessa's casual displays of power still blew me away.

"Impressive. From your world to here took maybe ten seconds," I said as Ione loped toward us with Quora next to him.

"Not as extraordinary as all that. It's why I built the portal." Daylight highlighted her cheeks. It might have been my imagination, but her skin still glowed from our lovemaking.

The snow leopard's nostrils quivered. Between sex and grime from the demon and vampire battles, I probably stank to high heaven. I ruffled his fur. "I need to clean up."

"We've been waiting for you," Quora yipped.

"Everyone else returned to the main guild house," Ione said. "Grigori made a point of finding me—"

"And me," Quora piped up.

"And you," Ione agreed. "He wanted to make certain you—"

"I have the picture," I cut in. "Front and center at the main guild house an hour ago."

"Actually, three hours ago, or even four." The snow leopard's whiskers twitched again.

"If you can deal with my luddite magic, I'll handle the transport part," I said to Tessa.

"Sure on the journey spell part, but what does luddite mean?"

"The modern use of the word means someone who's not especially computer savvy. I took a bit of license with the term."

My power was almost back up to 100 percent after the demon and vampire battles. I draped it around all of us and ignited it. The main guild house always takes a bit longer to reach since it's off world. Tessa leaned against me, and I wove an arm around her shoulders.

The urge to break into my journey spell and spirit us to a private island where no one could find us was strong. But Grigori was waiting. Aye, Grigori. My antipathy for taking orders was why I'd spent more time gone than present, but he needed me and my magic. More critically, the Circle needed Tessa's talents.

Since she'd revealed herself, it freed her to maximize her power.

The Circle would suffer repercussions from our work targeting seethes. What form it would take was unknown, but Grigori needed us all to remain vigilant. My destination was the courtyard; my intentions were to kill my spell, go inside, and clean up.

Except the courtyard wasn't empty. It teemed with mages

in full battle regalia. So much for a shower, clean clothes, and a leisurely breakfast.

Quinn ran toward us. "Excellent. You're in my group. We leave in five."

"Leave for where?" Tessa asked.

The earth mage's rugged features formed a frown. "You haven't been briefed?"

"We just got here," I told him.

He nodded tersely. "Grigori said this was your idea, so I figured you'd be up to speed. Remember the genetic freaks?"

"How could I forget?"

"Well, Grigori got a tip about the location of one of their labs. We're hoping it's the main one, and we're going to level it."

"Aren't we being hasty?" I asked.

"Why?" Quinn shot back. "You already wiped out one of them. You'll know right away if this one is related to it."

"The best way to deal with a problem is to go to the source," Tessa said.

"We're hoping this location will yield clues about the others. If there are any others." Quinn made a sour face.

I remembered all the banks of computers at the Russian installation. If I'd been quicker on the draw, I'd have culled data from them before I destroyed their hard drives.

"Where is it?" Ione asked.

"About a hundred miles north of Yellow Knife in the Northwest Territories."

My brows shot up. Another Arctic location. Probably not a total coincidence. I patted my sword. It would have to do as weapons went. The dead-man's blood still rattling around in a pocket wouldn't be much use. Or the silver stakes.

"Who is in our group?" Tessa asked.

"Ciara and me and the two of you." He stopped for a moment before continuing. "This isn't like our usual team delegations since we're all going to the same spot."

I nudged Quinn. "Does each team have an assignment once we get there?"

"Yeah, and ours is pulling information off the computers."

I rolled my eyes. "Grigori should have assigned someone younger."

"Speak for yourself," Quinn huffed. "I'm damned competent with electronics."

"Good because I'm close to worthless," Tessa said with a jaunty grin.

Quinn threaded his way through the crowded courtyard. We followed him.

"Spell's ready," Ciara announced. Tory, her eagle bondmate perched on her back.

Quinn whistled. An even larger eagle swooped down from where he'd been scribing circles in the air. Gwaihir was a worthy opponent with a taste for eyeballs. I'd fed him more than a few to stay on his good side.

Magic sizzled and hissed as Ciara added us to her casting. I remembered her from her days working as Poseidon's assassin. When she'd finally broken free of his net, I'd quietly cheered her on.

"Launch," Quinn shouted.

The courtyard dropped away replaced by the darkness of a journey channel. Ciara rummaged through her pockets and handed me an energy bar. She waved one under Tessa's nose. "Interested?"

While Tessa was thinking about it, I unwrapped mine and

inhaled it in a couple of bites. "If you don't want that one," I began, staring intently at the coconut, almond, walnut Perfect Bar.

Tessa snapped it out of Ciara's hand. "Thank you, but I'll never get used to eating something that's sat on a shelf for months."

"Sometimes years," Ciara noted cheerfully. Too cheerfully.

Tessa made a sour face. "Stop. I still have to choke it down."

"The rest of us cleaned up and ate," Quinn said pointedly.

I waited, but he didn't add a snarky comment about knowing what we'd been up to. He'd almost have to. The musky reek of sex was unmistakable. Every deep breath I took reminded me of being buried in the enchantment of Tessa's body. The stench that had settled around me like a shroud was also redolent of sulfur, courtesy of dead demons, and roadkill, courtesy of finally-really-and-truly-dead vampires.

"We're meeting up about a kilometer from our objective," Quinn said.

"Has anyone actually seen it?" I asked. "Like with Google Maps or something?"

"We tried," Ciara admitted, "but whoever owns the site blurred it out."

Interestingly, Quora had traded riding on Tessa's shoulders for catching a lift with Ione. Good the two of them were becoming friends. If Tessa and I formalized a commitment to one another, feuding bond animals could pose a problem.

Was I actually considering standing before Danu and opening myself to her binding magic, knowing full well the consequences if I broke my vows? It was the primary reason very few mages had Danu join them. The specter of being stripped of a goodly portion of your magic if the relationship fell apart was quite the deterrent. Matings occurred in Faery all the time, but Oberon and Titania officiating carried no penalties.

Sex among mages was fluid, commitments variable. I'd known any number of long-lived partnerships, but far more foundered after a century or two.

Quinn elbowed me. "Christ, dude. You're a million miles away. We're nearly there."

"Dude?"

He snorted. "Eh. Blame my tenure among mortals. Dude is one of those all-purpose words. You can manipulate it to fit almost any situation."

I heard the incessant howl of wind before Ciara's spell cracked and frittered to nothing. No trees this far north, so wind sweeps down from the North Pole unimpeded.

"Try not to waste magic on warming spells," Quinn warned. "If this goes well, we'll be inside soon enough."

Groups of mages popped out all around us. Grigori had sent everyone in residence at the primary guild house, a rare occurrence indeed. The eagles took to the air along with Aidyrth and a few hawk bondmates. Everyone else hustled forward after adjusting wards. With so many of us, if anyone was actually looking, they'd sense our energy rolling forward.

Maybe. Snow and ice pellets spit from the skies. Driven by wind, they hurt everywhere they connected with exposed flesh. I envied Ione's thick fur coat and his clear third eyelid.

A building came into view. Much like the one I'd encountered on Ellesmere Island, most of its bulk was sunk beneath the surface. The roof bristled with satellite equipment, but nothing moved outside. I risked a quick scan. Yup. Three floors just like last time.

Of course, nothing moved. No one but an idiot would volunteer to spend time outdoors in beastly weather like this. I tried for telepathy that would include everyone.

"Looks a lot like another of these I dismantled. If the layout is the same, computers are in the basement, lab on the middle floor, and living quarters on top."

"Which is why Grigori instructed us to wait for you," Quinn muttered. "What else did you find inside."

"One dark Fae."

"There are more than that within," Tessa said. "I checked."

"Do you know how many?" Ciara asked.

She shook her head. "More than ten, less than twenty."

The groups had aligned themselves into squads before Tessa and I arrived. Each was assigned a floor except they'd planned on four floors. We made adjustments since there were only three. Quinn's team might have drawn computer demolition, but two other groups provided backup to make certain we'd have ample time to do our jobs.

"In and out in half an hour," Xander cautioned. He and his team were working the middle floor.

"If you find blueprints for the genetic chaos," I said, "try to extract them intact."

"Wouldn't those be inside the computers?" The werewolf arched a silver brow.

"Depends how much the Fae trust one another," I muttered.

"Which would be not at all," Tessa commented.

Girding myself for the fallout from innocent creatures

who'd been captured for their DNA, I piggybacked onto the group spell to storm the fortress. This one practically had to be run by Russians too. If not, the same architects had built both installations.

Power arced between my hands. Better to come out swinging. Whoever said the best defense is a good offense wasn't lying. Quinn's aim was true, but his earth wizard skills are impeccable in situations like this, much like my magic is infallible in the sea.

A room that could have been cloned from the one I'd already been inside on Ellesmere Island popped into view. Unlike Ellesmere, three men and two dark Fae—glamored up as mortals—were working on something. The Fae's heads snapped around first. Clearly, they felt the fallout from our magic.

A bolt of white lightning flew from my hands, striking one dead in the chest. With a gurgling roar, he sank to his knees. Tessa yanked her sword from its scabbard and surged toward the fallen Fae, separating head from body. In a burst of courage, the other Fae charged her, skidding to a halt a couple of feet away.

"My lady." He bowed low.

Laughter burbled from Tessa. "Since when was I ever goddess to the likes of you?" Another sideways slice from her blade beheaded him. She ripped a length of fabric from his shirt to wipe her sword before dipping it into its sheath.

Meanwhile the three humans had frozen in place. The acrid stench of urine suggested at least one of the men had wet himself. We'd end them, but it could wait. They looked terrified enough to pony up information.

Maybe.

Quinn and Ciara moved through banks of computers filling flash drives before hitting the black plastic cases with enough juice to melt them. Ione growled a warning. The metal door slapped against its stops, admitting two more Fae and three burly men carting submachine guns. I didn't expect them to open fire in an enclosed space full of precious data. Never mind three of their own were helpless.

I'd have lost that bet handily.

The roar of gunfire was deafening. Bullets ricocheted off everything they hit, turning into a deadly game of double jeopardy. Meanwhile I felt the bite of Fae magic, hot and prickly, as they directed their puny magic our way.

Ha. The two other teams with us slathered magic over both Fae before dropping cages over them. We'd kill them too, but my human sources of potential information were dead or dying, cut down by what's euphemistically referred to as friendly fire.

Tessa was playing a game. Arms extended, fingers spread, she was deflecting bullets as quickly as they spat from the guns. Not just deflecting them, driving them back into the men wielding the guns.

"Aim for the throat and up," I yelled. "They have Kevlar vests on."

She gave me a quick thumbs up. Moments later, the men lay on the floor, life leaching out of their eyes. One still had his index finger on the trigger. I sliced it off with a burst of magic.

Silence reigned. Blessed silence.

"Progress?" I aimed my question at Quinn.

"Halfway," he said.

The eagles were munching on eyes. Aidyrth was probably

still outside. No room for her in here no matter how she shrank her bulk. She could pick off any stragglers trying to escape, though. When we left this place, I wasn't planning on leaving survivors.

Sauntering to a Fae, I said. "One chance to save your sorry ass. How many places like this are there?"

"Wouldn't you like to know," he sneered. Fae are usually the pretty ones, but his beauty had dried to wrinkles and rotten teeth. What in the holy hell had they done to him?

"Aye." I kept my tone conversational. "I would. Very much. I already told you I'll let you go."

"Pfft. So I can take my chances with the dragon who's been circling for the last half hour?"

"I'd tell her to spare you." I was lying through my teeth, but he couldn't know that.

"You're Poseidon's get," the Fae said.

Ione joined me, fangs bared, growling.

"Time's a funny thing," I said sweetly, bypassing his comment about my relationship to Poseidon. "You have the next five minutes to tell me everything you know about these gene-splicing experiments."

"Pass. I hated Poseidon."

"Yeah, me too."

His silvery eyes widened with surprise; he hadn't expected me to say that. The door to the room stood open, and my attention was glued to my quarry. Ione was already growling, so I didn't have that clue, either.

A booming voice blasted my eardrums. "You were not invited. Leave now."

My captive wasn't going anywhere. I spun around and came face to face with Satan. Unlike his princes and minions, he wore a man's form. No hoofs or scales or horns for him. Coppery tresses flowed down his back. Emerald eyes gleamed merrily, and he clapped his hands together as if he'd dropped in on a social gathering that pleased him.

Looking more like a stylized Jesus of Nazareth than Satan, he was garbed in a pale-blue robe sashed in white with sandals on his feet. Not exactly Arctic gear, but the route to his house led downward.

"We're not going anywhere," I told him.

"Eh, we'll see about that." He snapped his fingers. Searing pain traveled from my neck to my feet. When he pointed at the two captive dark Fae, they dropped like stones, their cages no longer necessary.

"Old habits die hard." Tessa stepped forward. "Still killing your own, I see."

"Darling," he gushed. "How lovely to see you again."

Air swooshed as she drew her blade. "Fond memories of when I tried to slay you, eh?"

"Sweetheart. That was foreplay. I'm up for a rematch anytime."

With an outraged howl, Quora bolted to her bondmate's side. Ione and I flanked them both.

"Done here," Quinn shouted.

"You may be," I snarled, "but I'm not."

❀ 18 ❀

"Yeah, you are." Satan's pleasant demeanor turned harsh. "I liked your sire far better. You'll never be the god he was." Raucous laughter spurted from the king of Hell. "Because you're not a god at all. Just a lousy half-breed."

"Better what I am than what you are," I shot back. "Besides, dear old Dad is dead."

It startled Satan. Clearly, he hadn't heard the latest from under the sea. "Didn't you wonder what the fuck happened to the army of mutants you sent to support him?" I went on.

He flapped a hand my way. "I have many minions. Keeping track of them all isn't possible."

Interesting. First time I'd come across a god with no idea if his armies had lived or died. Had he always been this way? Or was his power slipping? I cast a secret vote for door number two.

Quinn stomped forward. Guess he'd decided not to leave

after all. Gwaihir scribed circles in the air, squawking. "I just got a good look at the mess one floor up," Quinn gritted.

"Your point?" Satan furled both coppery brows.

"My point is what the fuck? You enslaved innocents for their DNA."

"I don't stick my nose in your business." An aggrieved note ran beneath Satan's words.

"I'm not engaged in the business of tampering with nature," Quinn retorted.

The king of Hell sneered. "Mr. Goody Two-Shoes. You piggyback onto mortal wars to feed your bloodlust. Who will ever notice ten more dead Taliban? Or fifty. Or a hundred."

"This isn't about who has the moral high ground," I inserted smoothly. "It's about you needing to shut down all these perverse operations."

Satan clapped his hands, banging the palms together slowly and deliberately. "Great performance, Kylian. I'll do what I please. You'll destroy some of it, but I'll always be two steps ahead."

In a pig's eye, you will.

Where was a unicorn when I needed one? Rhiana was here somewhere. So was Mother. If they hadn't done their work and left. We'd planned to regroup back at our staging area, so even if they weren't in this building they'd be close.

Satan would hear my telepathy. I didn't care. *Mother. Rhiana. First floor, now.*

More bitter, nasty laugher spewed from him. "Women? You're summoning women to stand against me? I should be outraged. Instead, I'm amused."

"Really? Hang onto your...amusement," Tessa said sweetly.

Ione chose that moment to tackle Satan from one side.

He and Quora and Gwaihir must have planned it because the fox grabbed hold of a calf, biting and cursing and biting again.

Ione sank his fangs into Satan's shoulder. He spat black blood on the ground. "Gah. Nasty."

The eagle dug his talons into Satan's head. Bone showed through rents in his scalp. A high, keening shriek rang from Satan, followed by a fountain of red-rimmed power that originated in his chest and blasted outward. The animals yelped and squealed, jumping away from the fallen god as if he'd turned into a high-voltage wire.

Mother and Rhiana sashayed through the door. Dorcha and Demelza were right behind them. Rhiana walked deliberately to where Satan was dusting himself off. Blood flowed from places teeth and a beak had broken through his skin.

Xander loped into the room in werewolf form.

"Don't bite him," Ione cautioned, still hawking and spitting bits of blood and flesh.

"But it would be so satisfying," the werewolf purred.

Rhiana planted herself in front of Satan and crossed her arms under her breasts. "Been a while."

Dark power shimmered as he warded himself. Guess he wasn't liking the odds. "Aye, you ladies should visit more often."

"In your dreams," Tessa sneered.

"Probably wet ones," Rhiana added.

"Only way he can get laid." Tessa chuckled.

The magic hovering around him thickened as he worked out a teleport spell. Fat chance. I reached downward. "Do not admit him," I ordered the earth.

"I second that," Quinn boomed. "By my bond with earth

and my vows as an earth mage, Satan shall not pass through your layers."

"But I must get home," Satan protested. If he was worried, it wasn't reflected in his voice or his demeanor.

"Why?" Tessa tossed her head.

"Your slaves probably like it a whole lot better when you're not there," I added.

"Subjects. They are my subjects," he corrected me.

I shrugged. "Potato, potahto. What's in a name?"

Dorcha had moved behind him. She prodded his back with her horn.

"Good luck with that, sweetheart," Satan hissed.

Good luck, indeed. Despite our numbers, we were at a stalemate. Even the unicorns couldn't kill Satan—and he knew as much.

"You said not to admit one, but others are coming. Many. Too late to stop them," a scratchy voice crooned deep in my mind. The earth was warning us. Good of her since very little roused her. Before I could alert the others, demons poured through rents in the dirt floor. The bond animals waded into the fray. Unicorn horns flashed as they killed whatever they could reach. Ione slit throats with his powerful jaws. The distant flare of light off Tessa's sword showed me where she fought.

That wily old bastard. No wonder he hadn't added voltage to his teleport spell. He'd already summoned reinforcements. When I looked for him, naturally he was gone. Not the bravest warrior in the battalion, he'd always prioritized his own hide over everyone else's.

The Earth knew not to allow him passage. It meant I should be able to find him. Should being the operative term. I've always been a sucker for lost causes. He wasn't an enemy

I could vanquish, but I wasn't done with him, not by a good big bunch.

"Ione!"

The big cat leapt over piles of bodies. "Aye?"

"We're going after Satan."

"I heard that," Tessa said into my mind. *"Want company?"*

"Sure."

A quick teleport spell moved us outside the building. If anything, the storm had grown worse. I shook my fist skyward and muttered, "Bring it on." Far above me, Aidyrth trumpeted. Clearly, she was still keeping watch. If Satan had passed through, she'd have circled him with fire.

Tessa popped out next to me with Quora curved around her neck. "What makes you think he's out here?"

"I leveraged my link with the earth to bar him entry. Means he'll have to use the sea to access Hell, and there are only a couple of spots that might come close to working. Where the earth's crust is thin enough for him to jump through it."

"What about all those tunnels he's dug?"

"They should bar his way, but I'm not certain they will. Depends how much demon magic they're imbued with. Earth shies away from high concentrations of wicked power."

Ione's nostrils quivered as he sampled the air. He took off at a dead run, still tracking. Tessa crafted a ball of amber light between her hands. After blowing into it, she barked a power word in old Gaelic and loosed her creation. It would search and report back.

I shook my head to clear the ringing in my ears from the word she'd uttered. Big magic requires sacrifice, though.

"We accomplished a lot," she said.

"We destroyed this undertaking," I agreed. "What else we achieved will depend on what Quinn and Ciara took off the computers. He came back, she didn't."

"Most everyone left for home," Tessa said. "I heard them talking. Ciara wanted to get all those little electronic boxes back to somewhere she could examine them."

"You can listen to everyone? Impressive."

"If I want to, aye."

Her enchanted construct barreled back to us. She caught it in an outstretched hand and interrogated it.

Ione raced back to where we stood. "I don't get it," he snarled. "Not a clue."

Tessa lowered the ball. It had stopped glowing. "He teleported from there"—she pointed at the dark stones of the building—"to the Arctic Ocean. Looks as if your theory about him using the sea as a path home was spot on. What are the two places he'd try?"

"Hang on. Let me tell the others what we're doing." I said and switched to telepathy. *"Quinn?"*

"Yeah?"

"We're going after Satan. See you back at the guild house. Be sure to blow this place up before you go."

Gentle laughter rang through my link with him. *"Not my first rodeo, dude. We'll handle it. Good hunting."*

"Should we split up?" Tessa interrupted the journey spell I'd started.

"Uh-uh."

"But if we guess wrong, he'll be gone."

I made a face and picked up the threads of my casting. "Gone is relative. We can always follow him."

"I don't think so. When I wanted to go after Satan's princes, Grigori forbade it."

There was that part. No difference between her being shot down and me wanting something similar.

I poured fire into my casting; it swept us into a psychic tunnel. We could bypass some of the geography because of my bond to the sea. Darkness ceded to the rush of water as I guided us to the first spot. Word travels fast in the ocean. Because we were in Arctic waters, the Kraken intercepted us. Ione lunged at his friend, and the Kraken batted playfully at him with his top set of arms.

"Any sign of Satan?" I asked.

The monster shook his head. "Should there have been?"

"We found another place that manufactures unnatural soldiers, like the ones we fought near the dungeon," Ione explained.

"Figures Satan would be behind it," the Kraken rumbled, "but why would he be here?"

"He's trying to get home," I said. "Quinn and I barred most of the earth routes to him."

"He wouldn't be here," the Kraken growled. "Poseidon built him a nice cushy channel from under the palace."

Disgust churned in my guts. "Fuck him. If he wasn't already dead, I'd kill him again."

The distinctive feel of the Kraken's sea-based power prickled as it wrapped around us. Moments later the deep blue of the Arctic changed into cerulean tones typical of the Mediterranean. Poseidon's erstwhile home reared before us. Lights still shone from many windows courtesy of the natural bioluminescence of ocean creatures. The three-story structure rose from sand. Crafted from coral, stones, and magic, it has always been lovely. I figured the Nereids designed it, since Poseidon lacked an eye for art.

"He's been here," Ione grunted.

I smelled Satan too.

"Hurry," the Kraken urged. The sea floor churned around him as we sank through layer after layer of sediment and limestone. Our exit point was an open doorway in the castle's foundation. In front of it lay a breach in the ocean floor.

Tessa stood over the chasm. Waves of the unmaking spell rolled from her hands as she sent her power through the tunnel. It was brilliant, but would it work? If he was still in the tunnel, her magic would shatter its walls stranding him in open sea.

Proactive could be my middle name. I called on the sea and the earth as I plumbed into the sea floor. "No demons," I exhorted. "Neither coming nor going."

I felt my way alongside the unmaking spell, careful to skirt its edges.

"Found it," the Kraken boomed so loud water sloshed around me. Somehow, he'd intuited I was hunting for the transition point where the tunnel made a full commitment to burrowing into dirt. Hell would be close then.

Could the combined power of sea and earth keep Satan out of his domain?

I skidded to a halt, treading water. Ione stood next to the Kraken. The door at this end was still shut. Did it mean the king of Hell was somewhere trapped in the unmaking spell? Or had he suddenly developed manners and closed a door behind him?

The first option got my vote.

"Got him." Tessa's voice brimmed with satisfaction.

With the Kraken and Ione ranged behind me, I yanked the door open, prepared to heave it shut if I caught so much as a glimpse of Satan.

Enhancing my voice with magic, I shouted, "You are barred from Hell forever. Destined to wander from place to place, all you meet shall loathe you. I, Kylian, have commanded both sea and earth to prohibit passage."

"Let's talk about this," a muted voice flowed toward me.

"No talking."

"I'll tell you where the other labs are."

"You'll do that anyway," Tessa called from the upper end of the unmaking spell. "If you don't, I'll wrap you so tightly in my power, you'll begin losing body parts."

The feel of her enchantment, fueled by grit and determination, barreled down the channel. Satan hesitated, but not for long, before wheezing out two more sets of coordinates. They were in the Arctic as well.

"I will stand guard over him," the Kraken announced.

"Are you sure?" I asked him. "It's not a favor I'd ask of anyone."

The Kraken laughed uproariously. "He'll call for help. They'll swarm through the hole, and I will eat them."

"Demons taste bad," Ione said.

"It's only the outer layer," the Kraken clarified. "Underneath, they taste like chicken."

"If you want to stay for the main course, it's all right," I told the snow leopard.

He licked my chin with his sandpaper tongue. "I want to spend time with my friend. If food shows up, fine. If not, there are plenty of fish here."

When I glanced at the Kraken, the monster was smiling.

"Tessa. Are you ready to leave?" I called.

"Give me five minutes to button this up, and I will be."

I set both hands on the castle's foundation. Someday, I'd be ready to go through its many rooms, but not for a while. "Make sure all sea dwellers know they are welcome in the palace," I told the Kraken. "Lot of rooms if anyone needs a home."

"That's kind of you, sire," the Kraken replied.

"Not sire. I will not be replacing Poseidon. No one in the sea needs a king or a god."

Tessa floated to where we stood with Quora next to her. "Ready."

"See you back at the guild house," I told Ione. "No rush. Stay here as long as you'd like."

Tessa's scent, vanilla and cinnamon, licked at my nostrils as she set a travel spell in motion. Once we'd left the sea behind, she murmured, "So, how much do we tell Grigori?"

"Everything. We followed the rules. We didn't go into Hell."

She hip-butted me. "Do you always follow the rules?"

I almost choked. "Not exactly. Not one of my specialties."

She wound her arms around my neck. The press of her body against mine wiped out everything. I was still trashed and dirty and starving, but everything else could wait.

I hugged her back and nibbled on an ear. My next words surprised me. "I am ready to stand before Danu and pledge myself to you."

Pulling me closer, she murmured, "Me too, but we can't go like this. She'd send us packing."

"I figured we'd shower and change and eat and report to Grigori."

"Whoa. Long list. Are you certain you won't have second thoughts?" She ran a grimy index finger down my cheek.

"Quite certain. You?"

"Not a chance."

We were still nestled in each other's arms, lips locked together, when the courtyard shimmered into being around us.

EPILOGUE

A month had passed. Tessa and I weren't any closer to finding Danu than we'd been the afternoon we returned to the main guild house. We'd cleaned up and joined the rest of the Circle for a meal. More like a sumptuous feast, but Grigori had ulterior motives.

Even with the Kraken standing guard, no one expected Satan would remain within Tessa's snare for long. The unmaking spell wouldn't do more than unravel a few edges. Sooner or later, he'd claw his way out.

"Now is the time to strike," Grigori had said.

He was right. If we were going to carve a swathe through Hell there'd never be a better time. Good soldiers, one and all, we'd been on nonstop maneuvers ever since. We'd stuck with our most recently assigned teams, which meant Quinn, Ciara, Tessa, me, and our bond animals had been fighting side by side.

A frisky spring rainstorm pummeled us as we returned to

the nearest guild house. In this case, it was the one located in the northern reaches of British Columbia. Smallest of the guild houses, this one has always reminded me of a rustic hunting lodge. Many miles of dirt road separated it from the nearest highway, and we buried it in magic when no one was there—which was most of the time.

We'd just returned from a sneak attack in a new spot, one that had gone particularly well. After several weeks of concerted effort, we had to be wearing the fuckers out. The animals left to hunt. Quinn clapped me across the back. "That went well."

I straightened, letting rain sluice grime and demon blood from my face. "What? No dude tacked on?"

"Not this time." He rolled his shoulders to the accompaniment of cracking bones. "We're done here from my perspective."

"Yeah, we are. One more trip would finish things, but we left enough wreckage to make them think twice."

"They didn't seem to fight back as hard today," Ciara added.

"If the other teams met with similar success, we should be able to move on." Tessa had joined us.

Ciara pulled out the energy bars that lived in her pockets, handing them around. I was starving and not nearly as picky about what went into my mouth, so I didn't bother reading the wrapper. A burst of almonds and raisins was a pleasant surprise.

"Either these things have gotten better, or I've grown used to them," I murmured around a mouthful.

"Maybe a little of both." Ciara laughed. Sea magic clung to her in ropy blue strands that tangled in her fair hair.

"So, the consensus is we're done?" Tessa glanced from Quinn to Ciara to me.

"I believe so," Quinn said.

Tessa's gaze locked with mine. "We need to jump on this. Before we go back and Grigori dumps another assignment in our laps."

"Jump on what?" Ciara's finely honed features sharpened as she probed my mind. She wasn't gentle or subtle, but I kept her out of my private places.

So far, the only ones who knew about Tessa and me were our bond animals, and we'd sworn them to secrecy. Not because we were ashamed, but because we had so much else to deal with. Hell hadn't been a walk in the park. We'd hit many dicey stretches where absolute concentration was a must. So was teamwork.

We'd fought and fought well. No one could accuse Tessa or me of daydreaming about each other rather than being fully present.

Quinn raised his dark brows. "Whatever this is, spill it now. I'm going to have to explain to Grigori why you aren't with us."

"If Tessa hasn't changed her mind—" I began.

"I haven't," she cut in.

Ciara angled her head to one side. "Oooh, this is sounding interesting."

"Ssht." Quinn held up a hand.

"Yes, dear." She patted his arm; her gaze flicked from me to Tessa and back.

"We will stand before Danu," Tessa said, "so she can bless our mating."

Ciara squealed and threw her arms around Tessa. "Wonderful news. I'm thrilled for you."

Quinn held out his hand. I shook it. "Congrats, old man. May all the years be good ones."

Ciara let go of Tessa. "Can we tell the others?"

"Of course." I hadn't realized I was smiling until tightness across my cheekbones gave it away.

"Hurry." Quinn made shooing motions.

"Aye. Best get moving," Ciara seconded. "Grigori's kept the assignments coming at a record pace ever since he nearly died—twice."

"We have the same problem we had last time we decided to find Danu," Tessa said. "We're filthy. She won't appreciate that."

"Easily remedied," I reminded her. Hooking a hand under her elbow, I guided us up the guild house steps. No electricity here, but we could heat water with magic.

Half an hour later we'd taken turns in the deep tub, draining the water each time it developed a dingy gray hue. A bit of rummaging through the wardrobe room yielded clean clothes. They made us look like extras from a grade B Western, but at least they weren't stained with blood and muck.

She was coaxing her damp hair into braids when I put my arms around her from behind. "You have no idea how tough it was not to ravish you when you were naked."

Twisting to look at me, she winked. "Rain check?"

"Double rain check."

She snorted. "We'll be lucky to cash one in. Grigori will have something else for us to do."

"What? No honeymoon? I was hoping we could retreat to

your world, shuck our clothes, and make love until we run out of magic."

"That could take a while." She smiled and blew me a kiss.

"My point exactly."

The steamy air from the bathroom had wafted into the bedroom blending with humidity that was always high in this part of the world. I stuffed my dirty clothes into a duffel I'd brought along. Tessa nudged hers into a pile and picked up her rucksack, slinging it across one shoulder.

"Don't you want the clothes?" I asked.

She gave a small shrug. "Eh. I can always come back for them. I'll leave them in the washing-up area."

"Shall I meet you back here or outside?"

"Outside. We need to collect Ione and Quora."

Whistling an old Gaelic folk tune, I enjoyed the clack of my bootheels on polished wood. Since I had a moment, I blitzed through the kitchen and tossed cheese and crackers into a sack. Sustenance for the trip.

By the time I closed up the guild house, sealing it with magic, Tessa and the animals were waiting. Quinn and Ciara and their eagles had left long since. Probably, they couldn't wait for a proper meal—and to spread the news. Mages are inveterate gossips. Don't ever let anyone tell you otherwise.

Blue-violet threads of power shot from Tessa in all directions. Her arms were extended in front of her, and her eyes closed. I wasn't certain what she was up to, but I kept quiet, waiting.

The magic stopped swirling and sank back into Tessa. She opened her eyes. "Found her," she exclaimed. "It wasn't easy."

I assumed her was Danu. "Where is she?"

"That's the humorous part. Hiding in plain sight. I started

with uber-distant worlds and gradually narrowed my search to closer locations. She has her own world too, and she moved it much nearer Earth than it used to be."

"Maybe she wants to keep an eye on things here?"

"Could be." Tessa held out a hand. "Ready?"

I walked to her side and laced my fingers with hers. "Aye. You?"

"This will be permanent," she warned.

"No backing out," I agreed. "Why would I want to? You're everything I've ever wanted."

Tessa laughed, the sound of her mirth reminiscent of the tiny bells in Faery. "You spent your wayward youth dreaming about tethering yourself to a bitch with a hideous temper? I think not."

"What I see is a skilled warrior. One who wants to win and won't give up until she does. Beyond that, you're bright and compassionate."

"Ssht. Do not spread that last part around. You'll ruin my image."

I muffled a snort. "The big question is what you see in me. You could have anyone."

She nodded solemnly. "You care about me for me. Not because I'm a goddess. Not because you want to leverage our association for your own ends. Beyond that, I could look at you forever." A corner of her mouth twitched. "And you're dynamite in bed."

"Thought you'd never get around to the important part." I patted my crotch. "My sidekick says thank you."

"Can we get moving?" Ione cast an indulgent look my way.

Tessa spun the hand I wasn't hanging onto in lazy circles. Quora jumped onto her shoulders and curled her body around her neck. Ione and I stood close. I didn't notice a transition point. One minute we were in British Columbia with rain pattering down. The next, we stood in a grand hall furnished with priceless antiques.

Or maybe they were custom pieces she'd had commissioned or crafted with magic. Sculptures and unique blades hung on the walls. Multihued crystals floated this way and that. The shiny wooden floor was crisscrossed with thick rugs in a rainbow of colors. No chairs. No couches. An altar of black onyx graced the far end of the room. Atop it sat a brazier with fire swirling above it.

Hands joined, we walked to the altar and waited. Ione stood by my side. Quora jumped down, took her Fae form, and stood on Tessa's other side.

Time slipped past. Apparently, this was a test of our patience, but I'd have waited forever to seal my bond with Tessa.

Wind blew through the chamber. Rush lanterns spaced at intervals in wall sconces flickered. The scents of flowers and damp earth wove into a spinning vortex. When it cleared, Danu stepped from it with a stag by her side. She always looked the same garbed in her flowing creamy robes embroidered with runes in a language so old it had fallen out of memory. Today, her robe was sashed in teal, and her silver-and-gold hair was unplaited.

The stag tossed his head. Golden horns caught the odd light in the chamber and reflected off passing crystals. Danu patted his rump.

The goddess turned onyx eyes on us. The stag chose that moment to morph into Gwydion, master enchanter and warrior magician. Fair hair was braided tight against his head, and he narrowed blue eyes our way.

"For what purpose have you come?" Danu asked.

"It had better be good," Gwydion cut in.

Tessa let go of my hand and bowed low. "Apologies for disturbing you. We ask your blessing on our mating."

Gwydion whistled. Coming close, he slugged me in the arm. "Strong work, sea god. We used to take bets about who'd hook up with Andraste."

"Really?" I slugged him back. "What'd you come up with."

"No one. She was always tough as nails."

"I am no longer Andraste," she announced. "My chosen name is Tessa."

"Why?" Danu thundered, clearly not pleased by the turn of events.

"I hid my identity for a long while. I rather grew to appreciate the new one. I'm no longer concealing my goddess ability, but I chose to retain my other name."

"I see." Danu exchanged a pointed glance with Gwydion. "Told you everything would change once we were less visible."

"About why we sought you out," I spoke up.

Danu cocked her head to one side. I swear she rolled her dark eyes. "For pity's sake, just fuck each other. This will be permanent. What if you change your minds five hundred years from now? I'd be forced to strip you of most of your magic."

"We'll deal with it." I said firmly. "Not the magic stripping part since it will never happen, but the figuring out how to love one another day by day."

"Not your choice to make for us." Tessa tilted her chin at a defiant angle. "Will you do this? Or shall we leave?"

Grumbling under her breath, Danu pulled a dirk from somewhere inside her robe. Chanting in Gaelic, she blessed us and called on the four seasons, the four directions, and all mages and animals to recognize our union. She warmed to the task and was actually smiling by the time she cut slices in each of our thumbs and smeared blood from Tessa on my forehead and blood from me on both her cheeks.

Birds had flown in from somewhere. Circling the hall, they serenaded us with sweet songs.

Danu pocketed the knife. "It is done," she said. "You will be joined forever more through all lives."

"Something within me shifted. My power slotted in with Tessa's, the strands undulating like a healthy vine that had just found nirvana.

"All the best to you both," Gwydion said. In the rare moments when he wasn't raging or joking or fighting, he was always sincere.

"Aye. I wish the best for you as well." Danu inclined her head. "What is done can never be set asunder. Be kind to one another."

Ione walked to the goddess and licked her arm. She ruffled his fur.

"Thank you," Quora bowed first toward Danu and then to Gwydion.

Danu narrowed her eyes. "I remember you."

"As do I remember your kindness to me," Quora said.

I made a mental note to ask after that story.

"Now that you've found me, visit occasionally," Danu invited.

"We will," Tessa assured her. "Thank you for blessing us."

"Aye, my thanks as well," I murmured.

"Andraste." Danu's voice was stern, and her use of Tessa's original name deliberate.

"Aye." Tessa locked gazes with her.

"I assume your, um, associates in the Circle of Assassins know who you are now."

"They do." Tessa nodded curtly. "I was discovered and had little choice."

"Of course, you had choices. You could have left, but because they are your family, I will not censure you for breaking our laws," Danu continued.

"Nor will I," Gwydion said. "Nothing is the same as it was. Danu and I both wish you well."

It was a smart time to take our leave. Before we wore out our welcome—or Danu rescinded her forgiveness—I called a journey spell aimed at the main guild house. With our power united, the transit was quick.

The courtyard formed around us under a sky shading to evening. A shout of, "They're here," was followed by a rush of mages surrounding us and shouting congratulations.

"Come inside," Grigori invited. "There's a wedding feast in your honor. I've been standing guard over it far too long."

"How did you know we'd be back today?" I asked.

He grinned, an uncharacteristic gesture coming from him. "Because I know Danu. No one remains in her company for long. I take it she forgave your Circle association?" The words were aimed at Tessa.

"She did, indeed. I hadn't planned to bring it up, but she and Gwydion already knew."

"Of course, they did," Grigori said. "Not much gets past them."

With my arm around Tessa and Ione by my side, we

mounted the steps into the guild house. Quora rode on Ione's furry shoulders. I felt like I'd come home after a long journey. Truly come home to friends and family and a mate.

"I'm happy," Tessa murmured near my ear.

"Me too," I told her. "Beyond that, I'm complete. Something was always missing from my life. I told myself it was a whole lot of things. More magic. More skill, enhanced resources to draw on. But none of them mattered at all. What I was missing was you."

She tossed her head back and laughed. "Check in with me a few years into this adventure."

"I'll still love you as much as I do right this moment."

Stopping amid the flow of mages, I swept her into my arms and kissed her.

You've reached the end of *Kylian*, fourth of the Circle of Assassin books. A fifth, *Grigori*, will be along at some point. Please leave a review for *Kylian*. Do it now while the story is fresh in your mind. I'd very much appreciate it. Doesn't have to be fancy. A line or two will do.

Have you explored my Magick and Misfits series? Read on for a sample from *Court of Rogues*.

Until next time, dear readers.

BOOK DESCRIPTION: COURT OF ROGUES

Urban fantasy and slow burn romance wrapped into a serial that will keep you up reading long into the night.

Strange bedfellows rock worlds.

Reluctant recruit to the nines, I became Faery's regent by default. Sure, I was next in line for the throne, but I never believed Oberon and Titania were gone for good until first a decade rolled by, and then two, and then ten.

They'll never be back, and the land is mourning. Or pissed. It's hard to tell which, and I'm not sure what difference it makes. I split my time between Faery and Earth searching for a way to mend the rift that's killing my realm. I haven't made much progress. Time is running through the glass, mocking my paltry efforts.

A sultry Witch is barely a blip on the radar. So what if she counts cards in the casino I run on Earth and makes my pit boss a little nuts? Out of the blue, she spits out the unbelievable, and I discover she's not a Witch after all. A glamour hid her Fae-Sidhe blood so well, she'd fooled me.

Her mixed blood is an affront. By rights, I should haul her before the Court to face justice. She understood the chance she took revealing herself to me, and her offer to join forces is tempting, but it could cost me my throne.

Some risks are worth the price. If I cross the line, there'll be no going back.

COURT OF ROGUES, CHAPTER ONE, CYN

The door to my cramped office slapped against its stops, rattling the frosted glass blazoned with Jedediah Rolfson, General Manager, Lady Luck Casino. The gilt lettering had faded, but everyone in the gaming house knew who I was and where to find me. Of course, Jedediah isn't my true name. Names hold immeasurable power. Even if mortals had been able to pronounce my real one, I'd never, never give them that sort of leverage over me.

My door was still vibrating. A knock would have been nice. Respectful, even, but manners had passed most mortals by. Fueled by irritation, my power simmered so close to the surface it took an effort to rein it in. No need to turn around to identify the man who'd disturbed what passed for peace in this place.

"What is it, Rudy?" I still hadn't swiveled my chair to face him.

"How'd you know it was me?" he demanded.

Because I can smell you, idiot...

I did twist then. The motion of my big body forced the ratty leather chair around almost as an afterthought. Stick-straight black hair fell across Rudy's face, and his white shirt was rolled to the elbows. His usual dark pants were rucked up over the tops of battered leather boots. He looked more like a kitchen knave than a pit boss—an underfed kitchen knave who'd stopped growing as a teenager. I made a point of hiring oddballs—freaks and losers. They weren't in a rush to use Lady Luck as a steppingstone for something better.

Angling a pointed look his way, I growled, "Never mind how I know things. What's gone wrong?" I snapped my fingers in the vain hope he might hurry things up.

He squeezed his bloodshot dark eyes shut for a count of two before opening them. "That infernal twit who counts cards is back."

Many patrons count cards, but only one had posed a challenge recently. Interest flickered as I constructed an image of the leggy red-haired Witch with an iridescent nimbus of power floating around her. "You mean the woman?"

"Of course I mean the blasted woman." A touch of his Russian accent slipped through. "She's the only one who's been able to beat our system."

"What exactly were you hoping I'd do?"

Color stained his sallow cheeks. It was such an unusual response, I delved into his mind and helped myself to his thoughts. Mortals were quite the superficial lot. Culling through their secrets saved me a lot of time.

"Well?" I snapped my fingers again, more out of frustration than actual hope it would move Rudy off the dime.

"Maybe you can tell her to leave." He drew himself up to his full five-foot-eight-inch height, but it didn't have the desired effect. He wanted me to respect him, to back his play, but I'd seen the whole sorry charade in his puny mind. He'd chased the Witch out the last time she stopped by the casino, but he'd also done his damnedest to fuck her.

She'd lured him with a fine set of tits, and then hexed him. Even though he had no concept of what she'd done, her sneaky spell had rendered him impotent. I smothered a chuckle. Witchy charms had a shelf-life. Eventually his little johnny would stand up and salute again, and—

A muted crash came through the audio on one of many screens I'd had mounted so I could see the entire gaming house. Not that I needed them, but they looked good and avoided explanations about how I knew jack concerning the brawl in the basement lounge. The patrons had no idea I spied on them—until I turned them over to the authorities for cheating the house. I've been called a lot of names since I was suckered into taking on this thankless job. So far, I've maintained my cool.

Eventually, though, some hapless mortal will find himself skewered by Fae magic. They'll beg for mercy, for the compassion of a human court, but it will be too late. Mortals never leave Faery unless we release them, not intact, anyway. Those who break free end up in institutions.

"Jed?" Rudy prodded.

"Yeah. Yeah. On my way." I flowed out of my seat. If Rudy weren't hovering in my doorway, I'd have teleported four floors down. Meanwhile, the ruckus was escalating amid the crash of breaking glassware.

"The thieving card counter?" Rudy's gaze skittered away.

"Is that why you're still standing there?" I made shooing motions with both hands. "Christ. Strap on a set. Get moving. I have bigger problems."

The color that had stained his face turned an ugly tomato shade before he spun and pelted down a nearby stairwell mumbling in Russian. He thought I'd never hear him, but he was whining about the fight that had broken out not being on his floor. If it were, the Witch would have beat a hasty retreat.

A snarl of frustration burbled past my throat. I'd never been able to pound the whole team player concept down everyone's throats. Rudy had risen to pit boss because he was honest—and loyal. Maybe it was too much to expect him—or any human in my employ—to show any initiative beyond the basics.

He didn't like me, but then none of the staff did. They sensed I was different, couldn't put their fingers on why that was, and felt uncomfortable in my presence.

Good. I'd never lift a finger to alter their instinctive dread of me.

The day humans can lounge in front of Fae royalty—never mind how far we've fallen—is the day for me to retire to the *Dreaming* and never resurface. A quick glance at the monitor reassured me the brawl was in full swing. No one would notice an unorthodox entrance, so I hopped on an enchanted conduit and emerged in the largest of five gaming halls in a blaze of light.

Muted light, but it still would have given someone pause. Not here, though, and not now. What looked like a motorcycle gang—leather and tatts and piercings—had faced off against a bunch of Asian street hoods who fancied themselves a modern-day version of the mob.

Ha! Bugsy and Al, two of my old buddies, would have laughed until they puked at the comparison. They'd understood how to be badasses because they'd borrowed liberally from Faery. Much of their wickedness never saw the light of day; they were too smart to reveal themselves, and I'd sworn them to silence. Most mortals wouldn't honor such a bond, but they did. They had no idea what I was, but they'd absorbed my lessons like mother's milk. I crossed a few lines—eh, more than a few—by teaching them gruesome ways to inflict pain and death. Even then, my kingdom was on its way out. What were a few more broken rules?

Turned out flaunting Fae law held a price beyond measure, but I'm getting ahead of things.

No one noticed me as I crunched over broken glass, my fury growing at the senseless destruction. The acrid stench of piss merged with the coppery tang of blood. If I didn't establish control over the situation, this room wouldn't be usable for a few days.

Unacceptable. The tables in this gambling hall raked in better than $50,000 a night.

Grunts and curses rained around me as men punched and knifed one another. I sent magic spiraling out, hunting for the telltale bite of metal. Lady Luck had a no-firearms-or-knives rule, and a metal detector sat at the main entrance. It netted us an impressive array of weapons that we stashed in a safe and turned over to the cops once a week.

Yeah. That's right. Bring a gun or a shiv into my club, and you have to petition the cops to get it back. Works great if the piece is legal, but most of them weren't. Ever since I'd established that brilliant bit of policy, we hadn't seized too many of them.

I'd made it to the front of the large hall. Not a dealer or croupier in sight. Either they were hiding in the shadows, or they'd fled at the first hint of trouble. I'd deal with that later. They were supposed to alert someone like Rudy. Or me. I employed half a dozen pit bosses who rotated through the club.

I'd heard from Rudy, but not about this mess.

Someone catapulted into me from the side brandishing a knife. I punched him squarely in the neck, and he dropped like a stone. Shouts told me I'd made someone happy by knocking out one of their enemies. Another dude decked out in black leather rushed me from the back. I knew he was coming, but I let him think he was getting away with something.

I swear, mortals' intelligence has been on the wane for the past hundred years. If Shit For Brains had any at all, he'd have recognized a dead-to-the-world five-year-old would have heard him bearing down on me. Timing is everything. I turned at the precise moment to hit him with a one-two combo to the gut and heart. I might have killed him, but I didn't care.

Once he was squealing and twitching at my feet, I cupped my hands around my mouth and amplified my voice with magic laced with you'd-better-do-what-I-say-or-your-days-will-be-numbered compulsion.

"Stop. Right Now." Three little words. No need to repeat them.

A slow lazy smile formed, stretching my face into an

unaccustomed configuration. Yay me. I still had it. Everyone had frozen in place.

"Excellent," I went on, smooth as melted butter. "Everyone get the fuck out of here except your top dogs. Take the fallen with you."

As the crowd cleared, shuffling toward the door, another of my pit bosses scuttled to my side and cleared her throat. "Sorry, boss," Tatiana mumbled. "I went to find you, but your office was empty."

Kind of like your head.

I'd learned to squelch comments like that long ago. Mortals were notoriously thin-skinned, and Tatiana reeked of fear. She hadn't pissed herself, but it had been nip-and-tuck. Her blonde hair was in an updo, and her skin pale under heavy makeup. She would have been pretty without all the war paint. Blue eyes, her best feature, were framed by thick lashes, and she wore Lady Luck's standard employee uniform: white shirt and black pants. Most of the shirts carried the Lady Luck logo, a phoenix sinking into a crater.

The symbolism escaped everyone except me, and I'd never been in a sharing mood when it came to questions like, "What's that mean, boss?" Besides, even if I told them it represented Faery's decline, they'd have thought I'd had too much to drink.

Meanwhile, four men had moved closer, but not too close. Like I said, I make humans nervous.

"Yeah?" One narrowed his eyes. "What'd you want us for?"

I nailed him with my gaze. I employ a glamour. It smooths the points of my ears and makes my eyes appear blue, rather than a mix of silver and gold with coppery centers. For the slightest of moments, I let it slip a notch, just a hint of a blur.

The dude rubbed his eyes. "Shit. Drunker than I thought." His words were slurred.

It was tempting to display more of what I really was. I shrugged it off. No point in making him yearn for the impossible. He'd be drawn to my deviant beauty. More than drawn. He'd twist himself into a pretzel for one more peek. If I'd wanted a lackey, sure, but I had other plans for him and his partners in crime.

"You have two choices," I told the men who were shifting from foot to foot as they looked mostly at the floor. "Grab mops and buckets and clean up the mess you made."

"Or?" One tried for a sneer, but didn't quite manage it.

"Or I hold you here and call the cops. Property damage is a felony. Bet you've had a few of those already."

I rocked back on my heels, waiting. Tatiana had drawn closer to me, not because I was warm and fuzzy, but because the thugs made her even more nervous than I did.

"Big talk. How are you planning to keep us from leaving?" Shit For Brains Number Two asked.

I swept an arm wide. "I don't have to. You're all on camera. I give the cops the feed and voila." I dusted my hands together. "I'm sure they know you already."

"We'll clean," he gritted out.

"It would go faster with more of us," another pointed out.

"Probably so, but I don't want 'more of you' in here," I told him. "While we're on that little topic, you and your gang members are barred from Lady Luck from here on in."

The one who'd said his life would be simpler with drones to order about drew himself up. "You can't do that, man."

"The hell I can't," I retorted and turned to Tatiana. "Show these fellows where the cleaning supplies are and oversee the work. They don't leave until you're satisfied they've done a good job."

Her blue eyes widened. "Erm. Maybe the head of janitorial would be better for that."

"He might be," I agreed, trying for an amiable tone, "but I assigned this job to you."

Something in my voice told her arguing was pointless. She'd run at the first whiff of fighting. That story about coming to find me had been pure fabrication. She rolled her shoulders back, barked, "Follow me," and loped across the expanse of parquet flooring.

After a pause a shade too long for my liking, the men turned to follow her. Just so there'd be no misunderstandings later, I called after them, "Don't even think about hassling her. If you do, I'll find out."

I left it there. No need to spell out what I'd do to their sorry, shitty asses if they made a grab for Tatiana's tits or any other part of her. I retreated to one side and wrapped myself in shadows. I wouldn't remain long, only until the cleanup project was underway.

I hadn't realized I'd clenched my hands into fists, and I uncurled my fingers one by one. Damn it, anyway. Everything was broken—and I didn't mean in this gaming room. I was here, straddling worlds, to mend what I could, but I hadn't made much progress.

Or any if I were honest.

Aye, and when I start lying to myself, I'm done for, a patronizing inner voice spouted off.

I wasn't the source of the original damage. It could be traced directly to the Fae court, who'd decided it would be a grand idea to kick Faery's gates open to mortals a century ago.

Not that any of us ever cared about humans. We've always held them in contempt, but we wanted their money.

They'd done a bang-up job stripping their world of everything salable and grown filthy rich in the process. My kinsmen are drawn by gold—and I'd be lying if I said it didn't sing to me as well. We all love wealth, which is strange since our creature needs are taken care of in Faery.

At first, around the end of the 1800s, everything appeared to be going smoothly. We provided something not unlike a circus attraction for the well-heeled. One element none of us had reckoned on was Faery herself. Our land is alive, and she rebelled at the presence of those without power. Not right away, but when it happened the backlash was swift, sure, and brutal...

Buckets clattered as they rolled across the faux wooden floor. Some establishments have carpet. Not mine. For just this reason. My impromptu work crew dug in. Two men looked as if they'd never seen a mop before, but after Tatiana taunted them for being inept dicks, they shaped up.

I heard cheers from the strip show one floor up. No reason for me to stay here. I'd have it out with the dealers and croupiers at the all-staff meeting tomorrow afternoon. Tucking my hands into my pockets, I strolled through a wall, angling until I intersected a stairwell. Rather than naming the deserters, perhaps I'd be better served reiterating club policies to everyone.

The more I considered it, the better I liked my idea. I'd gin up something and have everyone e-sign it. I started to head for the floor show. Getting a gander at bouncing breasts and shaved pussies always settled my mind. Or diverted it, anyway. My cock thickened where it was tucked into my trousers, and I curled my fingers around it, enjoying sensation as it skittered through me.

Sex served as a reminder of the Witch. My cock grew more distended as I remembered her striking face and generous curves. To hell with the dancers in the lounge. I wanted the Witch—up close and personal.

If she was still in Lady Luck, I'd weave a lust spell, make her see only me. My errant member twitched against my fingers. "Yes, yes," I told my sidekick. "She'll want you so much, she won't be able to contain herself."

Rudy managed the blackjack and poker tables. A magnet for card counters, they spanned two rooms on the second floor. I couldn't do much about my erection. It would be as useless as attempting to stuff a genie back into a bottle, so I crafted a diversion spell from my waist down. It would draw eyes away from the tented-out front of my pants.

I bounded into the nearest chamber, gratified by the small noises that verified Lady Luck was making money. Chips clicking, dealers calling for bets, and cries of delight as patrons raked in cash.

Rudy sidled up to me. "How'd it go?"

"It's handled. How about your assignment."

He screwed his face into an angry mask, adding ten years to his grizzled appearance. "I tried, but I'm not getting anywhere near that bitch ever again. She did something to her blackjack dealer."

"What do you mean, did something?" I added a jot of magical coercion to my question.

"He's not right. Won't look at me. Won't answer me."

Damn my eyes, it sure sounded like a hex. "Is she still at his table?"

Rudy nodded. "I told the dealer not to authorize payout, but—"

"Never mind. I'll take it from here."

"Thanks." For once, Rudy looked cowed, and embarrassed. Like most men, admitting defeat is right up there with swallowing glass shards.

The Witch wasn't in this room, so I crossed the hall and walked into the other one. The feel of her power smacked me mid-chest. Witch magic smells delightful. Aged whiskey and wildflowers with a touch of blood to blend everything together. This witch was old. I could tell from her scent and the extent of her power. It oozed from her and had wrapped around the dealer in visible strands.

Oberon's balls. She didn't need to count cards. She had the dealer in thrall. What did she think she was? A fucking Vampire? Whatever game she was running, she could damn well take it elsewhere.

I strode across the big room with its colorful tables. Horse races played on big screen televisions lining one wall. We took a bite out of bets placed on them too. Unlike a mortal, the Witch knew I was coming. I felt her attention, even though her back was turned.

A long skirt swirled around her sandal-clad feet. Made of a pale green sheer material, it offered tantalizing glances of long legs and made it clear she hadn't bothered with underwear. An equally sheer tunic made of silver fabric embroidered with violet runes covered her from shoulder to hip. Her shapely arms were bare. She told the dealer to hold up—in Gaelic—and he complied. I knew damn good and well Hector didn't speak Gaelic. He's Native American from a local reservation.

How deep in trance did she have him, anyway, that he responded to commands in a foreign tongue?

Slowly, tantalizingly, she twisted until she faced me, upper body first, followed by a two-step motion that bought her hips around. Her eyes were a pale, clear green, her face a study in perfection with high, slanted cheekbones, a regal forehead, and a strong chin.

When she smiled and ran her tongue over her lush lower lip, I dropped a hasty ward around myself. She could dupe a mortal—snare them in her spells—but I was Fae, and my interest in fucking her had staged a dramatic retreat.

The Witch angled her head to one side, still giving me come-hither vibes. "I know what you are," she purred.

Her words tossed still more cold water on my arousal. "Aye, and I know what ye are as well, Madame Witch," I growled back in Gaelic. "Get out of my casino."

Her full lips formed a pout. "You're no fun." Her magic intensified, pummeling my warding.

My control snapped and I grabbed her upper arm, squeezing hard. "Where is your coven? I will return you, as is my duty for any renegade Witch." I'd stuck to Gaelic, and an archaic form at that. Zero chance of anyone understanding it —other than Witchy-gal.

"No need to get tetchy." She yanked her arm, but I held fast.

"Your coven?" I added a whopping heap of compulsion to my query.

Her face twisted in pain, and I had a momentary twinge of conscience for forcing her. "Don't have one," she ground out.

Her reply had been true, but it shocked me. "Covens are a requirement," I lectured. "After the Witch uprising of 1943—"

A violent twist jerked her arm out of my grasp. "Don't lecture me on my own history," she hissed. "I'm...different."

"We all are, sweetheart," I told her tartly. "Misfits attract magic."

Her lips twitched into half a smile. "Hate to admit it, but that's catchy."

Fuckity-fuck. She was still trying to con me. "Yeah. Now beat it. And don't come back."

"But I need the money." Her pouty look was back.

"Not my problem, darling. Turn tricks. Get an honest job. Before you go, release my dealer from whatever you did to him."

"If I do, will you hire me?"

The question came out of left field, leaving me dumbstruck. Luckily, a loss for words never lasts long. I started to say hell would freeze over before I'd offer her work, but something stayed my tongue.

"Show up here at five tomorrow afternoon. We'll talk about it."

She tilted her chin and ran her gaze from my toes to my head. Something about her direct stare got me going all over again, even through my warding.

"Good enough." She nodded and walked to the dealer. Reaching into his pants pocket, she withdrew a charm, breathed on it, and we both watched it disintegrate into motes of light.

I eyed the dealer. He still stood motionless, a dreamy expression in place. "Get rid of the other ones too," I told her.

Breath swooshed from her mouth. "I was getting to them.

Can't hurry these things or he might turn into the village idiot."

Village idiots predated medieval times, so I asked, "How old are you?"

"Never ask a lady her age," she retorted and retrieved two more charms. By the time they were dead, the dealer was starting to look more like a man and less like a puppet.

She regarded him and spoke a few words before turning to me. "There. Give it a few and he won't remember a thing about any of this. See you tomorrow." Her hips swung enticingly as she strode away.

"What's your name?" I called after her.

"You'll find out tomorrow. When I complete the employment application," she replied in mind speech, not bothering to turn around.

I was still sorting how a Witch had mastered telepathy, not a skill native to their magic, when the dealer made a grunting noise. "Boss. What happened? I feel...off."

"Take a break," I told him. "Back to your table in fifteen."

Without waiting for more questions, I walked out of the card room. It was only an hour from closing time. I could skip the rest of tonight's never-ending drama and slip into Faery. My magic needed a boost, and my mind a rest. The mortal world dragged at me, drained my essence, and made me long for an earlier time.

One before we'd opened our doors to humankind...

Keep right on reading. Click here for information and buy links.

ABOUT THE AUTHOR

Ann Gimpel is a USA Today bestselling author. A lifelong aficionado of the unusual, she began writing speculative fiction a few years ago. Since then her short fiction has appeared in many webzines and anthologies. Her longer books run the gamut from urban fantasy to paranormal romance. Once upon a time, she nurtured clients. Now she nurtures dark, gritty fantasy stories that push hard against reality. When she's not writing, she's in the backcountry getting down and dirty with her camera. She's published over 100 books to date, with several more planned for 2021 and beyond. A husband, grown children, grandchildren, and wolf hybrids round out her family.

Keep up with her at www.anngimpel.com or http://anngimpel.blogspot.com

If you enjoyed what you read, get in line for special offers and pre-release special reads. Newsletter Signup!

Grigori

Coven Enforcers

Blood and Magic

Blood and Sorcery

Blood and Illusion

Demon Assassins

Witch's Bounty

Witch's Bane

Witches Rule

Dragon Heir

Dragon's Call

Dragon's Blood

Dragon's Heir

Dragon Lore

Highland Secrets

To Love a Highland Dragon

Dragon Maid

Dragon's Dare

Dragon Fury

Earth Reclaimed

Earth's Requiem

Earth's Blood

Earth's Hope

Elemental Witch

Timespell

Time's Curse

Time's Hostage

Gatekeeper

Shadow Reaper

Rebel Reaper

Untamed Reaper

GenTech Rebellion

Winning Glory

Honor Bound

Claiming Charity

Loving Hope

Keeping Faith

Ice Dragon

Feral Ice

Cursed Ice

Primal Ice

Magick and Misfits

Court of Rogues

Midnight Court

Court of the Fallen

Court of Destiny

Rubicon International

Garen

Lars

Soul Dance

Tarnished Beginnings

Tarnished Legacy

Tarnished Prophecy

Tarnished Journey

Soul Storm

Dark Prophecy

Dark Pursuit

Dark Promise

Underground Heat

Roman's Gold

Wolf Born

Blood Bond

Wayward Mage

Jinxed

Hunted

Salvaged

Wolf Clan Shifters

Alice's Alphas

Megan's Mates

Sophie's Shifters

Wylde Magick

Gemstone

Lion's Lair

Unbalanced

STANDALONE BOOKS

Branded, That Old Black Magic Romance (paranormal romance)

Edge of Night (short story collection, paranormal and horror)

Grit is a 4-Letter Word (nonfiction)

Heart's Flame (post-apocalyptic romance)

Icy Passage (science fiction romance)

Marked by Fortune (post-apocalyptic coming of age story)

Melis's Gambit (historical paranormal romance)

Midnight Magic (paranormal romance)

Red Dawn (post-apocalyptic paranormal romance)

Shadow Play (historical paranormal romance)

Shadows in Time (Highland time travel romance)

Since We Fell (contemporary romance)

Warin's War (paranormal romance)